# RAINBOW
# road

Also by Alex Sanchez
*Rainbow Boys*
*Rainbow High*

for younger readers
*So Hard to Say*

# RAINBOW road

*alex sanchez*

**SIMON & SCHUSTER**

New York      Toronto
London      Sydney

SIMON & SCHUSTER
1230 Avenue of the Americas, New York, New York 10020

Book design by Greg Stadnyk
The text for this book is set in Mrs. Eaves.
Manufactured in the United States of America

2 4 6 8 10 9 7 5 3 1

Library of Congress Cataloging-in-Publication Data
Sanchez, Alex.
Rainbow road / Alex Sanchez.— 1st ed.
p. cm.
Summary: While driving across the United States during the summer after high school
graduation, three young gay men encounter various bisexual and homosexual
people and make some decisions about their own relationships and lives.
ISBN-13: 978-0-689-86565-7
ISBN-10: 0-689-86565-1 (hardcover)
[1. Homosexuality—Fiction. 2. Vacations—Fiction.
3. Interpersonal relations—Fiction. 4. Automobile travel—Fiction.] I. Title.
PZ7.S19475Ram 2005
[Fic]—dc22 2004025980

FIRST
F
EDITION

# To love—and patience

## Acknowledgments
With gratitude to my editor, David Gale, my agent,
Miriam Altshuler, and all those who contributed to
the creation of this book with their encouragement,
feedback, and cross-country hospitality, including
Bruce Aufhammer, David Bissette, Roger Blanco and
Scott Connal, Scott Blades, Nancy Boutilier, Paul Bradley,
Bill Brockschmidt, Kevin Case, Christa Champion,
Clark Chandler, Jeremy Coleman, Alexandra Cooper,
Jann Darsie and Jorge Gattoni, Toby Emert, James Howe,
Toby Johnson and Kip Dollar, Chuck Jones, J. R. Key,
Erica Lazaro, Kevin Lewis, Mark Lyons and Joe Scavetta,
P. J. McCarthy, Myron Morris, Rob Phelps, John Porter,
J. Q. Quiñones, Bob Ripperger, Randy Rodriguez,
Nuttawoot (Nat) Sangsode, Cosper Scafidi,
Todd Schroeder and Michael Schultz, Short Mountain
Sanctuary, Steve Soucy, Spree and the Faeries
at IDA, Patty Talahongva and her son, Nick, Robby Tew,
Yingyord M. Visith, Mike Walker, and Joe Walseth
and Tim Bishop. Thank you all.

# chapter 1

**jason**        **kyle**

**nelson**

Kyle Meeks stirred from a sex dream, vaguely aware of a ring-ing phone.

"Kyle!" his mom's voice called from the hall. "It's Jason."

Blinking at the summer morning sunlight, Kyle grabbed the receiver on the nightstand and cleared his throat. "H-hello?"

"Hey, Sleeping Beauty!" replied the boy from his dream. "Wake up!"

Kyle had met Jason four years earlier, on the first day of high school. Kyle had jostled through the crowded halls, lost, till Jason helped him find his homeroom. But not till senior year, when Jason stepped into a gay youth meeting, did a chain of events unfold that led to their becoming friends and falling in love.

"You'll never guess what's happened," Jason now announced, rattling out something about going to high school in Los Angeles.

"You know I've always wanted to see the Pacific Ocean."

None of it made any sense to Kyle's groggy brain, especially since they'd graduated high school two months earlier. Not to mention that they lived in the suburbs of D.C., three thousand miles from L.A.

"Huh?" Kyle yawned and rolled over, wishing Jason were in bed beside him. "What're you talking about?"

"We need to talk about our camping trip," Jason replied.

Kyle sat up against the headboard, accidentally bumping his head. He was suddenly wide-awake. "Our camping trip?"

He'd been looking forward to that trip for weeks, hoping for at least a little magic with Jason in a summer that had somehow gotten eaten up by a drudge job at Chicken Little Rotisserie, boring family obligations, and freshman orientation at Princeton.

Both Jason and he had been so crazy busy they'd barely had time for romance. ("Hey, I just got home from work. My mom and dad went out. Come over, quick!")

The camping trip would be their last chance for quality time together before separating for college. Was Jason now canceling?

"Hurry over here and I'll explain," Jason told him before hanging up.

Kyle immediately speed-dialed his best friend Nelson, whose turn it was to drive them to work. "Hey, can you pick me up at Jason's? I think he's bailing on the camping trip."

"But you had your heart set on that."

"Tell me about it," Kyle grumbled and jumped out of bed.

# kyle

# jason

# nelson

Jason Carrillo hung up the phone with Kyle, grabbed the basketball from atop his dresser, and raced to the driveway, hoping a few hoops would help him figure a way out of his dilemma.

"Here's the deal . . ." Jason wiped the sweat from his forehead as Kyle strode up the driveway. "I got a call from this new high school for gay and lesbian kids in L.A. They heard about my coming out last semester."

In the spring, when Jason had come out to his coach and basketball team, the news had raced through school, and because of his varsity athlete status, he'd been interviewed on local TV. That story reached the Web—and the entire country.

"The school wants me to give a speech at their opening ceremony. They'll fly me to L.A., pay my hotel, and everything!"

"Jason, that's awesome!" Kyle high-fived him, leaping into the air.

"I know!" Jason agreed, relieved to hear Kyle's enthusiasm. "Can you imagine? Seeing the Pacific Ocean? Movie stars? I'm so psyched. Except . . . it's the same time as our camping trip."

"Oh." Kyle's smile fell.

Seeing Kyle so downcast, there was no way Jason could bail on their camping trip. "I'll tell them I can't do it."

"But you've got to go!" Kyle protested. "It's too important."

"So is our camping trip," Jason argued.

"We'll go the weekend before," Kyle suggested. "I'll switch my work schedule. I'm not going to miss our camping trip."

Jason smiled, thinking how Kyle always brimmed with support and enthusiasm. "You really think I should take them up on it?"

"Jason, they're inviting you to California!" Kyle gazed across the driveway at Jason, his hazel eyes full of encouragement. "I just wish I could be there to see you."

"I wish you could too." Jason suddenly wanted to kiss Kyle right there in front of his house beneath the basketball hoop. And he sensed Kyle felt it too.

But as the two boys moved toward each other, a car horn blared. Jason turned, instantly recognizing the figure behind the steering wheel pulling into the drive. He only knew one person nutty enough to dye his hair flaming pink—the same shade as stomach medicine.

# jason     kyle

# nelson

"You like it?" Nelson Glassman beamed, loving the stares on his friends' faces at his new pink hairdo.

"It's different." Kyle gazed into the car at Nelson.

"Yeah." Jason nodded slowly, as if stunned. "Definitely."

Nelson glanced at himself in the rearview for the millionth time, reveling in their reactions.

"Well . . ." Kyle checked his watch. "We'd better get to work."

Nelson popped open the passenger lock, but Kyle made no move, instead gazing at Jason. Nelson watched. Were they about to kiss?

Jason's eyes darted toward Nelson and noticed him. Turning red, he stepped away from Kyle and began dribbling his basketball. "Thanks for coming over," he told Kyle. "Catch you later."

"So tell me what happened!" Nelson asked Kyle as they

pulled out of the drive. "Did he bail on your camping trip?"

As Kyle explained about the school in California, a wave of anger rose inside Nelson. Was he hearing right? "Whoa! Miss Teen Closet-Case *finally* comes out during his last days of senior year and for that he wins a free trip to Hollywood?"

The injustice of it galled him. "How unfair is that? I've been out since kindergarten. Where the heck's my expenses-paid trip?"

Kyle failed to respond, gazing out the windshield with a far-away look. "I'd give a million dollars to be there with him. It'll be a huge moment in his life."

Nelson stuck a finger into his throat, pretending to gag, though it hurt to see Kyle so forlorn. Then suddenly an idea crashed into Nelson's brain.

"Hey! Why not ask the school if . . ." He snapped his fingers as a plan sprang into his mind. "If instead of an air ticket they'll give Jason the cash so the three of us can drive cross-country? Can you imagine how awesome that would be?"

"Drive to California?" Kyle turned from the window. "You serious? With what car?"

"This baby!" Nelson patted the dashboard of the Ford Taurus. It had been his mom's car till summer's start, when she'd bought herself a new one. "Kyle, it would be a blast! You, me, and the world famous basketball fag."

Kyle frowned but stayed silent, as if pondering the idea. "First of all," he finally said. "Like your mom's going to let you take her car cross-country? I don't think so."

"Kyle, it's *my* car. She gave it to me."

"Secondly . . ." Kyle shook his head. "You know how long driving to California would take?"

"We have time." Nelson shrugged. "You don't start school for three weeks."

"Yeah, but I have to work. I need the money for when I'm away."

"Hmm." Nelson emitted a loud, meaningful sigh. "I guess being in California with Jason isn't really worth a million dollars after all."

Kyle narrowed his eyes at Nelson. "Look, you realize how much hotels would cost?"

"Forget hotels! Weren't you going to camp anyway? Camping's cheap. We'd just need money for gas and food. Besides, I've saved money from my job."

Kyle shifted in his seat as they turned into the mall's parking lot. "Nelson, it wouldn't work."

"Why not?" Nelson insisted. He wasn't about to let go of the idea that easily.

"Because . . ." Kyle's mouth hung open as if to say something, then he quickly shook his head. "It just wouldn't work."

"But why not?" Nelson persisted, pulling the car into a parking space.

"Nelson, think about it." Kyle's voice became agitated as he flung open the door. "The three of us? Together? Camping? By week's end you'd toss each other out of the car window."

"We would not." Nelson followed Kyle across the scorching asphalt. "I've grown to like the old hoop-head."

"Forget it." Kyle flashed a scowl over his shoulder as they approached the mall. "Crazy—bad idea."

But Nelson sprinted ahead and swung open the glass door for Kyle, determined to convince him.

*chapter 4*

# jason    kyle

# nelson

Kyle stepped past Nelson into the air-cooled mall, determined
to resist being cajoled into the road trip.

"Oh, come on," Nelson pleaded. "Jay-jay and I love each
other now—as friends, of course. Why not ask him about the
trip and let him decide?"

"Nope," Kyle insisted, hurrying past shoppers staring at
Nelson's pink hair.

"Kyle," Nelson protested. "You're being controlling."

That was Nelson's latest shtick. If he couldn't get his way with
someone, he accused them of being controlling.

But Kyle stuck to his guns. "Yeah, right. I'm not the one
being controlling."

"Yes, you are!" Nelson called after him. "You're about to move
five hundred miles away to college and you're passing up this

amazing last chance for quality time with me and your boyfriend."

Kyle slowed his pace as he approached his workplace and checked his watch. He still had a few minutes before he'd be late.

Nelson lingered beside him silently, his jaw set, ignoring the darting glances of passersby. His disappointment about the trip was obviously genuine, for Nelson rarely turned away from attention and was almost never silent.

"Listen . . ." Kyle struggled with how to console him without giving in. "You're my best friend. Jason's my boyfriend. I love you both, but differently. You guys are just too different. That's why I know it wouldn't work." He reached for Nelson's shoulder and gave it a squeeze. "Okay? Have a good day."

"Whatever," Nelson mumbled and shuffled away, his pink tuft disappearing in the direction of the candle shop.

Kyle headed into work and pulled on his apron, resolved not to waste any more thought on Nelson's impossible idea.

Instead he focused on Jason. Kyle felt so proud of him for getting the invitation. More than anything in the world, he wished he could be with Jason to see him give his speech. But how? Kyle couldn't afford to blow that much money on a plane ticket. He'd already spent too much on camping stuff—a cozy tent, a sleeping bag, and a really cool Swiss Army knife with twelve different tools.

As Kyle prepared one dreary Chicken Little platter after another, Nelson's road trip idea began pecking and scratching at his thoughts. Maybe Kyle had been too quick to dismiss it. After all, it would give Jason and him a lot more time together. He could be with Jason not only in California, but also in places along the way: Carlsbad Caverns, the Grand Canyon . . . and each night sleep arm-in-arm with each other.

But what about Nelson? Would he and Jason really be able to stand each other all that time? Would Jason and Kyle be able to have any time alone? Could the three of them get along all the way across the country and back?

Of course, all three of them didn't have to be together every single hour of the *entire* trip. There were bound to be stops along the way when Kyle and Jason could be together without Nelson.

There remained the issue of wages Kyle would lose by taking the time off. But hadn't he slaved enough all summer?

In his mind he calculated how many platters he'd made this summer: three minutes per platter meant twenty platters per hour, times seven hours a day, times five days a week, times six weeks so far, equaled 12,600 dead chickens he'd prepared. No wonder he'd lost his appetite for chicken.

What was the point of such a pathetic existence if, at the end of it, he couldn't share a significant occasion in the life of the boy he loved?

That evening when Kyle finished work and peeled off his apron, Nelson waited for him, arms crossed, still sulking, neither speaking to him nor looking at him.

"Okay," Kyle announced. "I've changed my mind."

"About what?" Nelson asked, raising a pink eyebrow.

"About the three of us driving cross-country."

"Really?" Nelson's blue eyes grew wide. "You mean it?"

"Yeah." Kyle nodded, though hearing himself agree to the idea caused a sudden quiver in his stomach.

"Oh my God!" Nelson screamed, jumping up and down. "You are so awesome." He snapped his fingers and wrapped his arms around Kyle. "I love you, Kyle. I mean it."

As Nelson's warmth enveloped him, Kyle wondered:

Shouldn't he have waited to talk with Jason first? What if he nixed the idea?

On the way out of the mall, Kyle stopped at the candy shop and got some gummy bears for Jason, thinking they might come in handy.

## chapter 5

# jason        kyle
## nelson

"Hey, wha's up?" Jason opened the front door, happily surprised to see Kyle. "Come on in."

"Kyle!" Jason's little sister ran over, nearly tackling him. "Want to play my new video game?" She grabbed his hand, pulling him to the sofa to play Tomb Raider.

"Hey, thanks." Jason grinned as Kyle handed him the gummy bears. He felt even happier when his mom joined them for a moment, offering Kyle a Coke.

Jason loved how his sister and mom had taken to Kyle. It made him feel like the luckiest boy on earth—surrounded by people he loved and who loved him, a trip to California coming up, and a bag of gummy bears.

"I need to talk to you about something," Kyle whispered in Jason's ear as they finished the third video game.

Jason turned, searching Kyle's eyes. From the cryptic tone,

Jason could tell it was something private. Once they were able to pull away from Melissa and get to Jason's room, he closed the door. "What's going on?" he asked.

"Well . . ." Kyle sat down in the desk chair. "I told Nelson about—you know—you getting invited to L.A. and, um, he had an idea."

"Uh-oh." Jason gave a low laugh, sharing Kyle's obvious nervousness. "What's his idea?"

"Um . . ." Kyle continued. "If you could ask the school for money instead of a plane ticket? That way we could, um, *drive* to California?" He glanced up at Jason, eyebrows raised hopefully. "Then I could be with you at your speech. We could camp along the way. It wouldn't be expensive. I already have a tent and—"

"Awesome!" Jason interrupted. He'd always dreamed of a road trip. How better than with his boyfriend? Just the two of them. "It would be amazing!"

"Really?" Kyle's voice quivered. "You wouldn't mind?"

"Of course not!" Jason paced the room, excited. "We'd use your parents' car?"

"No. Nelson's."

Jason stopped in his tracks, confused. "He'd let us take his car?"

"Well, yeah." Kyle stared at Jason, studying him. "He'd be with us. It would be the three of us."

"The . . . *three* . . . of us?" Jason sat down on the bed opposite Kyle. "You're kidding, right?"

Kyle slowly shook his head. "No."

Jason stroked his chin, organizing his words. "Kyle, I know he's your friend, and you know I like him okay, but sometimes when he starts bobbing his head and snapping his fingers . . . I mean, if it was just you and me . . ."

"Yeah, I know," Kyle sighed. "But I thought—"

"And why'd he dye his hair *pink*?" Jason's voice grew frantic. "Doesn't he realize how ridiculous he looks?"

"That's just how he is." Kyle gave a shrug. "Look, let's just drop it."

"See?" Jason exclaimed. "We're already getting into a fight about him."

"No, we're not," Kyle protested. "I agree it was a bad idea." He walked over to the bed and sat beside Jason, wrapping an arm around him.

Jason felt himself relax again. It felt so good being with Kyle. He knew he'd miss him terribly when Kyle left for Princeton and he stayed behind at community college.

He turned to face Kyle. A split second later they were making out like crazy, forgetting about Nelson, and road trips, and college, till Kyle checked his watch.

"I'd better go," he told Jason, but then they began kissing again, till Kyle said, "I've got morning shift tomorrow."

At the front door Jason snuck Kyle one last kiss. Then he went to the kitchen, where his mom was rinsing dinner dishes.

"It was nice seeing Kyle again," she said cheerily. "I thought I'd see more of him this summer."

"Yeah," Jason agreed and helped load the dishwasher. "So did I. But between work and everything . . . I wish he could go with me to California."

When Jason had told his mom about the school invitation, she'd been excited for him, except she worried about his air trip. She always freaked out about flying.

He now mentioned the road trip idea and—just out of curiosity—asked her, "What do you think?"

"At least you wouldn't have to fly." She handed Jason the

**rainbow road**

last plate and dried her hands. "It might be a lot of fun for you guys."

"Yeah . . ." Jason nodded and closed the dishwasher. "Except . . . Nelson's kind of weird."

A slight smile creased his mom's lips. "Well, maybe if you got to know him better he wouldn't seem so weird."

"Or," Jason replied, "he might seem even weirder."

He didn't feel like talking about it anymore. Later, as he climbed into bed, he tried putting the road trip idea to rest. But thoughts of days *and nights* with Kyle and visiting places he'd never seen kept him tossing and turning.

Maybe his mom was right. Perhaps the time with Nelson wouldn't be so bad. In fact, hadn't Jason grown to like him okay? If only he'd stop pulling stunts like dyeing his hair pink.

The following day, thoughts about the road trip kept nagging Jason, till he decided to phone the L.A. school and see what they'd say.

His palm sweated beneath the receiver as he explained to the principal the idea of driving instead of flying. "But there's no way you could do that," he told her, "right?"

In his gut he hoped she'd say, "No way." But in his heart he hoped . . .

"Well . . ." She hesitated, as if considering. "Did your parents say it's okay?"

Jason switched the receiver to his other hand, wiping his palm on his pants. "Yeah. Actually, my mom's afraid of me flying."

His response apparently had an effect on the principal, for she turned silent a moment. "Well," she said at last. "I guess there's time. Are you sure that's what you want?"

Jason could feel his stomach grinding. But he thought of Kyle, took a deep breath, and replied, "Yes, ma'am."

As soon as he hung up, he phoned Kyle. "The school said they'd send a check."

"You called them?"

"Yeah. You said you wanted to come with me, right?"

"Yeah! But are you sure you can deal with Nelson?"

"Sure," Jason said, though he really wasn't sure at all. "You and I will have some time alone together, won't we?"

"Definitely," Kyle said.

"Okay, then." After hanging up Jason heaved a huge sigh, trying to foresee the worst that could happen. Nelson and he might end up killing each other. Kyle and he could come to hate each other and never speak again. The trip might be a total disaster. And yet in spite of all that, he let out a whoop of excitement.

# jason       kyle

# nelson

"Woo-hoo!" Nelson sprang into the air when Kyle called and told him that both Jason and the school had said yes. "See? I told you Jay-Jay and I are, like, best buds. You'll see how much he loves me after this trip. He'll never be the same again."

"That's supposed to reassure me?" Kyle asked.

"Lighten up, Kyle. Chillax. We're going to have the best road trip ever."

Only one catch: Nelson still had to tell his mom. He'd chosen to wait till after the trip was definite, since his mom had a tendency to freak out, like when he admitted to her he'd had unprotected sex ("You did *what*?"), or when he was dating an HIV-positive guy ("You're doing *what*?"), or that he'd decided to take a "gap year" between high school and college ("You decided *what*?").

This time he planned more strategically how he'd tell her. First, he held off till it was his night to make dinner. Then he

prepared soft-shell crabs, one of her favorites (and his, too; he loved seafood), and served her a glass of Chardonnay.

For dessert he made peach cobbler, and after that invited his mom to watch a chick flick he'd rented. She laughed, cried, and loved it. Now she was in the perfect mood for his news: happy, weepy, and a little bit tipsy.

"Mom?" he began. "Remember hearing about that new gay and lesbian high school opening in L.A.? Well, Jason got invited to give a speech at the ceremony, since he's a jock."

"That's wonderful!" his mom exclaimed. "You know, I should invite him to come speak to my PFLAG group."

Nelson cringed. How come she'd never asked her own son to speak to the group?

As if to add insult to injury, she asked, "How's it going with him and Kyle? They make such a cute couple."

"Whatever, mom." Nelson gripped the sofa arm. "Can you just listen, please?"

"Sweetie, I'm listening. I just want to know how it's going. I've hardly seen Kyle all summer."

"He's been busy with work," Nelson groaned. "He and Jason are fine. Everybody's fine. Now can I finish what I was saying?"

His mom nodded, and Nelson continued, "So, Jason needs to get to California. I told him the three of us could drive cross-country."

The statements sounded perfectly logical to Nelson, but his mom cocked her head to one side, as if his reasoning was faulty.

"If the school is inviting him to go there," she questioned, "why aren't they just flying him out?"

Nelson knew he had to evade the question, but he didn't want to lie. "Mom, you know all the states are cutting budgets. Anyway, so we're going to drive cross-country."

"Wait, wait, wait!" His mom waved her hands in the air. "Hold on. When is all this supposed to happen?"

"Next week," he said casually.

"Next week!" His mom's voice officially reached freak-out pitch. "What about your job? You can't just take off like that!"

"My manager said it was fine." Nelson gave a shrug, struggling to stay calm. "It's really not a big deal, Mom."

"Not a big deal? Driving across the continent? Where would you stay?"

"We'll camp. Kyle has a tent and stuff."

His mom raised an eyebrow. "And exactly whose car were you thinking of taking?"

Uh-oh. They'd reached the biggie. Nelson summoned all his theatrical brilliance to feign nonchalance. "Mine."

"*Yours?*" His mom looked him straight in the eye. "I haven't given permission for that."

"It's my car," Nelson retorted. "You gave it to me."

"To help you get to work each day, not to drive cross-country. I'm still the legal owner. And I'm the one who pays the insurance."

Well, duh! If he paid the insurance, he wouldn't have *any* salary left. "But I already told Kyle we could use it."

"Nelson! Don't pull that on me. You should've asked me first. Why didn't you?"

"Because I knew you'd freak out. What the heck's the big deal?"

"The big deal is something might happen. You could have an accident."

"Mom, most accidents happen three blocks from home." Or something like that. He'd heard it in Driver's Ed.

"I thought you were saving your money." His mom glared across the sofa at him, but he thought he heard a softening in her tone.

"Camping won't cost much. And the car doesn't eat gas."

His mom tapped her hand on the armrest, as if considering. "How long were you planning?"

"I don't know. A couple of weeks, I guess."

"Two weeks!" His mom sat up. "Absolutely not. I don't feel good about this, Nelson. It's not a wise idea."

In spite of her protest, Nelson sensed he was winning. Besides, how could she stop him? Call the cops for stealing her car? She'd never.

"Mom?" He drew breath and braced himself on the couch. "I'm eighteen now. You gave me the car. I want to do this. Plus, Kyle is going. You've always said how responsible he is."

If that didn't convince her, nothing would.

She stared across the length of the sofa at him. He stared back at her. After about a century, she gave an enormous sigh. "Before I say yes, you need to have the car checked out. Agreed?"

Nelson gulped. She was practically saying yes already. And he knew the car was fine, except for that scraping sound when he braked . . . and the rattle when he turned . . . and the shriek when it started.

"Everything will be great, Mom." He slid across the sofa and wrapped his arms around her. "You'll see."

"I hope so." She patted his back gently. "But I want to talk to Kyle before you guys leave."

# kyle

# jason

# nelson

Kyle was surfing the Web, checking mileages and charting possible cross-country routes, when the phone rang.

"My mom said we could use the car," Nelson announced.

Kyle's hands dropped from the keyboard. "You hadn't asked her yet?"

"Nah, I didn't want her to freak out till I was sure we were going."

"But Nelson, what if she'd said no?"

"She did say no. But I knew she'd come around."

Kyle never ceased to be amazed by Nelson's determination.

"Oh, and she wants to talk to you before we leave."

"About what?"

"I don't know. Probably to say how she's putting my life in your hands."

That was an ominous thought. Kyle leaned back in his desk chair, almost tipping over.

"How about *your* mom and dad?" Nelson asked. "What did they say?"

Kyle had talked to them about the trip on the evening Jason told him that the school had said yes. His parents had been in bed already, reading, when Kyle tapped softly on the door.

"Hi, honey." His mom put down her book. "How was work today?"

"Okay." Kyle shrugged. "Can I, um, talk to you guys about something?"

"Sure." His dad closed the *Sports Illustrated* he'd been reading. "What's up?"

Kyle told them about Jason's invitation to L.A., and his mom smiled. "That's wonderful, honey." Both she and his dad had come a long way since Kyle had come out to them the previous fall. And they both really liked Jason—especially his dad, a huge basketball fan.

"Yeah, it's pretty awesome," Kyle said. "I'd like to—you know—be there with him when he gives his speech, so, um, Nelson came up with an idea."

"Uh-oh." Kyle's dad shook his head, smiling. It had taken him a while to get to like Nelson, especially after Kyle came out and his dad blamed Nelson for it.

"Be nice." His mom patted his dad's arm. "Nelson's usually very creative." She turned to Kyle. "What's his idea?"

Kyle told them about the road trip, using Nelson's car, and camping on the way.

"But what about your job?" his dad asked, adjusting his glasses.

"They're okay with it. The manager said he wishes he could go with us."

Kyle's dad made a skeptical face. "I guess he hasn't met Nelson."

"Stop that." His mom gave his dad a swat on the arm and turned back to Kyle. "My concern is with you and Jason. This would be a big step for you."

"Huh?" Kyle sat down on the bed beside her. "What do you mean?"

"Well, you've only been dating a few months, right?"

"Yeah," Kyle said. He saw his dad pick up his *Sports Illustrated* and begin reading again. Kyle sensed that although his dad wholeheartedly accepted Jason as Kyle's friend, he felt uncomfortable with the thought of them being boyfriends.

"But we've hardly been able to spend any time together this summer," Kyle told his mom.

"That's what I mean," she replied. "Now you'll be spending twenty-four hours a day together. That's a mighty big step."

Without glancing up from the magazine, his dad asked, "Don't you need the money you'll give up by not working those days?"

"Life's not just about money, Dad."

"I didn't say it was."

"Okay, then," Kyle argued. "I think this is important too."

His mom laid a hand on Kyle's knee. "Well, I think you and Jason will definitely get to know each other much better by the end of the trip. Just remember every once in a while to take some time apart."

*Time apart?* Didn't she understand how much he wanted to be with Jason, how much the summer had sucked because they'd hardly had any time together, and how once he left for college they'd be constantly apart? Sometimes his mom and dad didn't seem to understand anything.

One night when he was free from work, Kyle invited both Jason and Nelson over to plan the trip.

Jason arrived on time, and once inside Kyle's bedroom handed him an envelope.

"What's this?" Kyle peered inside at a stack of twenties.

"The money from the school. My mom cashed the check for me." His coffee-colored eyes gazed at Kyle. "I think it's better if you handle it. You're the math expert. I'd probably spend it all the first day. I already bought my sister a going-away present with some of it."

"But *you're* the one going away." Kyle laughed. "She should give *you* the present."

"See what I mean?" Jason said.

"Okay." Kyle accepted the envelope. Actually, it felt good that Jason trusted him with the money, like it made them closer. He leaned forward and kissed Jason, but only for an instant, because he heard Nelson downstairs. Late, of course.

"God, it's so hot I'm wet—and not in a good way!" As he strode into the room, he kicked off his sandals, displaying emerald-painted toenails.

Kyle was already used to such things, but Jason gaped across the room, with a look somewhere between aversion and fascination.

It was then that Kyle realized he'd never actually had both his best friend and his boyfriend in his room at the same time. For some reason an image popped into his mind of a boxing ring—with him as referee.

"I checked the mileage on the Web," Kyle hurriedly said, tossing his dad's road atlas onto the carpet and plopping down alongside. "It's about 2,700 miles from D.C. to L.A. If we average eight hours a day, to leave time for sightseeing,

at sixty miles an hour, we can get there in six days."

"Oh, Kyle." Nelson sat beside him. "You're such a math geek."

"I know." Kyle continued, "Now, there are three routes we can take. Either I-64 and 70 this way through Kentucky and Kansas—"

"Woo-hoo, Kansas!" Nelson cheered sarcastically. "That sounds thrilling."

"—or this way . . ." Kyle pointed on the atlas. "Interstates 81 and 40 would take us through Tennessee and by the Grand Canyon."

"Let's do that!" Jason said. "We've got to see the Grand Canyon."

"Isn't Tennessee where Graceland is?" Nelson leaned over the map. "I want to go to Graceland."

"Yeah, we've got to go to Graceland," Jason agreed, nodding to Nelson.

"And New Orleans," Nelson told Jason. "We've got to do 'Nawlins.'"

Kyle watched his two friends, relieved they were getting along so easily. Yet he felt an uneasiness he couldn't quite pinpoint.

"Will it be Mardi Gras?" Jason asked.

"Oh my God!" Nelson raised his hand and high-fived Jason. "That would be so cool!"

"I hate to tell you," Kyle interjected. "Mardi Gras is in winter."

Nelson turned to him. "Kyle, don't be such a party pooper."

"Hey, don't blame me! I'm not the one who schedules Mardi Gras." His words came out more defensive than he intended. "Okay," he said more softly. "If we go to New Orleans we can continue on I-10 this way to Carlsbad Caverns."

"To where?" Jason asked.

"What do you want to go there for?" asked Nelson.

"Because they're the world's most amazing caves! I did a paper on them. We're not just going where you want to go. And we can't go everywhere, so you have to decide: Do you want to go this way?" He pointed. "Or this way? Or this way?"

Jason studied the map. "Well, what if we went to Graceland first, then this way to New Orleans?" His finger traced a zigzag across the map. "Then we go to those caverns, then to the Grand Canyon."

"Fine," Kyle said. "But I'll have to recalculate how long that would take." He stood and went to the computer, leaving Jason and Nelson with the map.

"Hey," Jason asked Nelson in a low voice. "You know where Yellowstone is?"

"I think it's in Vermont," Nelson replied.

"It's in Wyoming!" Kyle corrected. "That's nowhere near where we're going." He continued typing as fast as he could.

"Can we go to San Francisco?" Nelson asked. "We'll already be in California."

"No! You know how huge California is?"

"Oh, Kyle. You're so linear."

"Okay," Kyle announced. "If we do what you guys want, it'll take nine days just to get there."

"Does that include the caves?" Jason asked. "Those sound cool."

Kyle nodded. "The day after your speech in L.A., we'll have to hightail it back in four, so I can get here in time for Princeton. That's fourteen days altogether. We'll need to leave next week."

"Fine by me." Nelson shrugged. "My boss said I could take two weeks."

**rainbow road**

"Okay with me," Jason agreed. "As long as we have time to see the Pacific."

"We will," Kyle agreed. "We have a plan!"

They continued talking and organizing till midnight, when Nelson offered Jason a ride home. As Kyle watched them stroll down the driveway together, his uneasiness from earlier returned. He'd feared having to referee between Nelson and Jason. But what if instead they really did become—as Nelson had suggested—"best buds"?

*But that's silly*, he told himself. It could never happen.

*chapter 1*

# jason
# kyle
# nelson

Jason opened the passenger door to Nelson's car but found the seat already occupied by a mini Disney Aladdin doll.

"My first crush as a kid," Nelson explained. "Yep, I fell in love with a 'toon. Isn't he dreamy?"

Jason picked the figure off the seat, trying to figure out where to put it, and glanced around the car. Rainbow beads dangled from the rearview. A hula girl bobbed atop the dash. Below the radio a sticker read: I CAN'T EVEN DRIVE STRAIGHT.

And the car reeked of cigarettes. Was Nelson planning to smoke during the trip?

As Nelson turned the ignition, the engine shrieked.

"What's that noise?" Jason asked.

"Beats me." Nelson backed out of the driveway. "It started last week. I'll get it checked. Don't worry."

Jason buckled his seat belt. Although he'd enjoyed the time with Nelson at Kyle's, he now wondered if getting into a car with him was a good idea. How many miles had Kyle said it would be to California?

Jason's mom had gotten him a mail room job for the summer at the law office where she worked. The job was easy and the supervisor liked Jason, so it was no problem when he asked for time off for the trip.

But before he left, there were a couple of people Jason wanted to tell about the trip and say good-bye to. First and foremost was his coach.

Over the past four years Coach Cameron had become the most influential man in Jason's life. When Jason tearfully came out to him, Coach had accepted him, unlike his own dad. And when Jason lost his full scholarship to Tech because of coming out, Coach had stood by him.

He'd taught Jason about a lot more than basketball. He'd shown him that what Jason thought were weaknesses could sometimes be his biggest strengths, and what Jason often saw as defeats could turn out to be his greatest triumphs.

After endless phone calls and politicking, Coach had scored Jason a place on a local community college team that included a full tuition waiver. It wasn't Jason's Division-1 dream school by any means, but it allowed him to stay home and help his mom out with his little sister. All in all, Jason was grateful. He'd still be playing ball, he'd be part of a team—and he'd have a place to belong.

Since fall semester would be starting soon, when Jason stopped by Whitman High one day at lunchtime, Coach was already in his office, getting ready.

"Hey, Carrillo. Good to see you. How's it going? Take a seat."

Jason sank into the familiar green vinyl chair that faced Coach's desk and told him about being invited to speak at the L.A. school.

"Huh." Coach stroked his gray-stubbled chin. "That's pretty brave of you to stand up in front of strangers like that and talk about something . . . so personal. It's a good thing you're doing. I'm proud of you."

"Thanks," Jason said, and told him about the road trip.

"I'm sure that'll be a lot of fun." Coach gave a little smile. He was never a big smiler. "But remember to keep up your practice. You been practicing every day? You need to stay in form for next season. Did you already practice today?"

"Um, not yet. Actually, I'm on lunch break from my job."

"Well, come on." Coach stood up from his desk. "I'll give you a workout to do on the road. You can always find a court somewhere."

Jason followed him eagerly. The thought of stopping at a court every day to do what he knew best made the thought of traveling to unknown places feel a lot more comfortable.

During the next few minutes Coach led Jason through a series of individual drills. He began with a warm-up of dribbling, ball handling, and then some defensive slides. A series of toss-and-square shooting followed: straight-up jump shots, crossovers, spins, and step-backs. After each shot Jason was to chase down the rebound and put it back in with a power layup, then jog back out and toss it again.

"Make sure you give the toss plenty of backspin," Coach said. "So it'll bounce up nice and easy, and you can run onto it just as you'd catch a pass."

Jason nodded and tossed the ball out a few feet in front of

**rainbow road**

him with an upward flick of his wrists. He stepped forward to catch the ball, pivoted, and swished a jump shot.

By the time he returned to work, Jason was embarrassed by how sweaty he was, but fortunately his supervisor didn't notice. Nevertheless, he stayed in the mail room the rest of the day, memorizing the workout he'd gotten.

The other person Jason wanted to see before leaving was his ex, Debra.

Blond and beautiful, she'd been Jason's first love and first sexual partner. But from the start he'd secretly wanted to be with a guy, too. Eventually he'd realized he wasn't being fair to her. Yet even now, months after they'd broken up, the bisexuality thing still confused him. He continued to find girls attractive. And sometimes he deeply missed being with Debra.

"Oh my gosh!" She gave a crazy laugh when Jason now told her about the road trip one evening. "Nelson's going? I can just picture the three of you. That's going to be *very* interesting."

The cryptic way she said that made Jason squirm on her sofa.

"I can just imagine," she continued, "him in some bitty hick town with his million earrings and purple hair."

"Pink," Jason corrected. "Now he's dyed it pink."

"No way!" She giggled again. "You're going to have a blast. I wish I could go with you. How's it going with Kyle?"

"Okay. Good." Jason still felt uncomfortable talking about his boyfriend with his ex-girlfriend, but he was glad she asked about him.

"Well . . ." She grabbed hold of Jason's hand and gave it a gentle squeeze. "Remember to be patient with one another. There will probably be lots of times when you guys get on each other's nerves."

"Yeah," Jason said agreeably, feeling her soft fingers in his hand. He missed her warmth, her gentle touch, her understanding—all so similar and yet so different from Kyle's.

As they said good-bye, he wrapped his arms around her and she embraced him in turn. Her rose perfume brought back memories as she planted a tender kiss on his cheek.

That evening Jason sorted through his clothes, trying to figure out what to pack. Meanwhile his sister chattered and played with assorted Barbies, trolls, and Beanie Babies she'd carried onto his bed.

"Here." Melissa handed Jason an Asian Barbie. "She wants to go with you on the trip."

"But won't she miss you?" Jason smiled and tried to hand the doll back, but Melissa wouldn't take her.

"Nope, she wants to be with you for when you get lonely."

"Okay," Jason agreed, though he had no intention of actually taking the doll. How could he possibly be lonely with Kyle and Nelson around? But he played along, figuring his sister would forget about it later.

He set the doll on his desk chair, recalling Nelson's Aladdin doll, which led him to think about Debra's comment about being patient "when you guys get on each other's nerves."

Jason was glad to be taking time to say good-bye to everyone, but with each encounter, he was having more second thoughts about the trip.

# jason      kyle

## nelson

On his next morning off Nelson took his car to the service center for its checkup. Not till lunchtime did they finally inform him that the car needed new front brakes (the scraping sound) and a right axle (the rattle). They couldn't figure out the shrieking noise at ignition but suggested a tune-up and oil change. When the attendant quoted him the total estimate, Nelson made his own shrieking noise.

Panicked, he phoned his mom. "They told me it'll cost five hundred and thirty-seven dollars!" In a low voice he added, "I think they're trying to rip me off."

"No," she responded. "That sounds about right. Cars cost money."

That wasn't the response he'd expected. "Well," he said in his sweetest possible voice. "So . . . like . . . um . . . will they bill you?"

"Not me," his mom replied. "As you said, it's your car."

"You mean I have to pay for *all* that? Can't you at least pay half?"

"No. You decided you didn't want to start college next year and you wanted to work."

That wasn't exactly true. Putting off college had been his idea. Making him work had been *her* idea.

"I gave you the car," she continued, "and I'm paying the insurance. As far as I'm concerned, I'm already doing more than enough."

"But this is a chunk of change, Mom. It's half my savings."

"Nelson, you decided you could afford to take time off work for this trip."

As she spoke Nelson realized what this was really about. "You just don't want me to go, do you?"

"Well, it doesn't sound like you're in a financial position to."

"Thanks a lot, Mom." Nelson hung up on her, steaming. Why was she being such a witch? First she'd begun charging him rent because he hadn't wanted to go to college yet. Now he had to pay car repairs, too?

He thought about calling his dad and asking him for the money, but then the old fart would talk to his mom and Nelson would end up getting blamed for upsetting her.

Grudgingly, Nelson told the attendant to make the repairs.

That night his mom asked, "Is everything okay with the car now?"

"Yeah," Nelson grumbled. "But I still think they're crooks."

His mom offered no sympathy. "We got new health insurance cards in the mail. Here. Make sure you carry it with you on the trip."

"Mom, nothing's going to happen! Would you stop worrying?" But he took the card anyway.

The evening before they were to leave, Nelson picked Kyle up at his house. They loaded Kyle's stuff in the car and said good-bye to his parents. Then they drove to Nelson's to spend the night, so Kyle could help him pack.

"You're so good at anal stuff like that," Nelson reasoned. "And besides, without you how am I going to get up so early?"

They listened to CDs, deciding which ones to take on the trip, as Nelson danced around the room, plucking clothes from drawers and tossing them onto the queen-size bed while Kyle neatly folded them.

"How much are you taking?" Kyle asked. "There's not going to be any room for Jason's stuff."

"Good." Nelson grinned. "The less clothes he wears, the better."

Kyle did not return Nelson's grin.

"Just kidding, Kyle. That's why I need you—to help me decide what to take. It's hard being a supermodel."

While Kyle sorted out priority piles (definitely, maybe, and why this?), Nelson kept tossing stuff on the bed in between phoning friends to say good-bye.

Around nine o'clock Jeremy came over. So far he'd been the only boy Nelson could claim to actually have dated during his otherwise pathetically love-lacking life. But Jeremy was HIV positive and Nelson was HIV negative. They'd both decided the difference in status was too big an issue between them, but they also liked each other too much to stop being friends. And at moments Nelson wondered if they still couldn't somehow make a relationship work.

Now Jeremy handed Nelson a gift-wrapped box. "I tried to think of something just right for your drive through the sunny South."

Nelson tore off the wrapping and opened the box, revealing a vintage pair of sparkling 1950s women's cat's-eye sunglasses. "Woo-hoo!" Nelson jumped up and down, snapping his fingers. "Multi-multi snaps!" He put them on and smacked Jeremy a kiss. "What do you think, Kyle?"

Kyle glanced over from the piles of neatly folded clothes he'd organized. "I think they go great with your hair. The rednecks will love them."

Nelson gazed into the mirror, admiring the union of pink and green. "They do, don't they?"

Near midnight Kyle finally convinced Nelson that no more of his stuff would fit into the car, and Jeremy yawned that he needed to go home.

Both Nelson and Kyle hugged him good-bye, then Kyle unrolled his sleeping bag beside Nelson's bed.

"You don't have to sleep on the floor," Nelson told him. "You can sleep with me. Atticus can sleep on the floor."

Atticus was Nelson's black Labrador, currently lying on the bed.

"I want to try out my sleeping bag," Kyle replied. "I don't mind."

"Whatever," Nelson said, a little disappointed. When Kyle returned from the bathroom in his pajamas, Nelson had stripped down to his underwear and was pulling them off.

"Nelson, what're you doing?"

"Sleeping nude, like I always do."

"Since when?"

"Um, a while," Nelson said. "You can too if you want. I don't mind."

He'd seen Kyle in his underwear before, but had always been curious to take things to the next level.

"No, thanks," Kyle said, climbing into his sleeping bag.

"Oh, Kyle. You're such a prude." Nelson fell into bed beside Atticus. "I guess it's just you and me, pup. Our last night together."

But Atticus jumped to the floor, curling up next to Kyle's sleeping bag.

"Hey, where are you going?" Nelson protested.

"I set the alarm for seven," Kyle said, turning off the light. "Good night."

"Hey, Kyle?" Nelson whispered across the dark. "You think Jeremy and I could somehow make things work?"

"I think you should move on to someone else," Kyle whispered back.

"Yeah," Nelson said sarcastically. "All those hunky guys knocking down my door are starting to wear me out."

Kyle yawned. "You'll find someone."

Nelson closed his eyes, thinking about the trip, and wondered, *Will I?*

**jason** **kyle**

**nelson**

Next morning Kyle woke an hour before the alarm, too excited to sleep longer. He was about to spend the next two weeks *with his boyfriend!*

On the bed Nelson puffed sleepy breaths in harmony with Atticus. Kyle rolled his sleeping bag into a neat bundle, grabbed his clothes, and padded quietly down the hall to shower.

When he emerged from the bathroom, Mrs. Glassman's bedroom door had opened. Already dressed, she propped the last of a half-dozen throw pillows onto her bed.

"Good morning!" She smiled at Kyle. "How'd you sleep?"

"I woke so early, I guess I'm pretty excited."

"I bet you are. I don't suppose Nelson's up yet. How about you and I have some breakfast?"

Kyle recalled Nelson saying his mom wanted to talk to him. While Mrs. Glassman prepared eggs and turkey bacon, Kyle

toasted muffins and poured their orange juice. At seven the radio alarm began blaring music upstairs, but the sound elicited no stirrings of life.

"Nelson!" his mom shouted out the kitchen door.

No response.

She shook her head and sighed at her uneaten muffin.

"You know . . ." Her eyebrows rose trustingly toward Kyle. "I'm only letting Nelson go on this trip because you're going."

Kyle hadn't realized that, but it didn't surprise him. She'd often told him how glad she was that Nelson had him as a friend.

"I know how responsible you are, Kyle. Promise me you'll look after him, okay?"

"Oh, he'll be all right." Kyle tried to sound confident, though in truth he worried about Nelson nearly as much as she did. Eager to end the conversation, he told her, "I'd better wake him up."

As Kyle entered Nelson's bedroom, Atticus lifted his head off the bed to greet him, tail wagging to the radio. But Nelson still lay beneath the sheets, oblivious to the music.

"Hey, come on!" Kyle shook Nelson's shoulder. "I told Jason we'd be there by now."

That evoked merely a grunt. Only after Kyle tickled Nelson's ribs, yanked open the window blinds, pounded him with a pillow, and jumped on the bed did Nelson finally sit up, shielding his eyes from the sunlight. "All right already!" He blinked at the clock. "Why'd you let me sleep so late?"

"Yeah, right. Hurry up!" Kyle handed Nelson the big mug of coffee he'd brought up and grabbed the phone to call Jason.

"Hey, wha's up?" Jason asked. "Where are you?"

"Trying to get her majesty out of bed."

"He's not going to pull this all trip, is he?" Jason grumbled into the phone, so loud that Kyle pulled the receiver away

from his ear. "Tell him he'd better get his butt in gear."

"That's *royal* butt," Nelson corrected, carrying his coffee to the bathroom.

Meanwhile Kyle crammed his sleeping bag and pillow into the packed car. Even at this early hour, the August sun had already begun shining ferociously, though rain was forecast. When Kyle returned upstairs, Nelson stood in front of the full-length mirror, wearing Jeremy's dark glasses and buttoning a baggy Hawaiian shirt emblazoned with bright blue ocean waves and huge red hibiscus flowers.

"And for the final touch . . ." Nelson capped his pink hair with a Panama hat Kyle recalled from Nelson's junior-year English presentation on Truman Capote. "*Voilà!*"

"You have everything?" Mrs. Glassman asked when at last Nelson made it out the door. "Your cell phone? The charger?" Kyle could see her eyes were misting up. She hugged Nelson, squeezing him so hard his hat fell off.

"Mom!" he protested and climbed into the car.

"Call me tonight." She leaned in the window as Nelson started backing out of the drive. "Kyle, make sure he calls me!"

"I will," he told her as they waved and pulled onto the street. The mention of Nelson's cell phone charger reminded Kyle: "I think I forgot my toothbrush charger. I need to get it at my house."

That meant delaying their arrival at Jason's. But watching Nelson say good-bye to his mom had made Kyle secretly glad for any excuse to see his own mom again. And it turned out he hadn't forgotten his charger after all.

"Keep us posted, okay?" His mom wrapped her arms around Kyle, and he breathed in the clean smell of her hair. "Call us if anything happens."

"I will. And you have Nelson's cell phone number, right?"

"Yes, sir," his dad assured him and, after hugging him, pressed a fifty-dollar bill into his palm. "Here. Don't spend it all at once."

"That was worth going back for," Nelson remarked, as they waved good-bye and finally headed toward Jason's.

When they arrived, he was in the driveway shooting baskets, his duffle and sleeping bag on the stoop.

"What took you so long?" he asked Kyle, and then did a double take as Nelson emerged from the car in his straw hat, loud shirt, and '50 movie-star sunglasses.

"Hi, guys!" Mrs. Carrillo came out of the front door, along with Jason's little sister.

"Don't forget your Lacey!" She ran up to Jason, carrying the doll she'd given him.

"Aw, is she yours?" Nelson smiled at Jason. "I remember my first Barbie."

"She's not mine," Jason clarified. "She's my sister's. Let's get going."

"I'll help you with your stuff." Kyle walked up to the stoop with Jason. "Sorry we took so long."

"Why's he wearing those goofy clothes?" Jason asked, but Kyle wasn't sure how to answer, except to say, "That's just the way he is."

As Kyle helped Jason carry his stuff to the car trunk, Nelson played with Melissa, redoing her doll's hair.

"You'd better take that flag off," Jason told Nelson, pointing to a rainbow flag bumper sticker. "We're going through redneck country, you know."

"So?" Nelson gave a defiant shrug. "I'm not taking it off."

"It'll be all right," Kyle intervened. It seemed like they were

already getting off on the wrong foot, before they'd even left the driveway.

Jason hugged his mom and sister, then his mom hugged Kyle. It was the first time Mrs. Carrillo had ever done that, and it made Kyle feel even more a part of Jason's life.

After hugs were done, Nelson announced, "I'll drive first," and hopped into the driver's seat. "You two decide who rides shotgun."

"You can," Kyle told Jason. "I'll sit in back and navigate." Kyle's dad had gotten him auto club maps for all the states along the route and Kyle had carefully organized them.

"Woo-hoo!" Nelson turned the ignition and cranked the stereo up. "We're off!"

"You trying to blast us out?" Jason reached over and turned the volume down.

"Yeah," Kyle agreed as they pulled out of the driveway. "Can you turn it down?"

"Not so much!" Nelson nudged the volume back up. "I love this song." He began bouncing in the seat, clapping his hands above his head.

"Hey, would you keep your hands on the wheel, please?" Kyle protested. Why was Nelson acting like such a dork? Jason glanced over his shoulder at Kyle, his eyes dark and annoyed. And then Nelson shook a cigarette from his pack.

"You're not going to smoke that," Jason stated flatly.

"'Course not." Nelson glared back. "I'm going to stick it up my butt."

Jason smirked. "I'm not spending two weeks breathing in your secondhand smoke."

"Then don't breathe." Nelson lit up his cigarette.

**rainbow road**

Kyle leaned over the seat. "Can't you wait till we stop for a break?"

Nelson scowled into the rearview. "Smoke at a gas station? Brilliant, Kyle. Look, guys, it's my car and if I want to smoke, I'll smoke."

"Then at least open your window," Kyle suggested, trying to find a compromise.

But Nelson wouldn't. "It's too hot."

Instead Jason rolled down *his* window. In response, Nelson flicked the AC on full blast. In back, Kyle felt the cold stream of air, but inside, his blood was boiling.

# chapter 11

# jason     kyle

# nelson

Jason watched the Virginia suburbs blur past the window as they drove out I-66. The tension between him and Nelson hung thick as smoke.

*Stop the car!* he wanted to tell Nelson. *This won't work. Just drop me off at Dulles Airport. I'll catch the next plane to L.A.—alone.*

But instead he sat silent, wishing the road trip could've been just Kyle and him. As the stereo played none of the boys spoke, till the first sign for Shenandoah National Park came into view.

"Hey." Kyle nudged Nelson's shoulder. "Remember that fall we came to see the leaves turn color?"

"Oh my God!" Nelson snapped his fingers. "That was so amazing."

"Have you ever been to Shenandoah?" Kyle turned to Jason.

"No," Jason said somberly. He'd always wanted to, but his drunken dad never took their family anywhere on vacation, except to visit relatives.

"You haven't been to Shenandoah?" Nelson gasped. "You've *got* to see it. Let's go now!"

"No," Jason replied, though he wasn't exactly sure why. He would've liked to see the park, but it annoyed him that Nelson told him he *had* to see it, as if he felt sorry for him. He didn't like anyone pitying him.

"We don't have time," he told Nelson. "Since we started late."

"But it wouldn't take long," Kyle said cheerily. "Skyline Drive goes through the park in our direction."

"Come on, Jason." Nelson reached over and gave his shoulder a squeeze. "You're too tense. Chillax. Smell the roses."

Jason shook Nelson's hand off but decided not to protest further. "Whatever."

Nelson took the next exit, driving south toward the park's entrance gate, where a line of cars waited, edging slowly forward.

"Ten dollars," Jason grumbled, pointing to the admission fee sign.

"Here." Kyle handed Nelson a fifty. "It's my dad's treat."

"Woof!" Nelson exclaimed as he gaped at the ranger in the booth. "Isn't he adorable in his Smokey Bear hat?" Nelson grabbed his cell phone. "I want his picture."

"Dude, don't!" Jason tried to stop him, but too late.

As Nelson paid the ranger, he asked, "Mind a picture?"

Jason slunk down in the seat, hiding his face, while Nelson snapped the photo with the phone camera and drove away.

"Why do you pull crap like that?" Jason asked, sitting up again.

"'Cause I wanted his picture." Nelson handed Kyle his

**jason**    nelson    kyle                                        45

change and the cell phone. "Look! Isn't he totally lickable?"

Jason turned to Kyle, hoping for backup, but Kyle was looking at the photo image. "It came out great."

Jason groaned, crossing his arms, and turned to stare out the window, thinking there was no way he'd be able to endure this trip.

But as they wound up the mountain highway, he couldn't help admiring the tall trees and lush meadows. Deep valleys stretched far into the distance. Roadside waterfalls splashed suddenly into view. And deer were *everywhere.* He'd never seen so many.

"Isn't this great?" Kyle exclaimed.

In spite of himself, Jason nodded. "It's pretty cool."

At the next bend a bus marked FIRST EVANGELICAL CHURCH had pulled over onto the road shoulder. Alongside several parked cars, a crowd of people stood peering into a glade.

Out of curiosity, Nelson pulled over and the boys climbed out of the car.

"What's going on?" Kyle asked a group of middle-schoolers.

"Bears," replied a short girl with braces.

Jason gazed over the kids' shoulders. At a distance of about a hundred feet, mama bear stood beside two furry little cubs that rolled and tussled in the grass.

"Man!" Jason grabbed Kyle excitedly. "I wish Melissa could see this."

While watching the bears, he overheard the girl with braces tell Nelson, "I like your hair. That's so wild."

"I love your hat," another said.

"Where'd you get those cool sunglasses?" a third asked.

Nelson had barely started chatting with the girls when a moonfaced woman clapped her hands sharply and said, "Girls, stop bothering strangers!"

"They're not bothering me." Nelson smiled.

The woman's brow furrowed. "Then I'd appreciate if you'd stop bothering them. Come on, boys and girls, let's get back onto the bus."

"I wasn't *bothering* them!" Nelson pulled off his glasses and narrowed his eyes at the woman. "You got a problem with something?"

"Yes, with people like you." She turned and herded the kids toward the bus.

"Girlfriend?" Nelson snapped his fingers toward her and bobbed his head. "You need to get laid!"

Middle-schoolers spun around to stare at him, mouths agape with shock, then quickly covered to stifle giggles. As the woman rushed them onto the bus, Nelson turned to Kyle and Jason. "Can you believe her?"

"Maybe if you wouldn't dress so weird . . ." Jason replied, feeling no sympathy for Nelson. "Why do you always try to be so different?"

Nelson perched his dark glasses back onto his nose, his blue eyes peering across the top. "I don't try to be different, Jason. I just am. Try it sometime."

Jason wasn't sure what the heck Nelson meant by that, but he didn't care. "You always have a comeback for everything, don't you?"

"Guys?" Kyle stepped between them. "Why don't we get something to eat?"

Jason stood glaring at Nelson, unwilling to back down as Nelson stared back.

"Guys, stop it!" Kyle insisted, and pushed them away from each other, toward the car.

As they left the mama bear and cubs, Jason considered

sitting in back, but he didn't want to appear intimidated by Nelson. The fact was Jason could beat the crap out of him anytime. Didn't Nelson realize that? Then why didn't he act like it?

When they reached Big Meadows they stopped for lunch at the cafeteria and then continued toward the southern end of Shenandoah.

"So was the park worth it?" Kyle asked Jason as they exited the gate.

"Yeah." Jason nodded. In spite of his tiff with Nelson, he'd enjoyed it. "Those bears were the best part. My old man never took us anywhere."

"Neither did mine," Nelson said, turning toward I-81. That might've been the first time Jason could recall Nelson mentioning his dad, but Jason didn't feel like asking more about it.

Instead he watched the apple orchards and fields of baled hay pass by, as the sky began clouding. Around five o'clock they approached the exit for Tech, the university that had awarded Jason's scholarship. He watched the ramp lead off the highway and wondered, *What if they hadn't retracted their invitation?*

Kyle must've had the same thought, because he laid a hand gently on Jason's shoulder. Jason turned to look at him, thinking how different his life would be if he hadn't come out. He certainly wouldn't be driving across the continent with his boyfriend.

And he wouldn't be stuck in a car with Nelson.

*chapter 12*

# jason          kyle

# nelson

As they drove past the exit for Tech, Nelson watched Kyle quietly rest his hand on Jason's shoulder. That was just like Kyle: always knowing the right thing to do or say. Unlike himself, who seemed to constantly screw up.

"It sucked how they took your scholarship away," Nelson now told Jason, trying to be consoling. He lifted Melissa's Barbie off the seat beside him and imitated a little girl's voice: "Bad Tech!"

Jason turned and gave him a dirty look. "I'm over it, okay?"

Nelson put the doll down and glanced in the rearview mirror. Kyle was glowering at him, shaking his head. Nelson let out a sigh. Once again he'd messed up.

The three of them were silent after that, listening to the stereo and watching the clouds darken overhead. As they approached Pulaski, Kyle suggested they set up camp, "before it starts raining."

They checked into the High-N-Dry Campground, choosing a site near the basketball court. Kyle and Jason began unpacking the tent and sleeping bags, while Nelson grabbed a pine branch, sweeping the ground, clearing away sticks and rocks. "Let's put the tent down over here . . ." He pointed. "And the picnic table over there, so we'll a have prettier view of the mountains."

Kyle laid the tent where Nelson suggested and began assembling the poles.

"This is supposed to fit three people?" Jason stared at the tiny dome.

"Well . . ." Kyle shrugged. "I thought there'd only be two of us when I bought it. But the carton said 'Two to three people.'"

"It'll be cozy." Nelson winked at Jason, smiling.

Jason didn't smile back. Without another word, he grabbed his basketball from the car and headed toward the court.

"Why's he always so cranky?" Nelson whispered to Kyle.

"He's not," Kyle replied. "Why do you keep antagonizing him?"

"I don't! At least I don't try to."

"I think you do." Kyle pounded the tent stakes into the ground. "Ever since this morning—suggesting the doll was his, blasting your music, smoking even though you know it bothers him—"

Nelson crossed his arms. "Kyle, I've always smoked, I always listen to music loud, and his sister said it was his doll. He's the one who treats me like I'm a freak."

"He does not. And that's not the issue."

"Then what's"—Nelson raised his fingers into curved V-signs for quotation marks—"the Issue?"

"The issue is you keep teasing and provoking him. Don't deny it! I know you. And as for your smoking and music, can't

you think about someone besides yourself and what they might like for a change?"

Nelson clamped down on his jaw, feeling a twinge of guilt.

When Jason tramped back from the court, Nelson offered his cell phone. "You want to call your mom and sister and tell them about the bears?"

Jason eyed Nelson a moment, then accepted the phone. "Thanks."

"Sure. Talk as long as you want." Nelson flashed Kyle an exaggerated grin. "I'm going to shower."

When he reached the bathhouse, he found it a little decrepit, but clean. The shower curtain didn't close all the way, but Nelson didn't care. He was alone anyway.

He'd dried off and was dressing when Jason walked in.

"I left your phone with Kyle. Thanks for letting me use it."

"Sure. Anytime," Nelson replied, watching in the mirror as Jason pulled off his T-shirt, revealing his smooth olive-skinned chest.

Although Nelson had always considered Jason good-looking, he'd never been overly attracted to his straight-boy energy. But that was before seeing his tight pecs and ripped abs. Now he had to fight the urge to turn and gape.

"Is there hot water?" Jason asked, stepping into the shower stall in his boxers and pulling the curtain as closed as it would go.

"Yeah. It's great."

Nelson watched Jason's undies alight on the curtain rod and continued to stare into the mirror, rubbing moisturizer on his face till he'd probably clogged every pore. He felt like a total perv for hoping to snatch a glimpse of something, but he couldn't stop himself.

"Hey!" Jason shouted.

Nelson jumped, his heart skipping a beat.

"I forgot my shampoo." Jason pulled back the top of the shower curtain. Streams of water trickled down his soap-foamy chest while the plastic curtain covered his lower half. "You got some I can borrow?"

"Sure!" Nelson grabbed his shampoo, dropping it not once but twice as he stumbled toward Jason.

"Thanks." Jason grabbed the plastic bottle with his free hand and pulled the curtain closed behind him, but not before Nelson caught a peek at his glistening butt.

Okay, now he *really* felt like a perv. "Anything else you need?" Nelson shouted.

"No, thanks," Jason yelled back. "Kyle bought some food at the camp store. He can probably use your help with the fire."

*Kyle who?* Nelson wondered. Oh, yeah: Kyle, his best friend. Jason's *boyfriend.* Nelson watched himself turn red in the mirror, flooding with guilt. "Okay. I guess I'll go help him." Nelson hurried out of the bathhouse, although he did try to catch one last glimpse though the gap in the shower curtain.

*You're such a mess,* he told himself as he flip-flopped down the gravel path back to the campsite. *How could you try to check out your best friend's boyfriend like that?*

Kyle stood over the charcoal grill, trying to get the fire going. "What took you so long?" He glanced up. "Something wrong? You okay?"

Nelson stared back, his face burning with shame. "Kyle, I—Jason . . . I'm sorry. . . . It's just—God, he's beautiful. . . . I mean he's *really beautiful!*"

Kyle examined him a moment before proclaiming, "Well, duh! Like you never noticed that? Hel-lo! Can you hand me the lighter fluid?"

By the time Jason returned, Nelson had finally calmed down enough to eat his hot dog without envisioning Jason in the shower. As the boys ate, a couple of raindrops sprinkled, but not enough to stop them from roasting marshmallows for dessert.

"Oh, crap!" Nelson leaped up from the picnic table. "I totally forgot. You guys want some rum?" He ran to the trunk of the car and dug out a bottle.

"You never said you were bringing that," Kyle complained as Nelson opened the fifth.

"Can I have some?" Jason's eyes widened eagerly. "How'd you get it?"

"Paid some homeless dude." Nelson poured a generous shot into Jason's Coke can. "Want some?" he asked Kyle.

"No! I don't think they allow alcohol in the campground. Why'd you bring that?"

"Just have some, Kyle. It'll help you chillax." He tried to pour some into Kyle's Coke, but Kyle pulled his can away. "I told you, no! I wish you hadn't brought that."

But Nelson was glad he did. He loved the sense of acceptance drinking gave him. It helped him relax, made him feel like he belonged, and allowed him to say things he otherwise wouldn't. By the time he'd finished his first drink, he was admitting to Jason, "I was so jealous when you and Kyle first started going out."

And by the end of his second drink Nelson told Jason, "Dude, you've got such an awesome body."

Beneath the picnic table his foot accidentally bumped into Jason's, and Nelson let it stay there.

"I think you've had enough to drink," Kyle told him. "Come on, Jason. Let's get ready for bed."

Kyle stood up and Nelson realized it hadn't been Jason's foot he was stroking. It was Kyle's. Oops.

Nelson didn't feel like going to bed yet, but he didn't want to stay outside by himself either. Besides, it was starting to rain, so he went with Kyle and Jason to brush his teeth, merrily singing "Three Blind Mice" as he trailed along.

When they returned, Nelson climbed into the tent first.

"Excuse me," Kyle said as he and Jason crawled in after him. "Could you please move over to one side, so I can sleep next to my boyfriend?"

"But I wanted to be the sandwich," Nelson protested, giggling. He moved his sleeping bag over and all three boys began to peel off their clothes.

Kyle remained in shorts and T-shirt, Jason stripped to his boxers, and Nelson started to tug off his own underwear.

"I knew you'd try that." Kyle grabbed Nelson's wrist. "Don't even think about it."

"Kyle! You know I always sleep nude. It's roasting in here. Jason doesn't mind. Do you?"

"You're drunk," Jason said, and rolled over.

"Let go of my wrist," Nelson told Kyle, shaking him off.

"You're being a jerk," Kyle replied. "Now would you keep your shorts on?"

"Yes, Mommy," Nelson agreed and laid down.

Kyle switched off the battery lamp. Across the darkness, Nelson heard him kiss Jason.

"Go ahead," Nelson told them. "Don't mind me. I'll just lay quiet over here by myself."

He punched his pillow, unable to get comfortable, but the patter of rain and the rum in his brain put him to sleep within seconds.

# jason

# kyle

# nelson

Kyle refused to let Nelson's drunken craziness ruin his first night together with the boy of his dreams. He'd waited way too long for this moment. He wrapped his arms around Jason, something he yearned to repeat every night for the rest of his life, and breathed in his musky athletic scent.

His entire body ached to do more than merely hold Jason—but no way with nosy Nelson there. Instead Kyle contented himself with whispering into Jason's ear, "I love you."

"Back at you," Jason responded and turned to kiss Kyle, his breath still tasting faintly of alcohol.

That worried Kyle. What if Jason turned out to be an alcoholic like his dad? Kyle had heard the disease ran in families. And he knew how violent and abusive Jason's dad had been. What if Jason became like that?

Kyle hugged Jason tighter, trying to quell the troubling

thoughts, and Jason gripped Kyle's arm around his chest, reassuring him. The fact was Jason hadn't gotten drunk, or violent, or abusive tonight. He lay gently beside Kyle, the quiet thumping of his heart guiding Kyle to peaceful sleep amid the patter of raindrops.

Sometime later in the night, the rain subsided. In the ensuing calm, Kyle learned something new and unexpected about the boy he loved: Jason snored. Very. Loud. In fact, so thunderously loud that at first Kyle thought surely Jason must be awake and kidding around. But Jason gave no sign of joking. He lay on his back sound asleep.

Kyle's dreams about spending every night of his future life together with Jason had failed to include this detail. And he felt clueless as to what to do about it.

On the other side of Kyle, Nelson tossed and rolled in his sleeping bag. Finally he groaned, "Kyle!"

Even though Kyle clearly heard him, he lay silent, feigning sleep, while Jason rumbled and wheezed.

"Kyle!" Nelson insisted, his hand landing on Kyle's shoulder, shaking him. "I know you're awake. No one could sleep through that racket, so stop pretending."

"What do you expect me to do about it?" Kyle whispered. "It's probably 'cause of your rum."

"Do *something*!" Nelson brought his hands to his ears. "My head feels like a truck is roaring though it. How can anyone sleep like that? Shake him awake."

"I'm not going to wake him."

Even though Kyle said it in a whisper, Jason's cacophony abruptly stopped as he raised his head toward Kyle and Nelson. "Wha's up?"

"Nothing." Kyle gently patted his arm, not wanting Jason to

**rainbow road**

feel bad for waking them. But Nelson sat up and shouted, "You're snoring! Like, really, *really* loud."

"Oh," Jason mumbled. As if he'd been through this before, he rolled face down onto his stomach and returned to sleep.

Kyle waited, and he could tell that Nelson was listening too. But Jason's snoring was now replaced by soft rhythmic breathing.

"Thank God!" Nelson exclaimed. "He'd better not do that the whole trip."

Kyle's annoyance at Nelson returned, but, too exhausted to pursue it, he drifted once again to sleep till awakened by Nelson newly complaining, "Now what the hell is *that* noise?"

Kyle blinked his eyes open. Morning sunlight streamed through the mesh tent door, piercing the fog of Kyle's sleepy brain, as he tried to identify the pounding outside.

"Basketball," he told Nelson and sat up, putting on his glasses to peer out the door.

Kyle watched as Jason dribbled up and down the court, dodging sunlit pools of rainwater, his tanned skin glowing in the early morning sun.

"Do you ever have days," Nelson muttered, "when you wake up and just want to kill someone?"

Kyle ignored him and climbed from the tent, gazing admiringly at Jason's leaps and sprints. "Good morning!" He waved happily as he walked past Jason to the bathhouse to wash up and put his contacts in.

When he returned, Nelson was crawling out from the tent, scowling and pulling the hood of his pocketed red sweatshirt over his head. Grumbling something about murder, he pulled his cell phone out from the car charger and started toward the bathhouse.

"Hey, sorry about my snoring," Jason shouted as he dribbled

across the court. "At basketball camp my roomie mentioned it. You just have to tell me to roll over."

"Whatever." Nelson waved his hand, dismissing the apology.

"Hey, you want to shoot a few with me?" Jason asked.

Nelson stopped, put his hands on his hips, and glared from beneath his sweatshirt hood at Jason. "I do *not* play basketball."

"That's okay, I'll teach you." Jason gave an encouraging smile. "Hey, Kyle! Tell Nelson how I taught you to shoot!"

Kyle recalled how Jason had taught him to pitch crumpled scratch paper perfectly into the wastebasket, while Kyle helped Jason study math. It had been a step in their friendship.

Apparently, however, it wasn't going to be a part of Nelson's friendship. "Forget it!" he told Jason and started once more toward the bathhouse.

Jason watched him traipse away, then gave a shrug and tossed a perfect swoosh.

Kyle walked to the camp store, bought some milk and bananas, and returned to their site to prepare cereal. Beside the wooden picnic table he found the rum bottle from last night, still three-quarters full. An instant later he was pouring it out, watering a pine tree.

"What are you doing?" Jason asked, walking up from the court.

"I didn't come on this trip to watch Nelson get drunk every night." He tossed the empty bottle into the trash can. "Want some cereal?"

Kyle prepared them each a heaping bowl and said to Jason, "Can I ask. . . . How can you drink after everything that happened with your dad?"

He hoped Jason would respond with something like: *I'm sorry, Kyle. I can tell it worries you. I won't do it again.*

But instead Jason chomped hungrily on his Wheaties. "I'm not a drunk," he said simply. "I know when to stop."

"But I've heard," Kyle insisted, "that alcoholism runs in families."

Jason rested his spoon and gave Kyle a cold stare across the table. "I'm not my dad, okay?"

Kyle nodded and said softly, "Okay."

Nelson returned on the path from the bathhouse, carrying his toiletry kit in one hand while finishing a cigarette with the other.

"Want some cereal?" Kyle asked.

"God, no! I feel like a vulture is tearing out my stomach."

He raised the trash can lid to stub out his cigarette butt. "Hey, what's my rum—?" He pulled out the empty bottle and stared through the glass, obviously bewildered.

Kyle braced himself on the picnic table. "I poured it out."

Nelson stared at him openmouthed. "Do you know how much trouble I went through for this? It wasn't yours to throw out. Why'd you do that?"

Kyle's neck grew warm. "Because I'm not going to have you getting drunk every night."

"I wasn't drunk."

"Yeah, you were. You should've told me you were bringing alcohol so we could discuss it."

"And *you*"—Nelson tossed the bottle back into the trash can—"should've told me before you poured my rum out." He slammed the metal lid down. "I can't believe you. That is *so* controlling!"

Kyle bit into his lip, suddenly unsure. What had prompted him to throw out something that wasn't his? He'd never acted that way before. But then he'd never watched his best friend get drunk and put the make on his boyfriend, either.

As Nelson stormed toward the car, fuming and cursing, Kyle glanced at Jason, looking for help. But Jason merely shrugged. "Once my mom poured every bottle of my dad's booze down the toilet. And you know what? It didn't solve anything."

Kyle gazed across the table at the boy he'd spent the night holding in his arms. So what if Nelson had tried to put the make on him? Hadn't Jason quite plainly rebuffed his advances? And wasn't the whole notion of Nelson actually being able to score with Jason kind of ridiculous?

Kyle stirred his spoon in his soggy bowl of cereal, feeling pretty foolish.

# jason

# kyle

# nelson

Jason took down their tent while Kyle apologized to Nelson for pouring out his rum. "I'm sorry, okay?"

Jason had thought Kyle was acting crazy dumping out the booze, but the whole evening before had been crazy, with Nelson telling him he had an awesome body and wanting to get naked.

"Here." Jason handed Nelson a Coke as they packed up the car. "It'll help settle your stomach."

"Thanks," Nelson grumbled. "You want to drive? I'm too wiped." He tossed Jason the keys. "Just don't crash it, okay?"

As they climbed into the car, Jason bumped his knees on the steering column and had to slide the seat back to adjust for the height difference. He stood about half a foot taller than Nelson. Kyle hopped in front beside him, while Nelson climbed in back.

Jason liked being behind the wheel. He enjoyed driving and wished he had his own car. After adjusting the mirrors, he

pulled out of the campsite. As he drove past the basketball court, he glanced at Nelson in the rearview. "Hey, why wouldn't you shoot hoops with me?"

"I told you," Nelson snapped. "I don't play."

"But why not?"

"You really want to know?"

"Yeah." Jason nodded.

"Because it reminds me how much I hate ignoranus jocks."

Kyle shifted in his seat. "It's igno*ramus,* not ignoranus."

"No," Nelson insisted. "I mean igno*ranus.* They're not only ignorant, they're also assholes."

Jason felt his body tense. Was Nelson sideswiping him?

"All through school," Nelson continued, "whenever teams got chosen for some stupid game, I was always, always, always picked last. The jocks would say, 'I don't want him. You take him. He plays like a girl.' And after someone finally *had* to take me, they called me homo and faggot the entire game. And do you think any teachers ever stood up for me?" He smirked into the rearview at Jason. "I've got so *many* cheery memories of sports. Does that answer your question?"

"Yeah," Jason said quietly.

"I'm going to sleep," Nelson announced, laying down in the backseat. "Wake me when we get somewhere."

As they pulled onto I-81, Jason thought about what Nelson had said. He felt a little guilty recalling the many times in his own gym classes when he'd been elected team captain and picked teams. Naturally, he'd dreaded picking the Nelson-types. After all, wasn't the object of the game to win? Who wanted someone on the team who'd only help them lose? Jason remembered the name-calling, but didn't every boy get called names? Even he had. In his case it had made him work harder to prove he wasn't

gay. Now as he looked back, it all seemed so confusing.

"You okay?" Kyle asked from across the car seat.

"Yeah," Jason replied. He laid his palm next to Kyle and Kyle rested his own hand in it. As he tenderly stroked Kyle's fingers, Jason breathed a sigh of relief. Thank God high school was over.

A couple of hours later they approached the Tennessee border. Nelson sat up, wiping his eyes. "Where are we?" He yawned.

"About to cross into Tennessee."

"Woo-hoo!" Nelson reached forward across Jason and tooted the horn as they crossed the state line. Then he started searching the backseat. "Hey, do you guys see my cell phone up there?"

"No," Kyle replied. "Where did you put it?"

"I'm not sure." Nelson's brow furrowed. "This morning I took it to the bathhouse and called my mom. . . ."

"Did you bring it back?" Kyle asked.

"Oh my God!" Nelson pressed a hand to his forehead. "I think it's in the pocket of my sweatshirt. I must've left it hanging on the toilet stall door."

"Nelson!" Kyle exclaimed. "Are you sure?"

"Yes! I feel so stupid." Nelson banged his head against the back of Kyle's seat. "I can't believe I did that."

Jason glowered into the rearview at Nelson. "Dude, we've driven two hours already."

"Crap," Nelson muttered, shaking a cigarette from his pack.

"Well," Kyle grumbled. "We've got to go back for it."

Jason flicked the blinker on and turned around at the next exit, no longer feeling so guilty for the times he hadn't picked any pain-in-the-ass Nelsons for his teams.

During the return drive Nelson kept amazingly quiet in the backseat, probably because he realized Jason and Kyle

**jason**     nelson     kyle                                63

were too annoyed to talk to him. Two wasted hours later, they arrived at the campground.

Jason parked beside the bathhouse and Nelson raced inside. A moment later he returned empty-handed. No red sweatshirt. No phone. Only a peeved look on his face.

"Someone must've taken it. They're probably having a long-distance free-for-all."

"Let's ask at the office," Kyle suggested. "Maybe someone turned it in."

But at the registration desk, no one had turned in a red hooded sweatshirt or a cell phone.

"Are you sure that's where you left it?" Jason asked.

"You know," Kyle said, "we should check the trunk."

Jason opened the trunk. In a corner, wedged between Nelson's sleeping bag and duffle, was his sweatshirt, and inside the pocket, his cell.

Nelson clenched his teeth into a false grin. "Oops."

Jason gritted his teeth in turn. "That'll be four hours we wasted."

"Sorry?" Nelson whispered, slinking into the backseat. Once again Jason pulled out of the campground.

In order not to waste any more time, they opted for a McDonald's drive-through for lunch. Then they continued down I-81 to I-40, past fireworks stands, stores selling coon-skin caps, and mountains blanketed with kudzu.

Kyle read a book called *On the Road* by Jack Kerouac while Jason played CDs he'd brought (mostly hip-hop) and let his mind wander. That was part of what he loved about highway driving: letting his mind run free as the countryside drifted past.

A lot of Jason's thoughts focused on Kyle. It felt great to be with him and sleep beside him, though Jason wished he could've done more than just lie with his arm around him. They'd better

**rainbow road**

find some way to be alone together during this trip or the sexual tension was going to drive him crazy.

Their goal for that evening was some weird mountain place that Nelson had insisted on during the final days of plotting their route.

"I e-mailed them and they said we could camp for just ten bucks," he'd told Kyle and Jason. "It's like a sanctuary for gay and lesbian people."

Jason didn't know what Nelson meant by "sanctuary," but it sounded weird.

They would've made it there well before dusk, if not for Nelson's cell-phone-in-trunk delay. Instead they were still an hour away when it started getting dark. As Jason turned on the car lights, he glanced down at the gas gauge and realized he hadn't been paying attention. It was nearly at *E.*

He immediately began watching for a green exit sign. Fortunately, one soon appeared on the horizon and Jason flicked his blinker on.

"Where are you going?" Kyle asked, closing his book.

"We need gas." Jason slowed to a stop as they reached the end of the exit ramp, where a two-lane road stretched toward hills in both directions.

"I don't see any station," Nelson said. "Maybe we should try the next exit. Aren't we almost near the sanctuary turnoff?"

"We don't have enough gas," Jason informed them.

Kyle looked over his shoulder at the gauge. "It's empty."

"That's what I said," Jason told him. "That's why we need to look for a station."

"But there's nothing out here," Nelson complained, lighting up a cigarette.

Jason glared at him and rolled down his window, turning

left onto the narrow road. "There's got to be one nearby."

They drove past tobacco fields and trailers, rusting cars and winding creeks, but found no gas station. Meanwhile, the sky grew darker as night fell.

"Jason?" Kyle rested a hand on his shoulder. "I think we should go back to the highway."

Jason glanced down at the gas gauge, now well below the *E* mark. "I don't think we have enough gas."

"Well, there's plenty of gas out here," Nelson said sarcastically.

Around the next bend, the headlights illuminated an old bearded man standing beside a roadside mailbox, holding what looked like a shotgun.

"Jason?" Kyle squeezed his shoulder more insistently. "Can we go back? *Please?*"

"Oh my God!" Nelson said, exhaling a stream of smoke. "I saw a movie like this once, where people lay on the road and when you stopped to help them, they got up and ate you."

Jason grimaced into the rearview and noticed a pair of headlights approaching from behind.

"Oh my God!" Nelson exclaimed again, turning to follow Jason's gaze. "It's a pickup truck. What if they're rednecks? Or zombies?"

"Would you shut up?" Jason said as the truck loomed closer and began blaring its horn.

"You'd better let them pass," Kyle urged.

Jason gripped the steering wheel. "They've got room."

"Then why are they beeping at us?" Nelson asked as the truck drew nearer.

"Probably," Jason snapped, "because of your stupid rainbow flag."

"Jason, can you just pull over?" Kyle insisted. "*Please?*"

"You crazy?" Jason argued. "I'm not stopping."

But as he spoke, the car coughed and sputtered. The gas pedal gave out beneath his foot, and he had no choice but to turn the wheel toward the road shoulder. "That's it. We're out of gas."

The car bounced and coasted to a stop, the pickup pulling up behind them.

Nelson stared out the back window at the headlights. "Oh my God!" he screamed and grinned. "We're all going to die! We're going to die!"

"That's not funny," Kyle told him. "Lock your doors."

But Jason popped open his lock. "I'll handle this."

"No, don't!" Kyle reached for his arm but Jason stepped outside. Nelson climbed out after him.

Jason shielded his eyes from the headlight beams and braced himself for a confrontation. But as two figures emerged from the truck cab into the headlights, Jason tried to make sense of what he saw.

One guy looked to be in his early twenties. He was tall, good-looking, with a brown goatee, and . . . were those goat horns sticking out of his head? He reminded Jason of some mythological goat boy, with a pelt skirt, leather sandals, and a panpipe dangling from his neck.

The guy smiling beside him was equally young, but shorter, a little plump, and . . . dressed as a bug? Wire antennae with Styrofoam balls at the ends were sticking out of his head. He wore black polka-dot boxers with combat boots and a T-shirt that read: QUEEN OF THE UNIVERSE.

*This is totally bizarre,* Jason thought. Who the heck were these freaks? And what were they doing out here?

"We saw your rainbow flag," Goat Guy said, and Bug Dude smiled even wider. "You guys headed to the sanctuary?"

# chapter 15

# jason            kyle

# nelson

Nelson had first learned about the Radical Faerie sanctuary while surfing the Web one weekend. He immediately felt drawn to the images of guys living in the forest and wearing zany outfits: cheerleader skirts and military boots, women's wigs and cowboy chaps, or . . . barely anything at all.

And he identified with one description of the loosely knit group: "an anti-mainstream radical fringe of free-spirited queers." How like Nelson was *that*?

"You must be Faeries!" he now yelled excitedly at the guys who'd emerged from the pickup truck along this backwoods road.

"Yeah." The really cute one in the pelt gave Nelson a sexy smile. "This is Lady-Bugger and I'm Horn-Boy." He raised the panpipe dangling from his neck and blew a few notes while Lady-Bugger danced in the headlight beams, his cape flaring behind him.

The Faerie guys seemed exactly like Nelson had fantasized: crazy, wild, and cute. Lady-Bugger reached his arm out to swing Nelson, and he gladly joined in. "Hey, I'm Nelson and this is . . ."

He turned to see Jason staring warily, like the proverbial deer frozen in headlights. "This is Jason. We ran out of gas. Are you guys from the sanctuary?"

"Yeah, that's where we're headed," Horn-Boy said, ending his panpipe tune. "We've got gas. Out here we always carry a full can in the truck."

"Oh look, there's a third one!" Lady-Bugger waved and called "Yoo-hoo!" as Kyle emerged from the car, stepping up behind Jason.

"This is Kyle," Nelson said, and told Kyle, "These guys are from the sanctuary."

"Um, hi." Kyle extended his hand a little nervously.

*Why is he nervous?* Nelson wondered. These guys were awesome, especially supercute Horn-Boy.

After shaking hands with Kyle, the two Faeries searched the truck for the gas can.

Jason pulled Nelson over into a huddle with him and Kyle.

"Dude," he whispered to Nelson. "These guys are freaks. I'm not going to that place."

Kyle nodded in agreement. "Maybe we should go on to Nashville instead."

"They're not freaks," Nelson whispered back. "They're just gay people like us."

Jason rolled his eyes. "Like *you*, maybe. I'm not going with them."

"Here you are." Horn-Boy brought the gas can to Jason.

While they poured it in, Nelson pulled Kyle aside. "Would you chill your boyfriend, please? I want to see this place."

Kyle glanced over at Lady-Bugger flapping his cape mothlike in front of the headlights. "Are you sure these guys are safe?"

"Kyle, they're *Faeries*. What's the worst that can happen? They tie us up and perm our hair?"

Kyle didn't laugh. His eyes shifted among Horn-Boy, Lady-Bugger, Jason, and back to Nelson before he finally said, "Okay, I'll talk to him."

Nelson decided not to take any chances. When Jason finished pouring the gas and Horn-Boy said, "So, are you guys going to follow us?" Nelson told him, "Yeah, but can I ride with you?"

"Dude!" Jason hissed, but Nelson was already climbing into the truck cab, telling Horn-Boy, "Those horns are so cool."

He took a seat between the two guys and watched to make sure Kyle and Jason followed behind. As the pickup rolled down moonlit valleys and wound around blue hills, Lady-Bugger and Horn-Boy explained how Faeries existed all over the world, some in live-in communities like the sanctuary. Nelson listened eagerly, imagining a place where no one hassled you for being crazily queer, a place where you could be totally yourself.

After a while Lady-Bugger turned down a dirt road. Each time the truck bounced, Horn-Boy's leg gently bumped Nelson's knee and Nelson let it stay there. The touch was the biggest thrill Nelson had gotten since Jeremy. In fact, Horn-Boy's little goatee reminded him of Jeremy's and how the hairs had tickled when they kissed.

"So . . . like . . . are you two a couple?" Nelson asked.

Horn-Boy and Lady-Bugger gazed across Nelson at each other. Then Lady-Bugger winked at Nelson. "Mostly."

Horn-Boy followed with a mischievous grin, which looked even more impish with the horns atop his head. "We have an open relationship."

"Wow," Nelson said. He realized he sounded like a kid, but he'd never met anyone in an open relationship.

A lantern appeared on the dark road ahead of them, illuminating someone in white face paint and a shimmering red kimono. The figure gave a silent bow, welcoming them into a parking area, and Lady-Bugger explained, "That's Yoko Kim-Ono."

Jason parked Nelson's car alongside the truck, while Nelson climbed from the cab to see a half-dozen guys, ranging in age from late teens to sixties, giggling and chattering.

"Well, hey, cuties," said one in a pink miniskirt and cowboy boots.

"Welcome to Faerie Land," said another in overalls and high heels.

Nelson's skin tingled as if electrified. Ever since he was little, he'd loved to dress up, whether as a pirate, a sheik, or in his mom's gowns and heels.

"Isn't this place great?" He spun around excitedly to Kyle and Jason, only to find them pressed so nervously together they almost looked like conjoined twins.

"You guys want to find something to wear?" Horn-Boy asked, and led the boys past log cabin homes to a barn filled with dresses, skirts, and shoes. While Kyle and Jason watched, Horn-Boy held a black leather vest up to Nelson. "Take your shirt off and try this on."

Nelson hesitated to remove his shirt, confiding in a small voice, "My chest is too skinny."

"Naw!" Horn-Boy winked and smiled. "Skinny guys are cute." He persuaded Nelson and pulled him in front of a mirror. "See? You look great. Now how about a skirt?"

Nelson picked out a red pleated plaid skirt, monogrammed IMMACULATE CONCEPTION GIRLS' SCHOOL, while Jason rolled his

eyes, crossed his arms, and mumbled something in Kyle's ear.

"Stop being such goobers," Nelson scolded them. "Have some fun! Pick something out."

He convinced Kyle to wear a ruffled blue tuxedo shirt ("Very sexy!") but couldn't budge Jason into anything, not even a little white sailor's cap that would've looked adorable on his dark curly hair.

"You guys hungry?" Horn-Boy asked, casually taking Nelson's hand. "Let's go eat."

That marked the first time a guy had held Nelson's hand since Jeremy, though he tried not to show it. He didn't want to seem too eager. Besides, he wasn't quite sure how he felt about the "open relationship" thing.

Horn-Boy guided them to a clapboard house emanating music, with a sign on the door: WORK-FREE DRUG PLACE.

Inside, the rooms glowed in candlelight. Faerie shadows danced across the walls, cast by a crowd of uniquely dressed guys and women. Jason's eyes grew wide, as if in disbelief, whereas Kyle looked more curious.

At a buffet heaped with bowls of roasted tofu, summer squash, apple-raisin salad, and grapes, the boys piled their plates. Then Horn-Boy led them to a table where a bald guy wearing a bone through his nose introduced himself: "Hey, I'm Sonny Bone-Nose." And a bearded man in a nun's habit said, "I'm Sister Missionary Position."

Kyle moved his food around his plate and asked, "Um, so, like, can you tell us more about the Faeries?"

"Well," the bearded nun explained, "the group started with Harry Hay."

"The Harry Hay School!" Jason abruptly broke in. "That's the name of the school where I'm speaking in L.A.!"

**rainbow road**

"Harry pioneered the gay movement," Bone-Nose elaborated. "He believed that we as gay people see life through a different window. That's why the mainstream is scared of us."

Jason nodded as if trying to understand. It made Nelson feel glad for insisting on coming here.

After dinner and cleanup, the boys joined about a dozen Faeries on the rug of the living room for something called a "Heart Circle."

"Someone starts the circle," Horn-Boy explained, "by raising the talking stick."

In the center of the room lay a foot-long knobby piece of wood, worn smooth and dangling with multicolored beads and feathers.

"When the stick comes around, you either pass or speak about what's in your heart."

As the stick began going around, individuals talked about all sorts of life stuff. A guy with a Mohawk was scared because his sister had been diagnosed with breast cancer. A woman in a football jersey felt hurt because her girlfriend had moved back in with her parents. And an old white-haired guy was excited about going to trapeze school.

Nelson listened in amazement as people spoke so openly about their sorrows, dreams, and joys. When the stick reached him, Nelson rubbed his fingers along the smooth wood. "I think you guys are awesome," he told the group. "It's like *The Wizard of Oz* when you suddenly go from black-and-white to Technicolor. I haven't felt this excited since Madonna kissed Britney."

The crowd laughed and Nelson passed the stick to Kyle. "Um . . ." Kyle said. "Thanks for letting us stay with you." He passed the stick to Jason, who merely said, "Ditto. Thanks," and quickly passed it on.

When the circle ended, Horn-Boy helped the boys unpack the car. He guided them by flashlight to a meadow behind the cluster of houses and helped them set up their tent. "You'll have a glorious view of the valley in the morning." As he spoke, a drum began beating in the distance, quickly followed by another.

"The fire circle's starting. You guys want to come?"

"Of course!" Nelson said. He didn't want to miss anything.

But Jason complained, "We should go to sleep."

Kyle grabbed his hand. "Come on! I'd like to see it too."

Once again Horn-Boy took Nelson's hand, and Nelson wondered what had happened to Lady-Bugger. Was their relationship so open they parted ways that easily? Nelson appreciated how Horn-Boy had looked after them all evening and he definitely got Nelson horny, but Nelson couldn't help worrying. Didn't Lady-Bugger feel jealous and left out?

Horn-Boy led them along a forest path toward the slowly beating drums. Ahead in the darkness, Nelson began to make out silhouettes of men and women gathered around the flames of a blazing fire, like a primal tribe—some drumming, some swaying, some sitting on boulders.

As the boys stepped into a circle of several dozen Faeries, Nelson exclaimed, "This is so cool!"

"You mean weird," Jason muttered.

A young woman welcomed them. "Hi. I'm Voluptuous Clorox. Want to sit?"

She was conspicuously topless, except for a silver ring on her left boob. Nelson tended to get woozy at the sight of female breasts, but not Jason.

"Thanks!" Jason told the girl, suddenly more enthused than he'd been all evening.

**rainbow road**

As they sat beside her, Kyle whispered to Nelson, "What's that burnt smell?"

Nelson spotted a marijuana joint being passed around the circle. He'd tried pot before and liked how it made him laugh. It also made him even hornier, if such a thing was possible.

But when Horn-Boy passed Nelson the joint, Kyle nudged him in the ribs. "Don't! I think it's marijuana!"

"I hope so," Nelson replied, taking the reefer.

"Nelson!" Kyle reached out, trying to block him.

"Kyle, you're not my mom!" Nelson pulled away. "Stop acting like her."

He inhaled a toke. The smoke irritated his throat, but he held his breath anyway. His lungs burned like fire till he finally exhaled, trying not to cough.

Kyle shook his head in disapproval and passed the joint at arm's length past Jason, who was more preoccupied with seeing bare-breasted girls than with smoking weed.

Nelson's brain began tingling. After taking a couple of more hits off the circling reefer, he turned to Horn-Boy and burst out in uncontrollable giggles. The horns on his head suddenly looked so funny—and sexy. *Really* sexy. And all of a sudden Horn-Boy's relationship with Lady-Bugger seemed irrelevant.

"Hey." Nelson raised his hand, fondling the horns and giggling. "You want to go walk in the woods?"

"Sure." Horn-Boy grinned, standing up in his pelt.

"We're going with you," Kyle announced, yanking Jason away from Bare Boobs Girl.

The sight of it sent Nelson howling with laughter, till he finally calmed down enough to ask Kyle, "Why are you following us?"

"Dude, because you're totally stoned," Jason told him.

"You are both so controlling!" Nelson protested, but he couldn't stop laughing. He wrapped his arms around Kyle and whispered, "I'm so wicked horny." He gestured toward Horn-Boy. "And he is *so* cute."

Kyle leaned into Nelson's ear. "Don't! You'll end up doing something unsafe."

"Oh, Kyle! You're worse than my freaking mother!"

"Guys?" Horn-Boy stepped between them. "I'm going back to the fire."

"Don't go!" Nelson begged, and then cracked up again as he watched Horn-Boy stride away. "Kyle? Why are you ruining my life? You and Jason have each other. I don't have anyone!" He collapsed onto the dewy ground, wanting to cry but instead giggling. "All I want is what you have. Why won't you let me?"

Kyle sat beside him, wrapping an arm around his shoulder. "You're stoned. I don't want you to get hurt."

Nelson gazed up into Kyle's eyes, wanting more than anything to kiss those cute thin lips. But he wasn't so stoned as to have forgotten the time he'd tried kissing Kyle and gotten shoved away.

"I'm going back to the fire," Nelson now announced, pushing himself off the ground.

And Kyle followed him, with Jason in tow.

# kyle

# jason

# nelson

Kyle watched Nelson strip off his vest, toss it to the ground, and join the line of half-naked dancers circling the fire to the frenzied drumbeat.

For Kyle this whole Faerie experience seemed both over-the-top fascinating and also a little overwhelming—like coming upon a whole tribe of Nelsons. He'd always admired his best friend's outrageous individuality, but he never imagined an entire community like him.

Adding to Kyle's sense of being overwhelmed was the sight of female breasts for the first time in his life—live and in person.

Any doubts he'd ever had about his gayness were immediately dispelled as the bare boobs jiggled past, only inches away. Reflexively, he turned away. Yep, he was gay. No doubt about it.

In contrast, Jason grinned a full show of pearly whites each time a pair of girl-boobs paraded by, causing Kyle to squirm

nervously beside him. His boyfriend's sexual feelings toward girls had always been a source of confusion for Kyle. And after picking Nelson's vest off the ground, dusting it off, and folding it neatly on his lap, Kyle held tight to Jason as they waited for Nelson to tire out.

Around midnight the drumming reached a fever pitch. A guy with deer antlers strapped to his head, wearing only a bearskin cape and high-tops, leaped over the fire. Several young men in camouflage pants with ferns growing out of their pockets howled at the moon. And Voluptuous Clorox whirled bosomy circles around the flames.

Following that, the drumming and dancing waned as Faeries drifted off into the woods toward their houses.

"It's time for bed," Kyle told Nelson.

"But where's Horn-Boy?" Nelson asked.

"Forget him, dude," Jason said. "Let's go to sleep."

They stopped for water at the main house, then the three of them climbed inside their tent and crashed, exhausted.

A couple of times during the night, Kyle had to nudge Jason to roll over to stop his snoring. But other than that, he slept peacefully, his arms encircling the boy he loved.

And that's how he woke the next morning, watching the dawn's soft light slowly illuminate Jason's face. As birds cooed their morning songs, Kyle's entire being yearned to make morning love. But unfortunately that wasn't going to happen today, with Nelson there.

Kyle sat up and put on his glasses. Gazing out the door, he saw that their tent overlooked a seemingly endless valley, flanked by layer after layer of mountains. When Jason stirred behind him, Kyle whispered, "Look! That's like our life, stretching into the future."

**rainbow road**

"Huh?" Jason sat up, rubbing the sleep from his eyes. "That's pretty." He scratched his chest and pecked Kyle a kiss. "Hey, I wonder . . . You think maybe they've got a court here?"

They left Nelson sleeping and walked toward the houses. Along the way they came across a guy in an orange miniskirt chopping wood. Jason asked, "You guys got a hoop around here?"

Miniskirt Guy gave Jason a blank look. "You mean, like, for basketball?" He shook his head. "Nah."

"How can these guys not have a hoop?" Jason asked Kyle as they ambled on toward the bathhouse. After they showered and washed up, they continued on to the main house.

Breakfast consisted of yogurt, raisins, pomegranate juice, and applesauce pancakes made by Voluptuous Clorox, who—to Kyle's relief—now wore a tie-dyed T-shirt.

After Jason and he had eaten, Kyle carried a covered plate of pancakes and some juice back to the tent for Nelson, hoping to rouse him. But Nelson wouldn't budge.

"I'm not waiting for him," Jason complained. He unzipped Nelson's sleeping bag, grabbed his ankles, and dragged him out of the tent.

"What the hell!" Nelson woke up kicking and screaming. "Leave me alone!"

"Get your lazy butt up!" Jason dropped his ankles onto the ground. "I'm not waiting around for you every morning."

"Screw you!" Nelson shouted, pulling himself up.

"In your dreams." Jason grinned.

"No, in my nightmares," Nelson shot back.

To calm him down, Kyle handed Nelson the pancakes and juice. While Nelson sat beneath a tree to eat, Kyle rolled up their sleeping bags. Jason folded up the tent and disassembled the poles.

Then Nelson cleaned up at the bathhouse and they carried their stuff to the car. Jason asked him, "You sure this time you have your cell?"

Nelson quickly checked his pockets before grumbling, "Yeah."

As they finished loading the car, Horn-Boy walked up, hornless now. He looked almost normal in jeans and a tank top—except for the daisy behind his ear.

"Hey, good morning." He gently handed the daisy to Nelson. "How far are you guys going today?"

"Memphis," Kyle replied. "Can you tell us where's the nearest gas station?"

Horn-Boy gave them directions and explained how to get back to the interstate.

"Okay. Thanks, man," Jason shook Horn-Boy's hand.

"Yeah, thanks," Kyle shook hands too and followed Jason into the car, leaving Nelson to say good-bye privately. Yet Kyle and Jason couldn't help watching in the rearview as Horn-Boy rested his hand on Nelson's chest.

"What's he doing that for?" Jason asked.

"I don't know. He's saying something."

They both watched, curious, as Horn-Boy left his hand on Nelson's chest a moment before removing it. Then Nelson grinned and wrapped his arms around Horn-Boy, and they kissed . . . and kissed . . . till Jason punched the horn and shouted out the window, "We don't have all day!"

Nelson held up his middle finger at Jason, kissed Horn-Boy one last time, and climbed into the backseat of the car.

As they waved good-bye and began bouncing down the dirt entrance road, Kyle asked, "What was he doing with his hand?"

"He was praying for my heart." Nelson gave a wistful smile.

**rainbow road**

"He wished me peace, joy, love, and lots of hot, groovy sex!" Bringing the daisy to his nose, Nelson gazed out the rear window. "That place was so freaking amazing!"

"Weird," Jason corrected.

"No!" Nelson countered. "It's the rest of the world that's weird. Why shouldn't you be able to dress how you want, act how you want, and love who you want? If you're so straight-acting, then why don't you have the guts to just let yourself go and be who you are?"

Jason was quiet after that and Kyle said, "The place was definitely interesting."

At the gas station Jason filled up the tank and Kyle went inside to pay. Behind the register sat a woman with a long, thin face, pulled-back hair, and a gray T-shirt. Though she smiled a little, she seemed so plain compared with the people at the sanctuary. Kyle recalled Nelson's comment from the night before about *The Wizard of Oz* and Technicolor. It now felt like they'd stepped back into black-and-white.

An hour later they arrived in Nashville to see the sights. As they drove through downtown, Nelson stuck his head out the window, pink hair waving in the wind, shouting "Woo-hoo! Nashville!" as people on the sidewalk stared.

Kyle squirmed, but he knew there was no stopping Nelson.

"I want to go to the Grand Ole Opry first," Nelson announced as they parked the car. He'd been on a country music kick ever since Jeremy had taught him to two-step.

"You guys go," Jason said, grabbing his basketball. "I want to find a court."

Kyle suddenly got a hollow feeling in his stomach. "Don't you want to see the Opry and stuff? Isn't that the whole point

of this trip? To experience things together?"

"I've got to keep up my practice," Jason said, looking away. "I promised Coach."

"I know, but . . ." Kyle struggled for words, wanting to be supportive but also eager for Jason to see the sights with them.

Nevertheless, Jason insisted on finding a court. A parking lot attendant pointed him toward a school down the street. The boys agreed to meet back at the car in two hours. And Kyle watched in frustration as Jason dribbled his ball down the sidewalk.

Nelson chattered excitedly while he and Kyle toured the big red brick building that had been home to the original Grand Ole Opry, hosting performers ranging from Minnie Pearl to Patsy Cline to Bruce Springsteen. He insisted they get their souvenir picture taken on stage, paying for it himself. He grabbed the prop banjo and told Kyle, "Open your mouth like you're really singing!"

Kyle grabbed the guitar and they posed behind the stage mike while the tour attendant took their photo.

The picture came out great, except for the fact that Jason wasn't in it.

After the Opry the boys wandered along the honky-tonk shops and clubs on Broadway. Nelson took a camera phone photo of a cute cowboy playing his guitar on the sidewalk. After that he asked Kyle, "Why'd you stop me from getting laid with Horn-Boy last night?"

The question didn't surprise Kyle. He'd figured Nelson would bring it up eventually. "First of all," he explained, "because you'd just met the guy. You can't sleep with someone you just met."

"Why not? It's just sex."

"It's *not* just sex," Kyle said in a low voice, embarrassed that other tourists walking by might hear them. "It's *never* just sex. You're trusting a guy with one of the most special parts of you—and you need to know him first."

"Oh, Kyle!" Nelson swung his arm around him. "You're so old-fashioned."

"Plus," Kyle added, "you were stoned, giggling all nutty-like. First it's rum, then it's pot, what's it going to be next? Crack?"

"Yeah, boy crack." Nelson gave a sly grin. "You're over-reacting, Kyle."

"No, I'm not! Drugs screw up your judgment. You could've done something unsafe."

"I would've been safe." Nelson reached into his pocket and pulled out a condom. "See?"

"Would you put that away?" Kyle felt the color rushing into his face. "Even with a condom, he might've had some disease besides HIV. Every day the news reports some new drug-resistant STD."

"You are so controlling," Nelson groaned and shoved the condom back into his pocket. "Just like my mom. What did she tell you, anyway?"

"To look after you," Kyle answered. He was enjoying being with Nelson, just the two of them, in spite of having to chew him out—and even though he missed Jason.

He swung his arm around Nelson, and Nelson smirked. "So that means you'll decide if I get laid or not?"

"No." Kyle stopped at a DON'T WALK signal, holding Nelson back. "It means I'm not going to let you do something stupid."

Nelson darted a glance at him, then looked each way down the traffic-empty street.

"Kyle," he said at last, not bothering to keep his voice down. "I think you need to stop trying to control me. You and Jason better get laid. Soon!"

With that he stepped into the street, crossing against the signal, leaving Kyle amid the stares of the crowd.

But even though Kyle's cheeks grew hot, he remained lawfully on the curb, wondering if Nelson was right.

# jason      kyle

## nelson

As Jason had headed toward the school down the street from the boys' parked car, he'd seen in the distance a group of African-American guys playing full-court. Immediately he felt a connection, like family, and counted the number of players: five-on-five.

On the empty court beside them, Jason began the drills Coach Cameron had given him—a little self-conscious at first because of the guys on the next court, until he got into the flow of his shooting workout.

As he dribbled across the concrete, he tried to sort out his thoughts about the crazy Faeries and their sanctuary. He'd never experienced anything as wild as that before: the wacky clothes guys wore, the tribelike dancing around the fire, and the girls flaunting their boobs in his face.

That topless thing had totally crazed him. But why? Hadn't

he figured out he was gay? Then why'd he gotten so excited by bare girl titties? Kyle and Nelson obviously hadn't.

Jason began shooting free throws to calm his troubled mind. After about the tenth shot he began to feel his center, that integrity point inside his brain that Coach had taught him to identify.

"The eye in the hurricane," Coach had called it, the point where Jason could feel at peace with himself amid a stadium of cursing spectators, shouting referees, and his own conflicting inner voices.

"Hey, man!" someone abruptly called to him.

Jason turned. One of the players from the neighboring court stood watching him. "One of our guys left us short. Want to run?"

"Sure!" Jason set his ball down and joined the group.

"You're shirts," the boy told him. "Game's to eleven. Win by two."

Even though Jason knew none of these guys, he quickly felt at ease. Within seconds he'd hit his first shot and his teammates were clasping his hand. It felt great to be around *normal* guys again, who played by clear, established rules; guys who looked and acted like guys were supposed to look and act, in contrast to those wacky Faeries.

And yet Nelson's comment about having "the courage to let go and be who you are" kept nagging at him. Not wanting to think about it, Jason focused on the game at hand. And when it came time to go, he had to force himself to leave.

As he walked back to meet Kyle and Nelson, he thought what a relief it had been to take a break from 24/7 gayness. Between Nelson's finger snapping and Kyle's hand-holding, hardly a moment could pass that he wasn't reminded of it.

**rainbow road**

Like now, watching them approach, he could hear them bickering—not like most dudes his age, but almost sounding like a couple of old ladies.

He liked being with them, but . . . sometimes he felt so different from them. And yet he was different from the boys on the court, too. Would he ever feel like he fit in *anywhere*?

"How'd it go?" Kyle offered a tentative smile.

"Great." Jason smiled back. "How was the Opry?"

"Fabulous!" Nelson exclaimed. "You missed out big-time."

"I wish you'd come," Kyle told Jason. "Hey, check this out!"

Jason gazed at the photo of Kyle and Nelson on stage at the Opry. Now he wished he'd gone too. He bit his lip in regret.

Kyle must've noticed. "We can go back if you want."

"Nah." Jason shrugged. "That's okay." He handed back the photo.

"Well, you can't bag out on Graceland," Nelson told him as they started toward the car.

But Jason slowed his steps as he noticed the passenger door. Scratched into the paint, a word stood out: FAGGS!

"Assholes!" Nelson shouted at full voice. "The jerks can't even spell."

"Who would do this?" Kyle ran his fingers along the scratch. "How would they even know?"

"Probably that flag on the bumper," Jason speculated. "I told you to take it off."

"If it wasn't for that flag," Nelson pointed out, "we'd probably still be on the side of the road out of gas."

"Guys?" Kyle interjected. "There's nothing we can do about it now. Let's just go eat."

Grudgingly, Jason climbed into the car. As Nelson drove, Kyle guided them past the replica of the Greek Parthenon,

which was cool to look at from outside but cost too much to go in. A few blocks away from it, Kyle spotted a barbecue place and suggested, "Why don't we try that?"

Inside, the restaurant smelled like a hundred years' worth of wood smoke. As the gum-chewing hostess led them to their table, she stared suspiciously at Nelson's pink hair.

After they placed their order, Kyle asked Jason, "So did you find some guys to shoot with at the court?"

"Yeah." Jason nodded and sipped his water.

Nelson leaned eagerly across the table. "Were any of them cute?"

"Is that all you think about?"

Nelson put a finger to his chin as if thinking for a moment, then said, "Yeah. Were they?"

Jason set his water glass down. "I didn't notice."

But that wasn't entirely true. He had noticed a couple of the guys were good-looking, but he just hadn't given it much thought. He'd been concentrating on his game, not on hooking up. Besides, he didn't imagine any of them were gay.

In the middle of the waitress bringing their order, Nelson asked Jason, "So what's it like spending so much time with guys in the locker room? Don't you get totally horny?"

The waitress nearly dropped Jason's barbecue sandwich onto his lap. "Sorry. Anything else you need?"

*Yeah,* Jason wanted to say. *Some tape for his mouth.*

"Nelson!" Kyle hissed as the waitress walked away.

"Well, I'm curious," Nelson insisted and glanced back at Jason. "Have you ever gotten a woody in the locker room showers?"

"Dude, we're eating!" Jason chomped into his sandwich, hoping Nelson would shut up.

**rainbow road**

"So?" Nelson persisted. "How do you keep from popping a boner with all those naked guys around?"

Jason heaved a sigh and put his sandwich down. "They're my team. They're like family."

"Oh," Nelson said and bit into his sandwich, his brow furrowed in thought. "Well, I don't think that would stop me."

"Can we please change the subject?" Kyle asked. All three of them became quiet till Kyle asked Jason, "Have you thought about your speech?"

"Yeah," Jason said, but he neglected to add that every time the thought came into his head, he pushed it out again. He'd played ball and even kissed his boyfriend in front of thousands of spectators, but the thought of getting up to speak in front of total strangers stressed him too much to think about it.

He had no idea what on earth someone like him could possibly have to say at the opening of a gay and lesbian high school.

"I'll help you with it," Kyle offered. But Jason told him, "Maybe later."

And once again, he put it out of his mind.

*chapter 18*

# jason                    kyle

## nelson

Nelson lay down in the car's backseat as they left Nashville and continued west on I-40. He still felt tired from dancing around the Faerie fire the night before and wanted to take a nap so he'd arrive wide-awake to experience the full glory of Graceland. Besides, the road toward Memphis didn't have much to see: mostly a bunch of boring mountains covered with green stuff.

But as Nelson closed his eyes to sleep, Jason began reading mileage signs: "Memphis, 163 miles." Then "Memphis, 148 miles." And "Memphis, 128 miles."

"Dude!" Nelson sat up. "Could you please stop that?"

Thank God Jason shut up. When Nelson woke again, they'd reached the Memphis outskirts.

Elvis Presley Boulevard took them through a dumpy area of car washes, pawnshops, and used car lots.

"You sure this is the right way?" Nelson asked. It seemed like

a pretty sleazy neighborhood for the King to have lived in.

But amazingly enough, the Graceland Shops appeared on their right, advertising free parking. The boys pulled into a space, jumped from the car, and raced next door to the Graceland admission counter, just in time for the last tour.

They all agreed to splurge on platinum tickets, which got them into everything, beginning with the "mansion." It actually wasn't much bigger than Nelson's house, but it was definitely weirder.

For some reason, the TV room had mirrors on the ceiling. The Jungle Room had green shag carpeting on both the floor *and* ceiling. And the kitchen still smelled like bacon grease, even though it hadn't been used for thirty years.

Nelson sighed as he stared at the white fake fur bed. "Poor straight Elvis could've definitely used a queer makeover. Oh yeah. Uh-huh. Real bad."

But he thought the exhibits after the house were kind of cool, especially Elvis's collection of signature jumpsuits. "I'd kill for that gold lamé one."

"Isn't it weird," Kyle commented, "that this entire exhibit doesn't make a single mention of his drug use?"

"Kyle, stop being such a downer." Nelson strode away to look at Elvis's grave. At first he thought it was tacky how parents were taking photos of their kids in front of the gravestone, but then he decided, what the heck?

"Can you take one of me?" he asked Jason, handing him the cell phone. "I want to e-mail it to Jeremy. You want to send one of you to your mom?"

"Sure," Jason replied. Then Kyle asked a lady to take a photo of the three of them, smiling in front of dead Elvis.

Following the mansion they viewed Elvis's car collection and

airplanes. Jason thought they were the best part of the tour. Afterward they checked into the Graceland Campground. Nelson cleared some empty beer cans previous campers had left.

Kyle unpacked the tent and asked Jason, "Where are the tent poles? I can't find them."

Jason's face went blank. "They're not with the tent?"

"Nope." Kyle held up the empty tent bag as proof. "You packed them up this morning, right?"

Jason began rummaging through the trunk till he'd searched thoroughly. "I guess . . ." He shoved his hands in his pockets. "I must've left them behind."

"You *forgot* our tent poles?" Nelson asked gleefully, no longer feeling so stupid about his cell phone episode the day before. Then he got a brilliant idea. "Let's go back to the sanctuary for them."

"Yeah, right," Kyle protested. "It's four hours away."

"So?" Nelson flashed a grin. "We could spend the night again."

"No way," Jason said, "are we going back. We'll buy new poles."

They packed the tent back into the trunk and asked at the camp office for the location of the nearest discount store. After some driving around, they found the store and Nelson asked a silver-haired saleslady about tent poles.

"I'm sorry, miss." The old lady adjusted her trifocals, peering at Nelson's hair. "I don't know anywhere that sells poles without the tent."

The three boys stared at one another and Nelson whispered to Kyle, "Why'd she call me 'miss'?"

Kyle ignored his question and began looking through the half-dozen boxes on the shelf. "We'll have to get another tent."

"Do you have any bigger ones?" Jason asked the saleslady.

**rainbow road**

"This is all that's left." She wobbled her head. "It's the end of the season."

They decided to buy the cheapest box labeled as a two- to three-person tent and returned to the campground. But once assembled, the tent hardly looked big enough for two.

"It's even smaller than the last one," Jason complained.

"Well, maybe we can use the poles from this tent with our old tent," Kyle suggested. They proceeded to try that, but the poles were too short.

"I think we should go back and get our old poles," Nelson suggested again.

"I told you," Jason cut him a sharp look. "We're not going back there."

Kyle agreed: "We don't have time."

Nelson lit a cigarette, annoyed, and took a walk to phone his mom. He'd never imagined he would miss her, but he did, a little.

When he returned to the campsite, Kyle and Jason were sitting at the picnic table, staring at the dinky tent as if hoping it would somehow grow bigger.

"Let's do something!" Nelson told them. "Not just sit around moping. Isn't the Mississippi somewhere around here? I want to go see it. You guys coming?"

Jason drove and Nelson sat beside him while Kyle navigated from the backseat.

"There it is!" Jason yelled as they drove up Riverside Drive. "Let's stop and look at it."

But in trying to cross over, he accidentally turned onto a ramp for I-40 West. Suddenly they were on a bridge across the river headed toward Arkansas. In both directions, the Mississippi stretched golden in the sunset.

"Woo-hoo!" Nelson leaned out the car window. "The

Mighty Mississippi!" he shouted, the wind rushing through his hair. "Mark Twain!"

Jason tugged at Nelson's belt, yanking him back inside. "Are you trying to get yourself killed?"

Nelson sat down, grinning. "I didn't think you cared, Jay-Jay."

Once they crossed back over the river, they drove past the Pyramid sports arena and then downtown. At Beale Street Kyle informed them, "This is where the blues started."

They stopped for dinner at McDonald's. Upon glimpsing the tall African-American cashier, Nelson's gaydar began to ping like crazy. But the teenage boy didn't notice him at all. Instead he gazed directly at Jason, with a huge welcoming smile.

"Hi. I'm Nate." His voice was soft and deep. "What can I get for you this evening?"

Nelson's translation: *Big Mac, fries, or me?*

But Jason remained oblivious, ordering the Big Mac and fries. It wasn't fair. Jason already had Kyle.

Nelson realized there was a problem with this trip. Alongside gorgeous Jason, Nelson would *always* be the ugly stepsister—or at best the less cute guy.

"You from around here?" Nate asked Jason.

Nelson's translation: *Are you gay?*

Kyle stepped in, explaining that they were only passing through. Nate's smile fell in disappointment.

"He was *so* trying to pick you up," Nelson told Jason when they sat down.

"Huh?" Jason said, unwrapping his burger. "He was not." But then he turned to Kyle. "Was he?"

Kyle nodded, sipping his Coke. "He didn't take his eyes off you."

Nelson could hear a hint of jealousy in Kyle's voice.

Jason glanced toward the counter at Nate, then back at Nelson and Kyle. "For real?"

A moment later Nate strode out with a broom and long-handled dustpan, pretending to sweep invisible crumbs near the boys.

"How is everything?" He said it like he was addressing the group, but his eyes gazed only at Jason, as if really asking: *Do you think I'm cute?*

Jason's gaze darted nervously at Kyle. Nelson thrust his face in front of Jason's, hoping Nate would finally notice him, and smiled as big as he could. "Everything's great!"

For an instant, Nate did seem to notice Nelson. And Nelson's heart caromed against his chest. But then Jason pushed Nelson's head aside.

Nate strode away, and Nelson's heart crashed back into place.

Once back at the campground, the three boys squeezed into their new tent, packed even more tightly than before, all elbows and knees.

Atop his sleeping bag, Nelson thought about Horn-Boy and Nate. And he wondered how on earth—between Kyle trying to protect him and Jason stealing attention away—he would ever find love.

# chapter 19

## jason    kyle
## nelson

The following day Kyle woke up soaked with sweat. The morning sun had turned the tiny tent into an oven. Next to him, Jason's sleeping bag lay empty. No doubt he'd gone to shoot baskets.

On the other side of him Nelson groaned, kicking open his sleeping bag. "What time is it? How can it be so hot already?"

Kyle squinted at the Star Trek hologram watch Nelson had given him last Christmas. "It's eight already. Come on! The civil rights museum opens at nine."

"You go!" Nelson pulled his pillow over his head. "Pick me up afterward."

"No!" Kyle pulled the pillow off Nelson. "We're *all* going."

During the past four years, as Kyle had gradually come out and learned to accept himself as gay, he'd become more and more interested in social justice stuff. He'd learned about the

National Civil Rights Museum while plotting their trip.

"We went to Graceland like you guys wanted," he told Nelson. "Now I want you guys to go to the museum with me. It's a lot more important than Graceland."

"That's blasphemy," Nelson moaned. But he crawled from the tent anyway.

The museum was located in the two-story Lorraine Motel, on whose balcony Martin Luther King Jr., leader of the civil rights movement, had been shot in 1968. As Kyle pulled into the parking lot, Jason looked out the window at the other people emerging from their cars.

"Hey, Kyle," Jason said in a low voice. "I think this is for black people."

Kyle stared at him, unsure what to make of the comment. "Jason, it's the *Civil Rights* Museum. It's for everyone."

It irritated him that Nelson and Jason were so unenthusiastic. Didn't they understand how important civil rights were? To avoid any further arguments, he paid for everyone's admission tickets with the money that was left from his dad's fifty.

Once inside, Kyle couldn't help notice they were about the only nonblack people in the place. Nelson and Jason yawned through most of the exhibits, until they stepped into the 1955 Montgomery city bus.

Behind the wheel, a bus driver statue faced a Rosa Parks statue sitting near the front. As Nelson and Jason slouched into empty seats, the bus driver abruptly barked, "Move to the back of the bus!"

Nelson and Jason jumped.

"That scared the crap out of me," Nelson gasped, staring at the driver statue.

Then the Rosa Parks statue replied that she wasn't moving.

As Jason descended from the bus, he asked Kyle, "You mean that really happened?"

"Yeah," Kyle replied, and told them the story of Rosa Parks. He was happy to see Jason and Nelson starting to take an interest. Their curiosity grew even more when they saw another bus with its firebombed blasted-out window.

"How can people hate so much?" Jason asked, shaking his head in amazement.

By the time the boys reached the restored motel room where Martin Luther King stayed the night before being assassinated, Nelson and Jason stared solemnly at the historic balcony.

"Hey, Kyle?" Jason asked as they slowly walked back to the lobby. "If this is a civil rights museum, shouldn't they mention the hatred toward gay people, too?"

"Yeah!" Nelson agreed. "They have a whole frickin' exhibit about the Little Rock black kids getting called names and being beaten up for going to a white high school. What about all the gay kids who still get beat up every day?"

"Well . . ." Kyle nodded in agreement, excited by Nelson and Jason's newfound enthusiasm. "We could put that in the suggestion box."

"We should do something better than that," Nelson argued, "like stage a kiss-in."

Jason's brow furrowed and Kyle persuaded Nelson to settle for the suggestion box. They each wrote their own note and turned them in.

"You think they'll really pay any attention?" Jason asked as they walked back outside into the heat.

"At least we spoke up," Kyle replied. "Isn't that what the museum is about?"

**rainbow road**

Jason bit his bottom lip, as if thinking, and Kyle asked, "What?"

"I was thinking about my speech."

"You want to work on it now?" Kyle asked as they reached the car. He was getting nervous that Jason still hadn't begun work on it.

"I'll help you too!" Nelson chimed in.

"Maybe later," Jason said.

"We can work on it while we're driving," Kyle insisted, climbing into the front seat beside Jason.

"Let me drive," Nelson interjected.

"Look, I don't want to work on it now," Jason snapped.

"Fine!" Kyle barked. "If you want to wait till the last minute, that's your problem." He climbed out of the front seat, no longer wanting to sit beside Jason, and tossed the keys to Nelson.

Just like that, all three of them suddenly got in a bad mood. As they headed south on I-55 through Mississippi toward New Orleans, Jason and Nelson argued about CDs. Jason wanted to play one of his headbanger albums, whereas Nelson wanted to play "Redneck Woman" for the millionth time.

"Why can't you just take turns?" Kyle intervened. "You two act like kids sometimes."

He returned to reading *On the Road* but got annoyed every time the author used words like "fags" or "queers"—and not in a good way. He finally closed the book and stared out the window at a flock of buzzards circling overhead.

"I'm getting hungry," Jason announced.

Nelson pointed to a billboard of doe-eyed women and suggested, "Let's stop at the 'XXX Barely Legal All-You-Can-Eat Topless Truck Stop.'"

But instead they stopped at a Burger King and walked

inside to stretch their legs. Upon placing their order Kyle reached for his wallet, but his back pocket was empty. His pulse quickened as he checked his front pocket. "I think I left my wallet in the car."

"I'll pay." Nelson pulled out his own billfold.

"I'm going to look for it," Kyle said and hurried outside. The wallet contained his driver's license and half of Jason's money.

His heart pounded as he searched under the seats, in the CD compartment, and everywhere else the wallet could've gone to. How could he tell Jason he'd lost two hundred bucks of his money? And how could he drive without his license?

"I can't find it," he announced to Jason and Nelson as they carried their drinks and food across the hot blacktop to the car.

"Oh my God!" Nelson screamed. "You lost it?"

"Where'd you have it last?" Jason asked.

"At the museum . . ." Kyle thought back. "Buying our tickets. I'm sure I put it back in my pocket." He felt his pants as if he could've somehow overlooked the leather lump. "Half your money was in there. I'll pay you back."

He watched guiltily as Jason's forehead furrowed with worry lines. "Where's the other half?"

"In the glove compartment." Kyle reached down and flipped open the latch, pulling out the envelope to prove he still had it.

"That's a clever hiding place." Nelson pulled a French fry out of the bag and chomped on it. "No thief would ever think to look there."

"I'm *really* sorry," Kyle told Jason. "I don't know how I lost it."

Jason took a deep breath and let it out again. "Well, you didn't mean to lose it."

"Maybe the museum found it." Nelson handed Kyle his cell phone. "Call them."

They went back into the air conditioning and sat at a booth. While Nelson and Jason ate, Kyle dialed the number on the museum brochure. He spoke to several sympathetic people, but none reported a found wallet.

"Eat something," Jason said as Kyle hung up the phone.

"My stomach's too tense," Kyle replied. He knew he'd screwed up big-time.

"Can I have your fries then?" Nelson poured them onto his tray. "So, how much money do we have if we put all our money together?" He pulled out his wallet and withdrew its bills.

"That's not enough to get us to California and back," Kyle told them.

"Then I'll phone my old lady," Nelson offered. "Can I have your burger?"

Kyle nodded. He had no appetite whatsoever.

"I can phone my mom," Jason suggested.

"No," Kyle mumbled. "I'll phone my dad. I'm responsible for this. Besides, he gave me his credit card in case of emergency. I'll ask if we can use it."

"He gave you *what*?" Nelson's eyes grew huge as Kyle pulled the card from the envelope with the second half of Jason's money. "Then what're you so worried about?"

"Because it was supposed to be for emergencies. That's why I left it in the envelope."

"This is an emergency," Jason argued.

"No, this was stupid." Kyle stared at the card, recalling his dad's concern about money even before the trip started.

"Kyle, you're human." Nelson covered his mouth to burp. "Get over it."

"Hey, I lost the tent poles." Jason tapped Kyle's foot beneath the table. His brown eyes gazed at him, reassuring. "Just call and tell him."

"And what am I going to do about my license?" Kyle thought about how much farther they still had to travel. "I won't be able to drive."

"Jay-Jay and I will drive. You've hardly driven anyway."

"Stop calling me Jay-Jay." Jason snapped a look at him. "I don't like it."

Kyle picked up Nelson's cell phone and dialed his dad's office. When Kyle told him about the lost wallet, his dad said, "You need to be more careful, son. How'd you lose it?"

"I don't know," Kyle told him. Didn't his dad realize how bad he felt screwing up like this?

"Well, that's why I gave you the card." His dad gave an audible sigh. "Just remember the bill will be waiting for you when you get back."

"I know," Kyle said, exhaling relief.

"How's everything else going?" his dad asked. "Everyone getting along?"

Kyle glanced across the table at Jason and Nelson. So far, four days had gone by and even though at times it seemed like they wanted to kill each other, they hadn't—yet.

"Everybody's fine," Kyle replied.

"All right. Call your mom tonight. She'll be worried about this. Okay? Love you."

"Love you, too," Kyle echoed and hung up, announcing, "He said okay."

"Woo-hoo!" Nelson thrust his hand in the air to high-five Kyle. "How much is the credit card limit?" He clapped his

hands and bobbed his head, chanting, "Party! Party! I wonder if they have an ATM here."

Kyle scowled at him and asked Jason, "You're not mad at me?"

"No." Jason gave a vague shrug. "It's kind of reassuring when you screw up."

Kyle pondered that and leaned back in his seat, still wishing he hadn't lost the wallet.

# chapter 20

## jason

## kyle

## nelson

Jason wasn't exactly thrilled that Kyle had lost his money, but at least now he felt less dumb for running out of gas, leaving behind the tent poles, and not having known who Rosa Parks was.

Up till now this trip had reinforced Jason's image of Kyle: intelligent, thoughtful, caring, and well organized. Jason admired him, but at moments he felt inferior by comparison.

That unease had never come up in his relationship with Debra. Because she was a girl, he never felt like he had to compete with her. But because Kyle was a guy, Jason sometimes felt like they were competing—and Jason was the loser.

As Jason drove out of the Burger King parking lot, Kyle gently laid a hand on Jason's shoulder. "Sure you're okay about the money?"

"I'm good," Jason replied. He wished he could articulate his

**rainbow road**

complicated thoughts. Instead he reached up to Kyle's hand and gave it a reassuring squeeze.

For the next hour he focused on the road, until he told Kyle and Nelson, "I need to take a dump."

"How fascinating," Nelson replied. "You know, Kyle and I take a huge interest in your bowel movements."

Jason ignored the remark, scanning the horizon for an exit sign, but Kyle spoke up: "Nelson, would you cut it out? Please?"

Nelson opened his mouth in mock shock. "Kyle, don't deny it! You know we wonder every day about Jason's poop."

"Nelson!" Kyle shouted. "Would you shut *up*?"

Jason realized it was the first time he'd heard Kyle tell—or at least ask—Nelson to shut up. Fortunately, Nelson did.

"About time," Jason muttered as an exit came into view.

At the bottom of the ramp, a lonely road offered up a solitary gas station with a beat-up tow truck and a couple of service bays. Jason parked beside a pump so Kyle could fill the tank, and he hurried inside for the restroom key.

Pushing through the door, he stopped in astonishment. At the counter, brushing her hair, sat Britney Spears—or at least a teenage girl who looked exactly like the singer: sexy brown eyes, silky blond hair, luscious lips.

"Um . . ." Jason hesitated. "Men's room key?"

"Sure." The girl flashed a bright white smile and handed Jason the key, her soft fingers grazing his.

When Jason came back out of the restroom, Nelson was standing at the counter, talking to Britney and borrowing her lip gloss.

"Everything come out all right?" He grinned at Jason.

Jason pretended not to hear and handed the girl the key. "Thanks."

She smiled like the photo on a CD. "You're welcome."

Outside, Kyle was squeegeeing the windshield.

"Did you see her?" Jason asked in a stage whisper.

"Yeah." Kyle nodded. "There's a Britney look-alike contest in New Orleans tonight. She asked if we could give her a ride, so she won't have to wait for the bus."

"Oh, I get it." Jason gazed through the plate glass window. Even the girl's figure resembled Britney's, slim and shapely. "Fine with me," he told Kyle.

Kyle gave him a slant-eyed look. "Okay." After returning the squeegee he went inside, with Jason following.

"I'm BJ." The girl extended her hand to Jason.

"I'm Jason." He gently shook her hand, smiling.

When Kyle told her she could come with them, BJ cheered, clapping her hands. She ran to tell a gray-haired mechanic in the service bay. He looked over at the three boys. BJ returned saying he'd asked her to write down their license numbers and addresses. "In case you guys turn out to be ax murderers." She grinned.

Once the boys had done that, BJ returned to kiss the old man on the cheek. Then she grabbed her bag from behind the counter and climbed into the car's backseat with Nelson.

"Put on one of my Britney CDs," Nelson told Kyle as they pulled back onto the interstate. "I *worship* Britney," he said to BJ. "She's a great look for you. So what's it like out here in the sticks growing up gay?"

Jason flashed a glance in the rearview. Was the girl in the backseat a lesbian? Wow. He'd never have guessed.

"Well, the truth is . . ." BJ hesitated, her voice quivering a little. "I never really thought of myself as gay."

Jason listened carefully. Was BJ saying she *wasn't* a lesbian?

**rainbow road**

"Not that I have anything against gay people. But for as long as I can remember, I've always known I was a girl."

Jason didn't understand. What was she trying to say?

"Is it okay if I smoke?" BJ asked, and Nelson gave her a cigarette from his pack.

Jason frowned into the mirror at the two of them smoking. To make matters worse, it had starting raining, so he could open the window only a bit.

"In school I always played with the other girls," BJ continued and puffed on her cigarette. "And I always wanted to wear my sister's clothes, though my mama and papa tried to stop me."

BJ raised her chin to exhale a stream of smoke and Jason noticed something weird from the rearview. Did BJ have an Adam's apple?

"The problem," she said, "was I'd been given the body parts of a boy."

"Watch out!" Kyle shouted, reaching over to grab the steering wheel.

Jason swerved, barely missing a truck that had braked ahead of them. His heart pounded as he refocused on the road ahead, while trying to keep from staring at the boy/girl in back.

"The school I went to hadn't a clue what to do with me," BJ resumed. "They sent me home for wearing skirts I borrowed from other girls. My papa took a strap to me, telling me he'd die before any son of his wore a skirt."

As BJ spoke, Jason darted glances in the rearview, both curious and a little repulsed. Why would a guy dress up like a girl except as a joke? With the Faeries' zany outfits at least it had seemed like they were half-kidding. This wasn't joking. Jason felt the urge to wipe off BJ's makeup and tell him to stop it. But at the same time, she looked so beautiful.

"I knew in my heart I was a girl." BJ's cigarette trembled in her hand. "I just couldn't understand why nobody believed me. The county found out papa was beating me and called social services. They brought me to live with my grandmama and granddad. That was him at the gas station. They didn't know what to do with me either, but they pretty much let me stay home, grow my hair long, and help Granny around the house—until the county said I had to be in school. But when I showed up in a dress, the school sent me home saying I couldn't come to school like that because it caused too much disturbance. I don't know why it made the boys so crazy."

Jason glanced over at Kyle. Had he known BJ was a guy? Kyle glanced back at him and shrugged.

"Finally grandmama tried to put me in a Christian school across the county, telling them I was a girl. She put them off from getting my school records. For a whole week everybody treated me like a girl. It was the happiest week of my entire life."

BJ smiled at the green fields beyond the rain-spattered window.

"Then this horrible PE teacher said I had to change clothes like the other girls. Well, I said I couldn't do that. And it made them figure things out. The principal nearly had a heart attack. He yanked me into his office and made me kneel beside him, reciting Bible verses and telling me to repent or I was going straight to hell."

BJ flicked her cigarette butt out the window. "Well, I knew I'd already been to hell and it couldn't get any worse. Besides, I'd never hurt anyone. They're the ones who'd beat me and called me names, calling me gay. I'm not gay. I'm a *girl*."

Jason felt sorry hearing the story, but the whole thing still creeped him out. What made the guy want to be a girl in the first place?

"Anyway . . ." BJ smoothed her skirt. "That was the last time I went to school. Now I'm working on my GED. I found a doctor in Jackson who let me start taking hormone pills. And one day I'll save enough money to get my SRS—that's Sexual Reassignment Surgery—and it'll be settled, once and for all."

Jason glanced back at her. Was she serious?

"I'm sorry." BJ blushed. "I didn't mean to talk all y'all's ears off. I don't get a chance to unload like this very often."

"That's okay." Nelson patted her hand.

Everyone was quiet after that as Britney sang on the CD, "Oops, I did it again. . . ."

By the time they reached Lake Pontchartrain, north of New Orleans, dark gray thunderheads were pelting the car with rain as Kyle searched for a campground on their map.

"Y'all can't camp in this rain," BJ told them. "Come stay with me at my friends'. They've got plenty of room."

"Awesome!" Nelson exclaimed. "I'm so sick of camping."

"Sounds good to me," Kyle agreed.

But Jason still felt weird about this Britney boy/girl. And what would his/her friends be like?

"No, thanks," he said. "It should stop raining soon."

"Oh, I wouldn't be so sure," BJ warned. "Storms down here can last for *weeks!*"

Jason gazed at the sheets of rain blowing across the lake. Should he go along? His knuckles clenched the steering wheel as he nodded. "Okay."

# chapter 21

# jason     kyle

# nelson

Nelson had met a couple of transgender teens before, at the queer youth group he sometimes attended. But they'd been superbutch girls who dressed as boys, with baseball caps and baggy jeans. He'd never met a male-to-female tranny, especially one who loved Britney.

The house BJ directed them to looked right out of *Gone with the Wind:* tall white columns, green-shuttered windows, a gaslight over the front door.

"Toot the horn!" BJ told Jason, and her friends ran out with open umbrellas, greeting BJ and the boys with smiles and hugs.

Although BJ introduced her two friends as Clarissa and Charlotte, Nelson decided he'd better not jump to conclusions. Were they truly women? Clarissa had short hair and was heavyset, with breasts that could've belonged to either an overweight man or a woman. Charlotte was thin, with long blond-

highlighted hair. Both wore blouses but also wore pants.

"These boys are driving to California," BJ explained. "Isn't that exciting? This butch one is Jason." She tapped his shoulder. "He and Kyle are a couple. And Nelson is on a quest for love."

Inside, the house had the highest ceilings Nelson had ever seen, with lazily turning fans and walls lined with slightly crooked paintings.

"Tonight you boys can sleep on the foldout couch," BJ told Kyle and Jason. She led Nelson into a side bedroom. "We girls can sleep in here."

Nelson and the other femmy guys at youth group had often called each other "girl" or "girlfriend," as if to champion their queenyness to the world. But unlike BJ, Nelson had never seriously desired to become a *real* girl.

On numerous occasions when he was little, he did get into his mom's makeup to smear lipstick across his mouth and smudge eye shadow on. Then he clomped around in her heels, draped in pearls. But beneath his mom's blue chiffon dress, Nelson knew he was a boy. And he had no wish to alter that. It was the *illusion* of being female (and freaking out his dad) that had thrilled Nelson. He shuddered at the thought of ever slicing off his lifelong pubic friend. They had *way* too much romantic history.

While Jason, Kyle, and Nelson unloaded their stuff from the car, BJ's friends heated a pot of steaming seafood gumbo—a rich red stew of shrimp, crabs, crawdads, okra, and tomato broth, served with rice. When they started eating, Nelson relished every spoonful. "It's the best meal I've had since home."

"Enjoy! There's plenty." Clarissa smiled, and Charlotte asked, "Are you boys entering the Britney contest too?"

At the suggestion Jason nearly choked on a crawdad. Kyle

patted his back, but Nelson sparked to the idea. After all, hadn't he danced to Britney's videos nearly a million times?

"Could I?" he asked BJ excitedly.

"Oh, that would be such fun!" BJ exclaimed. "I'd love to dress you up. We're about the same size."

Much as Nelson loved the gumbo, he could barely sit still for another spoonful.

"First let me run you a nice hot bath," BJ instructed as they hurried to the bedroom. She handed Nelson a fresh towel and glanced at his legs. "And you'll need a razor, maybe two."

Nelson gazed down. "I've never shaved them before."

"Well, use plenty of shaving cream." BJ handed him the can. "And go real slow, so you don't cut yourself. All the way up, and in back too. Use the mirror. You want everything silky smooth, even where you can't see."

A thrill sparked through Nelson at the thought of his transformation. Could he really pull off looking like a girl?

He didn't actually have much leg hair yet, but he slid the razor up in careful straight lines and only nicked himself a couple of times. By the end of his bath, the tub was clogged with hair. He spread lotion over every inch of his smooth skin, admiring his hairless body in the bathroom mirror. Already he looked more feminine.

"Look what legs!" BJ whistled as Nelson stepped from the bathroom in the black satin shorty robe she'd given him. "Now let's do your face."

She sat him at her vanity and began working on his eyebrows. "This may sting a little. Hold still or my line will go crooked."

Nelson gritted his teeth. The tweezers hurt more than just a little.

"Good," BJ told him. "You can open your eyes now."

**rainbow road**

Nelson gazed in the mirror at his new, thin brow-line—a little red, but already making him look femme.

"You've got beautiful skin." BJ ran the back of her fingers across his cheek. "Now for a little foundation." She dusted the cream-colored powder across his face and pulled open the collar of his robe. "A little on your chest too."

Nelson watched as his chin-line magically grew softer, more girlish. "How'd you learn all this?" he asked.

"Watching my mom when I was little." BJ brushed soft pink rouge across Nelson's cheeks, giving his face a radiant glow. "And Granny had been a beautician. . . . Now, the eyes are the trickiest part." BJ smiled enthusiastically, picking out a brown liner from her makeup case. "They can make or break all the magic."

With a steady hand and a combination of liner and brush, BJ defined Nelson's upper and lower eyelash line, finally smudging them with a Q-tip.

Nelson watched as his blue eyes grew delicate and ladylike. "Are you going to put on false lashes?" he asked excitedly.

"I don't think you need them, hon." She blew a puff of breath across his face. "You've already got gorgeous lashes—like a baby doe."

"Really?" Nelson asked eagerly.

"Indeed!" BJ drew back, perching a hand on her hip. "Now surely I'm not the first one to tell you that."

"Yeah." Nelson shrugged. "Except for my mom."

BJ shook her head in disbelief and picked up a lip liner pencil. "Well, don't you worry. By the end of this trip, you're going to find a man who'll see you for the beautiful person you are, both inside and out. I know that's your destiny."

"You really think so?" Nelson gazed up into her chocolate-

colored eyes, wondering if she really could see his future.

"Without a doubt." BJ's voice rang with confidence. "Just like I always knew my destiny was to be a woman." She filled in his lips with a soft red, then folded a tissue in front of his mouth. "Now press your lips together."

He did as she told him, lifting his chin and holding his head high. The image in the mirror, with a boy's body and a girl's face, looked oddly strong and soft, vulnerable and confident.

"You're a caterpillar about to become a butterfly." She clapped her hands like a magician, reached into a drawer, and pulled out a bra and two nylon balls that looked like stuffed panty hose.

"Nature's little helpers," BJ explained, as Nelson took off the robe and put on the bra. "What I used before hormones—birdseed boobs."

Nelson gave a nervous laugh as she filled the bra cups with the instant breasts. They looked so real. He couldn't help running his hands across the smooth nylon bra, turning sideways in the mirror, enchanted by his evolving female self.

"Now for the tuck," she announced, holding a pair of rose-colored panties. "You shaved your boy parts, I hope? Take off your briefs. Now, don't be shy. You don't have nothing I ain't seen before."

Nelson stepped out of his underwear, feeling oddly like he was standing in front of his mom.

"Okay, now pull everything back between your legs," BJ ordered, unrolling a length of duct tape.

"Are you serious?" Nelson's voice quavered. "What if I have to pee?"

"You'd better go now," BJ said, matter-of-factly.

"But won't it hurt, to peel that off later?"

"That's why you shaved, hon."

"Do I have to?" Nelson hesitated. "Okay, let's just do it!" He shut his eyes, then opened them as BJ showed him how to strap himself down. It really wasn't *that* bad, except when he moved . . . or laughed . . . or breathed.

For Nelson's Britney outfit, BJ suggested a tight black miniskirt, with a huge black belt, boots, and a slinky black crossover blouse, cut high above the midriff. But in spite of the mock boobs, his body didn't look quite as shapely as Britney's.

"I think I need a birdseed butt."

Last came the blond Britney wig.

"Close your eyes," BJ told him as she adjusted the wig on his head. She stood close and he breathed in her clean, perfumed smell.

"Okay, Miss Butterfly," she said softly, her breath tickling his ear. "Spread your wings and soar."

Nelson opened his eyes. At first the girl in the mirror startled him. Then she mesmerized him. It was hard to believe she *was* him. He slowly raised a hand and the image followed. He really was her . . . if he'd been born female.

He glanced at BJ's reflection as she came to stand beside him. And suddenly Nelson understood how displaced BJ must feel trapped in the wrong body, unable to peel off the male masquerade nature had mistakenly given her.

"Okay, now." BJ folded Nelson's long blond hair over his shoulders. "A few quick lessons on being a girl. First, don't stroke your hair away with your hand. Instead, flick it with the back of your fingertips. Like this!" She showed him.

"Second, when you sit down . . ." She moved to the chair. "Brush your skirt from behind to make sure it comes forward. I like to sit diagonal, crossing my legs at the ankle. Of course,

never *ever* sit with your legs apart. Let's see you do it."

"Great! Next, for the walk. If you notice, guys walk from the legs. Girls walk from the hips. Stand up straight, look up and forward, smiling, relaxed, and confident. Say to yourself: 'I'm a girl, getting the attention she deserves.'"

The walk took a little work, but with BJ's coaching, Nelson finally got it.

"Ready to show the boys?" BJ asked.

Nelson swallowed, took a breath, and nodded. BJ turned the doorknob and Nelson stepped out.

The events that followed that evening unfolded as though Nelson were watching himself move through a dream.

Jason stared at him, mouth agape, then gazed at him, with a gentle, sheepish smile such as Nelson had never before experienced from him. Meanwhile, Kyle laughed and kept repeating: "This is wicked freaky."

The Saint Charles streetcar whisked them like a carriage past stately oaks and balconies ribboned with Mardi Gras beads.

Once in the French Quarter, they jaunted by topless strip clubs and restaurants with petticoated Southern belles, past drunken college frat boys, spilling their super-size cups of beer, and around street musicians dancing with trombones.

Their destination, the Rendezvous Bar, was Nelson's first gay club ever. The walls pulsed with music and the floor was thronged with men—white, black, old, young, bald, tall, paunchy, skinny, in jeans, leather, sports coats. And everywhere, there were beads.

Kyle pulled Nelson by the hand, as they rose with a cloud of smoke upstairs, past a sign reading BATTLE OF THE BRITNEYS to a room packed with Britney blondes everywhere—black Britneys,

old Britneys, Asian Britneys, plump Britneys. . . . The crowd cheered as onstage a wheelchair Britney crooned "Toxic."

And then somehow Nelson was being passed arm by arm up to lights shining in his eyes. Voices cheered as he lip-synched "Boys" and danced the steps he'd watched a gazillion times on MTV, and he looked down to see Jason clapping for him.

Nelson felt like a star: beautiful, applauded. He wished he could stay on that stage forever. But he came down and Kyle hugged him. Strangers told him, "You're a fabulous Britney." And a muscled guy in a tight tank top marked STUD whispered, "I wish I was as brave as you."

Then it was BJ on stage, lip-synching "Slave 4 U," except you could've sworn it really was Britney singing. She won first prize, and Nelson thought, *She's a girl, getting the attention she deserves.*

Then they were walking down the street, trying to wave down a taxi, past a drunk yodeling to a lamppost.

"I'm cold!" BJ gave herself a hug and asked Kyle, "Can I borrow him a minute?"

She draped Jason's arm around her waist, telling him, "Someday I'm going to find myself a tall sweet muscley guy just like you, Jason."

And Kyle smiled, though it looked a little forced.

All the way home Nelson thought how much fun it had been to be a girl—at least for a little while.

Then he was sitting in front of the mirror, wiping his face with cold cream as he returned to being a boy.

"Yeow!" he screamed, as he tore off his tuck tape. "I've got to pee so bad! How do you do this all the time?"

"One day I won't have to," BJ said hopefully, gazing down at her own freed masculinity.

And soon they were asleep, breathing softly, side by side.

# chapter 22

## jason    kyle
## nelson

Arriving back at the New Orleans house, Kyle had quickly undressed and climbed into the foldout couch, exhausted and eager to sleep. But once beneath the sheets, he lay wide awake in the dark beside Jason, his mind replaying the day's wild ride of events: picking up a Britney wannabe at a backwoods gas station, finding out she was a he, seeing his best friend shape-shifted into a girl, going to his first gay bar ever, and watching as his boyfriend put his arm around BJ's waist. Kyle had been able to deal with everything except that last item.

He now snaked his own arm across Jason's chest, trying to reassure himself that Jason's action with BJ hadn't really meant anything. Kyle felt silly for his jealousy, except he knew Jason had been attracted to girls and had a special weakness for blondes. Didn't that make BJ the best of all worlds—boy, girl, and blonde?

"You still awake?" Kyle whispered, unable to contain his thoughts any longer.

"Just thinking," Jason replied from the pillow beside him. "About everything that happened today."

"Me too." Kyle stroked his fingers along Jason's arm, working up his courage. "Can I ask you something? Do you, um . . . are you attracted to BJ?"

While he nervously waited for Jason's response, his fingertips brushed the soft hairs of Jason's arm. Would Jason be honest? What if he said he *was* attracted to BJ?

Jason yawned and the couch springs squeaked noisily beneath him. "She's cute. It's freaky how much she looks like Britney."

Across the darkness Kyle eyed Jason guardedly. He hadn't exactly answered Kyle's question. "So are you attracted to her?"

Jason remained silent, then turned onto his side to face Kyle, as the couch squeaked again. "You're nutty."

Kyle propped his head up to explain. "Well, I mean, you used to like girls, right? And she's both a boy and a girl."

"Yeah . . ." Jason said, as if pondering. "But I think it would be too freaky, too confusing. This whole day was bizarre enough."

The response helped reassure Kyle. He wrapped his arm tighter across Jason's chest, listening as Jason continued.

"I kind of feel sorry for her, you know? Can you imagine growing up with the wrong body parts? It's hard enough with the right body parts."

Was Jason becoming more understanding—or at least less freaked out—than he'd been at the sanctuary? Maybe he hadn't felt as overwhelmed by one teen tranny as he'd been by the throng of older gender-bender Faeries. Or maybe he really was becoming more accepting.

In any case, Kyle rested easier now. He leaned across the

pillow, kissing Jason tenderly on the lips. Jason kissed him back and slid a hand beneath the elastic of Kyle's underwear.

"Hey," Kyle whispered nervously. "What if someone walks in?"

"Everyone's asleep," Jason whispered back, pressing against Kyle.

"They won't be for long." Kyle giggled as the couch squeaked and creaked beneath them.

"Crap," Jason muttered. "Let's get on the floor."

Kyle thought surely Jason was joking, but Jason pulled him by the hand as the couch squealed louder than ever.

The two boys crawled off the mattress and lay on the hard floor, softened only by a rug. The circumstances weren't the greatest, but after three nights spent lying beside Jason in unrequited anguish, Kyle wasn't about to complain.

The next morning sunshine sliced through the window shutters as Kyle woke. To his amazement, Nelson's voice carried from the kitchen, chattering and laughing with BJ and her friends. Had Nelson actually gotten up before Kyle and Jason?

On the couch beside Kyle, Jason lay snoring softly. Kyle gazed at him, recalling their rug romance of several hours earlier. And he couldn't stop grinning, even when he walked into the kitchen for breakfast.

After beignets and coffee came good-byes. Nelson gave BJ an Elvis key chain he'd bought at Graceland and BJ's eyes teared up. She gave Nelson, Jason, and Kyle each a hug. And to Kyle it no longer seemed the least bit odd that she was really biologically male. She was their friend; that was all that mattered.

Kyle guided them onto I-10 and Jason drove down the elevated highway over the bayou.

"You two sure are smiley today." Nelson gave them a devilish grin. "Did you finally bone last night?"

Jason flashed a red-faced glance in the rearview at Kyle.

"None of your business," Kyle told Nelson.

"You did, didn't you?" Nelson gave Jason a playful nudge on the shoulder. "I'm so jealous. I hate you both. I wish we could've stayed longer in that bar. All those men! What a waste."

At the bar Kyle had watched Nelson revel in the attention from guys. Fortunately the bartenders hadn't served Nelson any alcohol, and BJ had kept him focused.

For Kyle, the bar experience had been a little unnerving because of all the guys staring at him, and even more stared at Jason. And at the same time it had given Kyle a rush to watch how Jason turned heads—and to put his arm around Jason, letting everyone know this guy was his.

"I want to go out again tonight," Nelson said, running his hands over his hairless bare legs. "As a boy this time. It's my turn to get laid."

Kyle stared out the window at the cypress trees, half-wishing Nelson would get laid so he'd shut up about it, but also worried. More than anything he wished Nelson could find someone good for him.

For lunch they stopped at a "Gator-to-Go" place where Nelson bought alligator-on-a-stick, Kyle got a burger, and Jason got chicken, though it all tasted nearly the same.

After lunch Nelson took the wheel, and when they crossed into Texas, he beeped the horn and shouted, "Woo-hoo!"

East Texas passed by the window, uneventful and hot. The sun still shone brightly when they arrived in Austin and checked into the Lone Star Campground. After the boys unloaded the

car, Jason grabbed his basketball to go practice. "Come partner with me," he told Kyle.

Kyle hesitated, still tired from the night before and also the drive, but then he decided maybe the exercise would help wake him up. Besides, how could he turn down Jason's suggestion to "partner" with him?

The word echoed in Kyle's ears as he rebounded and passed for Jason, watching him run in, gather up the rebound, and go up strong for the put-back. He loved being with Jason, watching him.

They practiced for over an hour before returning to the campsite, where Nelson was waking from a snooze. They all showered at the bathhouse, then they bought hot dogs and chips at the camp store. While grilling the dogs, Nelson said, "I want to go dancing."

Especially after basketball practice, the last thing Kyle wanted to do was dance. "I'm beat," he said, serving himself a wiener. "Can't we just relax for one night?"

"No way!" Nelson protested. "This is our vacation! I don't want to spend it sleeping."

Kyle chewed his hot dog, debating. He could tell by Nelson's insistence that it was probably pointless to try to keep him from going out. Maybe he should just let him go by himself. But that worried him. Who would Nelson end up meeting? What little drama would he get into next?

Nevertheless, it would give Kyle and Jason time alone—and their sleeping bags would be a lot more comfortable than the floor of the New Orleans house had been.

However, just then Jason announced, "I want to go too."

"Aren't you tired?" Kyle asked.

"Yeah, but we might never be here again. I want to see where we are."

**rainbow road**

Kyle grabbed a handful of chips, feeling outnumbered, and chewed on them, trying to decide what to do.

"Or," Nelson proposed, slathering his hot dog with mustard, "if you don't want to go, then Jason and I will go alone."

Jason flinched as if startled by the idea of going alone with Nelson. He turned to Kyle, his brown eyes beseeching. "Come on, Kyle. Come with us."

Though he really didn't want to, Kyle agreed. After dinner, the boys dressed to go out.

At the camp office a beefy registration guy was reading a college textbook. Nelson asked, "You know where we can find a dance club?"

"There's lots of places around Sixth Street," the guy replied.

"Isn't he delicious?" Nelson commented, returning to the car.

Kyle unfolded his map, searching for Sixth Street. Then he guided them on a quick tour of the city, past the university's tower and the pink granite capitol.

"I love it!" Nelson observed. "This butch cowboy state has a pink capitol!"

Then they headed to Sixth Street, an area lined with neon signs, nightclubs, and people spilling onto the sidewalk. At a stoplight three teenage girls—a black chick, a blonde, and a brunette—waited at the crosswalk. The black girl pointed at the boys' car and waved, so Nelson rolled down the window to hear her yell, "I like y'all's rainbow flag!"

"Thanks!" Nelson shouted back. "Where's a good club to go to?"

"We're going to Score!" The blonde chick grinned as though fully aware of her double meaning.

"That's the name of the club," explained the brunette, pointing down the street.

"It's eighteen and over," added the black girl.

The stoplight had changed to green and a car beeped behind them.

"Meet us there!" The blonde smiled again, and it seemed to Kyle like she was smiling especially at Jason, in more than just a friendly way.

As Nelson proceeded down the street to search for parking, he proclaimed, "They're family!" That was one of Nelson's code terms for "gay."

"No way!" Jason exclaimed. "Really?" He gazed over his shoulder back toward the girls and asked Kyle, "You think they are?"

"I hope so," Kyle said.

Outside Score, a line of older teens and twenty-somethings stretched from the door.

"We're over here," the black girl called. She introduced herself as Keesha and the brunette as Evie. The blonde was Leah. With her Texas drawl she pronounced it "Lay-ya."

"I saw ya'll's license plate," she told Jason. "Ya'll sure came a long way from Virginia." She smiled like she was checking Jason out.

"We're driving cross-country." Jason unabashedly smiled back.

The girls said they were sophomores at UT, originally from Dallas.

"So is this place gay?" Nelson asked, scoping out the line.

"Mixed." Evie giggled, darting her eyes at Keesha.

"Are *you* gay?" Nelson followed up.

"Heteroflexible." Keesha laughed, draping her arm around Evie.

Kyle had never heard that term before. Did it mean the same as "bi"?

**rainbow road**

"I like that," Jason said, laughing too as they shuffled along the line toward the door.

"At first," Keesha explained, "I thought kissing a girl would be nasty."

"But then she met me," Evie interjected.

"And I totally flip-flopped!" Keesha continued. "You see, girls understand how girls think. So they can be there for you emotionally."

"My mom thinks I seem happier with girls," Evie added. "She says I'm better off."

Leah suddenly spoke up: "Well, I'm definitely straight."

"Oh, yeah?" Keesha teased. "What about you and Alyson last year?"

"That was an exception." Leah grinned and turned to Jason. "What about y'all?"

Even though they were in public, Kyle quickly took hold of Jason's hand. "Jason and I are boyfriends."

He hoped that would put to rest any designs Leah might have, but Jason slipped his hand out of Kyle's. Kyle wasn't sure if he did that because they were in public, but he saw Leah notice it.

"Well, I'm a hundred percent queer!" Nelson jumped in, obviously feeling left out of the conversation.

When they finally reached the club entrance, a bouncer with a snake tattoo told them, "There's a five-dollar cover."

Kyle hadn't planned on that. It worried him to spend money they hadn't budgeted.

Inside, the music blared so loudly you could hardly talk. Evie led their group through wall-to-wall bodies onto the packed dance floor, where they all jumped and jostled together

till Nelson started dancing with some cute tan-skinned guy.

Kyle had hoped to be able to dance at least somewhat alone with Jason, like they had at prom. But the place was way too hot and crowded, with everyone bumping into everyone. So he kept getting pushed away from Jason.

"I'm going to take a break outside," he finally shouted over the music to Jason. "Want to come?"

Jason glanced at Leah and the other girls. "I want to dance some more," he yelled back to Kyle. "I really like this music. Hey, can I have some money?"

"We don't have much," Kyle shouted, but gave him a ten anyway. Then he got his hand stamped and walked outside. He wandered down Sixth Street, past the other clubs, wishing he and Jason had stayed at the campground.

When he got back to Score, he found out he had to wait in line again.

"Why?" he argued with the bouncer. "I got my hand stamped."

"Yeah, but it's too crowded inside. You've got to wait till someone leaves."

Kyle folded his arms and waited, thinking about Jason.

When at last he got in, a slow song was playing, and Leah was pressed against Jason, slow-dancing.

"Hey!" Nelson appeared beside Kyle, holding the tan-skinned boy's hand. "This is Arturo," Nelson shouted over the music. "I asked him to come back to camp with us."

Kyle smiled faintly at Arturo, who smiled back eagerly. He looked nice enough, but Kyle leaned into Nelson's ear and yelled, "Where's he going to sleep? The tent barely fits three."

Nelson gave a shrug. "He can sleep in the car with me."

"Nelson, that's crazy."

**rainbow road**

"What else can I do? He lives in a dorm, with a 'phobe roommate." He grinned at Arturo and told Kyle, "Isn't he a total lust-magnet? We've been making out. Awesome kisser! And I *so* need to get laid."

"Whatever," Kyle said, less concerned about Nelson getting laid than he was about Leah hanging all over his boyfriend.

"I'm going to go find my friends," Arturo told Nelson. "Let me know what you guys decide."

Nelson watched him walk away. "See what you did?" he told Kyle.

"I didn't do anything!" Kyle shouted over the music. Then he glanced back toward the dance floor, totally unprepared for what he saw: Was Jason kissing Leah?

# chapter 23

# jason     kyle

# nelson

Jason hadn't meant to let Leah kiss him. It just . . . happened.

When Kyle had said he was going outside, Jason merely planned to keep dancing. He liked the music the DJ was playing—mostly house. And he liked this club a lot more than that bar in New Orleans.

For one thing, the crowd was a lot closer to his age. He'd felt like a kid among all the older guys at the Rendezvous. The way they kept checking him out, darting their eyes between Kyle and him had given Jason the creeps.

And he liked the fact that Score had a mixed crowd of gays and straights. You couldn't easily tell who was what. Jason felt more comfortable that way. Plus, after spending five days cooped up in a car with two guys, he was enjoying the female company of Leah and the other girls. He'd liked BJ, too, but that was different, more complex. This was simpler.

He thought it was interesting what Keesha and Evie had said about being "heteroflexible." He could identify with that. He liked watching them dance together. And when they started making out during one song, right there in the middle of the dance floor, it totally turned him on.

"You like that?" Leah shouted over the music to Jason.

He felt the blood rush into his face, embarrassed that she'd caught him staring. He wasn't sure exactly what she was asking, but he nodded. "Yeah."

Keesha finally pulled out of her lip-lock with Evie, giggling because of all the boys staring at them. Evie asked Jason and Leah, "Y'all want to get something to drink?"

Keesha led the way through the crowd, holding Evie's hand. In turn, Evie held Leah's hand. And when Leah reached for Jason's hand, he took it without a second thought.

He'd realized earlier Leah was checking him out from the way she let her blue eyes linger on him. He didn't mind; he was flattered. He thought she was cute too. But even though she was blonde, she wasn't really his type. For one thing, he didn't like how strong she came on. And for another thing, she wasn't Kyle. Even though Kyle wasn't blond, he was Jason's boyfriend, and Jason had no desire to change that.

Nevertheless, at the bar Jason bought all the girls soft drinks with the ten dollars Kyle had given him.

"You're a great dancer!" Leah shouted, leaning toward Jason's ear, so that her breasts brushed his arm.

"Thanks!" he replied and backed up, even though her boobs were quite nice. "You're a good dancer too!" he yelled.

A grin played across Leah's lips. "You're sweet!" She leaned into him again, this time resting her hand softly on his arm. "You know, I never would've guessed you were gay."

Jason wasn't sure how she meant that. Was it a compliment or a put-down?

"Did you ever try girls?" Keesha asked, apparently overhearing Jason and Leah.

"Yeah. Before Kyle I had a girlfriend for two years," he yelled to the group.

"You're bi?" Evie said. "That's cool."

Jason shrugged and sipped some of his Coke. He didn't really like to label himself as "bi" because it made him feel like he didn't belong in either group, straight or gay. Besides, he was boyfriends with Kyle, so didn't that mean he was gay? He wanted to ask Evie and Keesha more about how they dealt with their "heteroflexibility." Were they still attracted to guys? Did they feel like they fit in with hundred-percent lesbians?

"When was the last time you were with a girl?" Leah shouted.

From her coy smile Jason got a strange sense of where that question was headed and he didn't want to pursue it. Instead he glanced away toward the crowd, hoping Kyle would appear.

"I hope you don't mind my asking." Leah leaned into his shoulder as though they were intimate friends. "I'm just curious. I guess I'm weird that way."

Later, Jason would realize that this would've been the moment to excuse himself and get the heck away. But at the time it seemed like leaving her would be like agreeing she was weird. He didn't want to hurt her feelings, especially since she obviously liked him.

Fortunately, the song changed and Keesha yelled, "Let's dance! I love this song." She led them all back to the dance floor and Jason sighed with relief at having dodged the Leah bullet. But where was Kyle? Why was he taking so long? And where had Nelson gone?

Jason was about to tell the girls he was going to look for his

friends when the music changed to a slow song. Evie took hold of Keesha and Leah leaned into Jason. Without even asking if he wanted to, she suddenly had her arms wrapped around him, slow-dancing. He could smell her spicy citrus perfume.

Jason hadn't slow-danced with a girl since nearly a year before—at senior year Homecoming with Debra. Leah's soft warm body pressed gently against his and he decided there was nothing really wrong with just dancing. And it wasn't his fault Kyle wasn't around.

He gazed over Leah's shoulder at Keesha and Evie. As they danced, they started making out again. Jason's throat tightened as he watched. His heart beat faster. Then Leah tilted her face up to him, gazing into his eyes, her lips a little apart.

*Oh, crap,* Jason thought. Why was she doing this?

And next thing he knew, her moist lips were reaching up and resting on his.

They only kissed an instant before Jason pulled away. "Look, I can't." He slid out from her arms. "Sorry."

Without waiting for a response he turned, muttering under his breath. Why had she done that? And why had *he* done that?

At the edge of the dance floor he spotted Nelson and Kyle staring at him. Jason's heart dropped to his stomach.

Casually, he walked over, praying they hadn't seen him. "You guys ready to go?"

A flicker of pain crossed Kyle's face and his tone was definitely angry. "What were you doing?"

Jason bit into his lip, then answered, "Nothing." His voice sounded false, even to him.

"Tell me what happened," Kyle insisted, his voice breaking.

Jason gave a groan of resignation. "She made a pass at me and I walked away. That's all!"

"*Ew!*" Nelson butted in.

Jason wanted to slug him.

"You smell like her perfume," Kyle said, his voice full of hurt. "What did you do with her? I want to know."

"Nothing, I told you. She kissed me. That's all. You saw me walk away, didn't you?" Shouldn't Kyle feel proud of him for that, instead of grilling him?

"Then why'd you let her kiss you in the first place?"

"Because you weren't around!" He immediately realized that hadn't come out like he meant it.

Kyle's mouth drooped into a brooding look. "I want to go!"

"What about Arturo?" Nelson asked, but Kyle was already storming out of the club.

On the drive back to the campground none of the boys spoke. Nelson was pissed because he'd missed out on getting naked with Arturo. Kyle was ticked off at Jason. And Jason was equally PO'ed at Kyle.

When they got to the campsite and climbed from the car, Jason tried to put his arm around Kyle and accidentally brushed his cheek. Was it damp? Or was it just Jason's imagination?

Kyle pulled away. "You need to figure this out!" His tone left no doubt he'd been crying. He bent into the tent and gathered his sleeping bag, dragging it out. "I'm going to sleep in the car."

"Kyle, you're being ridiculous." Jason grabbed his arm, trying to stop him, but Kyle pulled away again, climbing inside the car.

Jason sat on the picnic table and stared at the car, frustrated by how unreasonable Kyle was being, and angry at himself for getting into this mess. Finally, he crawled into the tent.

Nelson yawned. "I guess it's just you and me tonight, huh?"

Jason undressed and slid into his sleeping bag, ignoring him, but Nelson kept at it. "I can't believe you kissed her. That is so totally *ew!*"

"Shut the hell up," Jason muttered.

"Oh, yeah." Nelson yawned again. "I'm so scared."

Jason wanted to shove his pillow over Nelson's face, but soon his thoughts returned to Kyle. Didn't he realize how much Jason loved him?

# chapter 24

## jason

## kyle

## nelson

Nelson hardly slept that night, roused time and again by Jason's snoring.

"Hey, Pavarotti, roll over!" he grumbled and lay awake, thinking about the past day's events.

He'd liked the heteroflexible girls and had had a fun time dancing with them.

He wished he'd been able to get naked with the boy he'd met at the club, *mucho* yummy Arturo. But at least they'd been able to make out a little. And what an awesome kisser!

Then there was the incident of Jason kissing the skeezer. Nelson understood Kyle's fury at Jason. Nelson would be angry too if his boyfriend did that to him. But Kyle had known Jason was confused about girls before they'd become boyfriends. Jason was now probably going through one of those insecurity things by which bi guys reassured themselves they weren't *completely* gay.

But of course Jason was gay. Nelson had told Kyle that Jason was a closet case long before Jason even showed up at the queer youth group meeting.

Why would Jason have become boyfriends with Kyle if he wasn't gay? Kyle could give Jason the masculine affection no female could compete with. So why was Kyle taking on such a jilted wife role, complete with drama-queeny exit from the tent to sleep in the car?

Nelson turned to face Jason, sleeping inches from his face. The more time he spent with the big dolt, the more he was growing to like him. Not that he'd ever admit that. He'd always thought Jason's thick eyebrows were sexy, and he loved the olive color of his skin. His shoulders stuck out of the sleeping bag, broad and muscled. His lips looked so tender and inviting. Nelson really couldn't blame Leah for going after him.

An idea began worming its way into Nelson's brain. Kyle had always said Jason was a great kisser. What would it feel like to kiss him now? Sleeping soundly as he was, would Jason even notice?

Jason gurgled a snore, rattling Nelson back to sanity. Was he nuts? He drew a deep breath, trying to calm himself. He'd better get laid pronto and stop lusting after his best friend's boyfriend or this trip was really going to turn into a disaster.

Rather than wake Jason from his snoring, Nelson left him alone. He decided it was better to lie awake wanting to clobber the noisy goon than hoping to ravish him. And with that thought, he somehow fell asleep.

The following morning Nelson awoke to find Jason's sleeping bag empty. No doubt he'd gone to shoot hoops. Although Nelson didn't envy Jason's dedication, he admired him for it.

Nelson emerged from the tent, curious how Kyle had made out in the backseat of the car. When he saw Kyle was still sleeping, he tried to extricate his toothbrush, soap, and towel from the front seat as quietly as possible.

Nevertheless, Kyle blinked awake, groggily glaring at his watch. "I'm so exhausted. I couldn't sleep out here." He gazed toward the tent and whispered, "Is he awake?"

"You mean the skank? He's shooting baskets, I think. I couldn't sleep either. I kept having to tell him to roll over."

"Get used to it," Kyle replied, climbing out of the car. "'Cause I'm not sleeping with him anymore."

"Kyle, I think you're overreacting. You knew Jason liked girls when you met him. Just because he hit on some blondie doesn't mean he's dumping you. You're just cheesed off because you can't control him."

"You know, I'm really getting sick of your control crap." Kyle slammed the car door.

"Well, you *are* controlling," Nelson said. He grabbed his cell phone and set off for the bathroom, dialing his mom as he walked. Big mistake. She yelled at him for not calling back the previous day after she'd left a message.

Nelson sat on the toilet seat, listening to her rant and wishing he could dump her into the bowl, though not really. He knew she cared about him or she wouldn't give him such a hard time.

He stood up from the seat, done with his stinky business, and cupped the phone beneath his chin while he reached for the roll of toilet paper. As he did that, the small metal phone slipped out from beneath his chin. Immediately, he grabbed for it, his fingers brushing the metal, but he missed.

The phone plunged directly into his morning labors. Plop!

"Damn it!" Nelson banged the butt of his hand against the stall partition. "Damn it!" He stared at the sunken phone at the bottom of the bowl. "Damn it! Damn it!"

He stomped his feet, debating. Should he stick his hand in to get it back? How nasty was that? He'd be touching not only his own germs, but those of a million other people who'd ever . . . yuck! Besides, he wasn't about to use that phone again. It probably wouldn't even work anymore.

As he pulled his shorts up, trying to decide what to do, someone shuffled into the stall next door and farted. *Oh, great.*

Out of frustration Nelson reached for the toilet handle. He'd just flush the stupid thing and buy a new one. But what if the phone clogged the toilet and flooded the entire bathhouse?

Besides, with the car repairs and all the money he was spending on this trip, he couldn't afford to buy a new phone. And this one might still work. Once before it had gotten wet in a rainstorm—though not this wet.

Holding his breath, Nelson leaned over the bowl and extended his arm, his fingers breaking the cold water.

"Gross, gross, gross," he muttered to himself, as he deftly plucked the metal phone from its resting place.

He let out his breath and quickly bundled the phone in toilet paper to dry it off. Flushing the toilet, he tried to decide: Now what? Should he wash it?

He couldn't use it like it was. Since it was already wet, a little more water couldn't hurt. He carried it to the faucet, soaped it up, rinsed, and held it beneath the hand dryer till it was fully dry.

Now, the test. As he left the bathhouse, he pressed the ON button and waited. Nothing. He tried again. Still nothing. After all that? Crap.

At the campsite Kyle and Jason were sitting at opposite ends of the picnic table, eating their bowls of milk and cereal, not speaking.

"Can I use the phone?" Kyle asked. "I want to call my mom."

Nelson sat down between Kyle and Jason. Should he tell them?

"It's not working," he said simply. "See?" He pressed the ON button again but the phone failed to light up.

"What happened to it?" Kyle asked.

"I don't know," Nelson lied.

"Well, here." Kyle reached for it. "Let me look at it."

Nelson lifted the phone away from his grasp. Even though Kyle was pretty good at fixing things, shouldn't Nelson first tell him where the phone had been? But how could he?

Silently he handed the phone to Kyle.

Kyle pulled the battery cover off and set it next to his cereal bowl. "It's wet. How'd it get wet?"

"I don't know." Nelson looked beyond the picnic table, avoiding Kyle's gaze.

"Nelson, what did you do to it?"

"Nothing."

"Nelson!" Kyle's voice rose with annoyance. "Would you just tell me what happened?"

Nelson glanced at Kyle, then at Jason, unable to keep his secret any longer. "It fell in the toilet."

"Oh, gross, man!" Jason bolted up, yanking his cereal bowl and spoon off the table.

"Why didn't you tell me?" Kyle asked, glancing down at the phone in his hands.

"I washed it off with soap," Nelson said lamely.

"This is great." Kyle dropped the phone onto the table and wiped his hands across his shorts. "Not only don't we

have enough money, now we don't have a phone."

Nelson stared down at the ground, feeling like a total dumb-ass. How would they manage?

None of the three boys said much after that. Each sullenly rolled up his own sleeping bag. They took down the tent and packed up the car.

"I'll drive," Nelson offered, once they were ready. "Where are we heading today?"

"We're going to San Antonio, aren't we?" Jason asked Kyle. "You said you wanted to see the Alamo."

"No, let's just skip it," Kyle replied, climbing into the backseat.

"But you said it's supposed to be really cool." Nelson turned the ignition.

Kyle glared at him straight on. "I don't feel like it anymore, all right? I want to keep going."

Boy, was he cranky.

As Nelson pulled onto the two-lane road outside the camp-ground, he got caught behind a dump truck.

"Don't follow so close," Kyle cautioned him.

"But he's going, like, five miles an hour!" Nelson shifted impatiently in his seat.

"You're too close!" Kyle insisted.

The next instant, a pebble catapulted from the truck, flying onto the windshield. Smack!

Nelson winced, clutching the steering wheel. The rock chipped the glass and bounced off, continuing its flight.

"Crap!" Jason reached over and felt the inside of the win-dow where the stone had left its mark.

"He cracked my windshield!" Nelson began beeping his horn. "What should I do? Should I stop him?"

"His insurance isn't going to pay for that," Kyle said. "I told you not to follow so close."

"But it's his fault!" Nelson argued.

Jason shook his head, staring at the dime-size crack. "I just hope it doesn't grow any bigger or you're screwed, dude."

"Asshole!" Nelson shouted at the truck. This was starting to be the suckiest day of his life.

# jason
# kyle
# nelson

Kyle stared out the backseat window at the receding Austin skyline, angry at Nelson—not for one thing in particular, but for everything: for letting the windshield get chipped, for dropping the phone into the toilet, for insisting they go dancing the night before, and for suggesting this stupid trip in the first place.

And he was even angrier at Jason for kissing Leah. He'd always worried Jason might someday go back to girls. And where would that leave Kyle? Maybe Jason wasn't The One for him after all. But how could he not be? Kyle had been so certain.

From the instant Kyle had seen him that first day of high school, he'd sensed Jason was going to have a special place in his life. And wasn't it amazing how Jason had walked into the gay youth meeting? Everything had been so perfect: how they

became friends first and then boyfriends. How could Jason betray him like this?

As the car drove westward, up and down the rolling hills of central Texas, Kyle felt his heart lurching and plunging. One moment he wanted to shake Jason and the next minute he wanted to cling to him.

In the front seat Nelson pulled out a cigarette and Jason turned toward him, glaring.

"Don't scowl at me that way." Nelson's hand trembled as he lit up. "I'm upset about the windshield."

Jason shook his head in disgust and rolled down his window. In the backseat, Kyle got blasted by both the hot air from outside and Nelson's cigarette smoke from inside.

"Put it out," he told Nelson.

"Huh?" Nelson glanced in the rearview.

"I said," Kyle repeated, "Put. It. Out. I'm sick of breathing in your smoke. I don't care if this is your car. I'm sick of smelling like tobacco all the time. You can smoke when we stop."

Kyle's heart pounded as he braced for an argument. But Nelson's face puckered into a pout. He tossed the cigarette out the window, muttering something Kyle couldn't hear because of the wind.

Jason glanced over his shoulder at Kyle. "Thanks."

Kyle turned away from him, still angry, as they reached I-10, where a sign welcomed them to WONDERFUL WEST TEXAS—DRIVE FRIENDLY. After that the landscape became flatter and the sky seemed to grow taller before their eyes. The oak trees got scrubbier, and the ground cover faded from vivid green to pale brown. Patches of flat nopal cactus began to appear alongside pinwheel windmills.

"It looks like we're in a cowboy movie." Jason pointed at a

huge flat-topped mesa and turned toward Kyle. But Kyle remained coolly silent, taking in the desert sights without Jason's help.

"Hey, look!" Nelson exclaimed, passing an RV. "They've got a rainbow flag!" He beeped the horn and waved.

Two older guys, one light-complexioned and the other cinnamon-skinned, waved back from the front seats of the RV.

That was just about the most exciting event of the next couple of hours. After a while the monotonous landscape of washed-out creek beds and recurring mesas seemed like a film background that kept repeating. The interstate stretched boringly ahead of them, cutting through limestone cliffs. And Jason began reading mileage signs: "Fort Stockton 139 miles," "Fort Stockton 102 miles," "Fort Stockton 86 miles."

"Would you stop?" Nelson finally shouted at him. "It's like dripping water torture. You're driving me crazy."

Jason gave a wounded frown. "I need to take a—" He stopped and corrected himself. "I need to use the bathroom."

"We may as well stop for lunch," Kyle suggested.

Outside Ozona a billboard advertised the Halfway Café, and they decided to try that.

"Yeah, it looks halfway decent," Nelson quipped as he drove into the crowded parking lot.

Inside, the café walls were lined with a bizarre collection of paintings—of a beagle eating at a bowl, a lone brown horse grazing on a green hillside, and a goat devouring a hat. In the corner hung a photo of the World Trade Center with the caption: PRAY. And at the center of each table stood a single cowboy boot, serving as a vase stuffed with plastic flowers.

While Jason headed to the restroom, Kyle scanned the packed restaurant. Weathered-looking men in jeans, every one with

either a cowboy hat, a baseball cap, or hat hair, occupied each table.

"Hi, boys," said a mint-uniformed waitress. "A table should clear in a sec."

"I wonder if her name's Flo," Nelson whispered.

Kyle ignored him, watching out the window. The RV they'd passed earlier was pulling into the parking lot. Once parked, the two older guys climbed out and walked into the café. Their hair was graying and tiny wrinkle lines showed at their eye corners.

"Hi." Kyle gave them a friendly nod and the men smiled back.

"Aren't you the boys with the rainbow flag?" the darker man asked and introductions followed. "I'm Miguel and this is Todd, my partner."

Todd's gaze moved between Kyle and Nelson. "And are the two of you . . . ?"

"We're just friends," Kyle clarified.

"*Best* friends," Nelson corrected. "His boyfriend is . . . this guy." Nelson pointed with his thumb as Jason walked up. Todd and Miguel introduced themselves again.

"Y'all together?" the waitress asked.

Kyle turned to the men. "You want to sit with us?"

After spending so much time around people his own age these past few days, Kyle eagerly welcomed the opportunity to be around adults.

"We'd love to," Miguel said, and Todd smiled. "Are you sure it's okay with you guys?"

"We don't want to intrude," Miguel added.

"It would be great," Kyle assured them.

The waitress led them to a freshly cleared round table. Kyle was glad to be sitting with the guys. It took his mind off Jason and Nelson, even though Nelson hardly let anyone else say any-

thing as he recounted tales of the Faerie Sanctuary, Graceland, the Britney contest, the windshield crack . . .

After the waitress returned and took their orders, Kyle seized the opportunity to jump into the conversation. "How long have you two been together?"

Todd and Miguel gazed at each other, smiling.

"Twenty years," Todd said softly.

"Twenty years today," Miguel specified, nodding happily at Todd.

Kyle realized that these two guys had been together as long as his parents had.

"This is our anniversary trip."

"Touring the West."

"We've been planning it for years."

"Since the first night we met."

"We talked about our dreams."

"Twenty *years*?" Nelson's jaw dropped. "I'm lucky if I can get a guy's attention for twenty minutes."

Jason moved the boot with the flowers aside to get a better view of the guys. "So, like, what's your secret?"

"Our secret?" Miguel asked.

"Yeah, you know, for staying together."

Miguel glanced at Todd. "I don't think there's any one secret, do you?"

"We share the same values," Todd replied. "Trust. Communication. Commitment."

Miguel chuckled. "We like the same food."

Kyle had noticed they both ordered the tuna salad platter, whereas Kyle had ordered grilled cheese with coleslaw and Jason ordered a burger with fries. Was that a sign that their relationship was doomed?

"We not only finish each other's sentences," Todd continued.

"We also answer each other's questions—"

"Before we even ask them."

As the food arrived, Nelson argued, "But I always heard opposites attract."

"Yeah." Miguel grinned. "But similars stay together."

Kyle swallowed a bite of his grilled cheese and asked, "How'd you each know the other was The One?"

"I knew the moment I laid eyes on him." Todd poked his fork into a tomato. "I swear my heart leaped inside my chest."

Kyle recalled the first moment he'd laid eyes on Jason. He'd been rendered speechless.

"In my case," Miguel contrasted, "I didn't have a clue. I'd kissed so many frogs that I'd given up ever finding Prince Charming."

Nelson laughed at the joke, though his laugh had a nervous ring.

"And how about you two?" Todd's gaze shifted across the table between Kyle and Jason. "What attracted you two to each other?"

Jason looked across the table at Kyle. Kyle glanced away uneasily, still too miffed at Jason to admit anything.

"His smile," Jason answered.

"My smile?" Kyle blurted out, incredulous. "What're you talking about? I wore braces."

"I know," Jason replied. "And you always tried to hide them with your shy little smile."

Kyle narrowed his eyes at Jason, refusing to let himself be sweet-talked.

But Jason stared right back at him. "And I liked how smart he was—I mean *is*—and I liked his body."

"His *body*?" Nelson protested. "He's skinnier than I am!"

"And what did you like about Jason?" Miguel asked Kyle.

Kyle frowned, answering reluctantly, "His eyes . . ." Even now, furious at Jason, he still loved those brooding deep brown eyes. "And his strength." Kyle always felt protected around Jason, with good reason: Jason had rescued him from a fight during senior year.

"And his passion . . ." Kyle admired the unwavering determination Jason showed toward basketball, the same steady persistence with which he'd approached Kyle, and that he demonstrated each time they made love. How could he not feel infuriated at Jason for sharing that passion with some girl at a bar?

"I'm not sure I could spend twenty years with anyone," Nelson interjected.

"At first I couldn't imagine it either," Miguel responded. "You just take it one day at a time."

"And before you know it," Todd said, "twenty years have passed." He smiled at Kyle and Jason. "You guys are lucky to be getting such a young start."

Kyle clenched his jaw. He wasn't feeling very lucky today.

When the bill came, Todd and Miguel insisted on paying for the boys' meals. The boys thanked them and said good-bye. Outside, beneath the shade of the front awning, Kyle watched the RV pull out of the parking lot.

While Nelson smoked a cigarette, Kyle returned inside to call his mom collect from a pay phone next to the rest room.

"What's happened, honey? Why aren't you using Nelson's cell phone?"

"He dropped it in the toilet."

Kyle's mom was quiet a moment, then asked, "Well, is everything all right? Where are you?"

"I don't know. Somewhere in Texas. I got into a fight with Jason."

He heard his mom take in a little breath. "You mean a fight-fight or an argument?"

"An argument," Kyle clarified.

"Do you want to talk about it?" his mom asked.

"No. It's about a girl. I don't want to talk about it."

"Okay . . . well . . . you and Jason both are still young. You're both growing. You're both changing."

That wasn't what Kyle wanted to hear.

"Have you taken some time apart, like I suggested?"

"Yeah," Kyle said, thinking about having left the club for a walk. And look what had happened. Instead of helping, this conversation was only adding to his anxiety. "Look, I've got to go," he told her.

"Well, just remember, you're both having new experiences that might change you and your relationship."

"Mom, I've really got to go, okay?"

"Okay, honey. I love you."

"Love you, too." He hung up and returned outside.

Nelson was finishing his cigarette. Jason was waiting beside him. Kyle asked Nelson for the keys and crossed the parking lot to the car, even though it was broiling.

He turned on the engine and cranked the AC full blast. A moment later Jason climbed in. Kyle didn't look over at him. They both sat silent, listening to the whir of the air-conditioning till Jason said, "I'm sorry, Kyle. I made a mistake, okay?"

Kyle squinted his eyes at him, refusing to give in. "I need to be able to trust you, Jason."

"You don't trust me?"

"How can I after last night? How do I know you really want to be with me?"

Jason gave a shrug. "I'm here, aren't I?"

Kyle shook his head, unconvinced.

"Do you want to break up?" Jason asked. "Is that it?"

Kyle stared at Jason, stunned. As angry as he'd gotten, the thought of breaking up had never entered his mind.

"No, I don't want to break up!" A shudder ran down his spine. "Do *you* want to break up?"

"No." Jason shook his head.

Kyle probed into those deep brown eyes that held such power to both anger and move him. He thought about what his mom had said about being young and changing. And he wondered: Could Jason and he ever possibly make it to twenty years?

# chapter 26

## jason    kyle
## nelson

At first Jason had been a little wary about the older guys they'd met at the Half-Way Café. He worried they'd be like some of the guys at that bar in New Orleans—checking out Kyle and him as if wanting something. But in fact they'd been just the opposite—they seemed to want the best for the three boys. It had been really nice of them to buy them lunch and to share their experience.

It amazed Jason that the guys had been together twenty years. It made him feel a lot more hopeful about Kyle and him, especially after the whole kissing Leah thing.

On one hand he thought Kyle was being unfair for not giving him more credit for walking away from Leah. But he also wished he could somehow convey to Kyle how much he regretted having let Leah kiss him.

He wanted to buy Kyle an apology gift. He'd noticed at the

café counter that they sold packs of Mexican jumping beans. They looked like they'd make a cool present.

But Kyle held all their cash. He might ask Jason what he wanted the money for. That would ruin the whole sense of a gift. Maybe giving Kyle all the money hadn't been such a good idea. But now didn't seem like the best time to ask for it back.

As they turned back onto I-10, Jason was relieved that at least Kyle didn't want to break up, but it bothered him that Kyle had said he didn't trust him.

Mile after empty desert mile whisked by, and Jason recalled what the two older guys at the café had claimed as their secret to staying together: Trust. Communication . . .

"Hey!" He glanced over at the speedometer and saw that Nelson was going ninety. "Take it easy, man!"

Kyle leaned forward across the seat. "Are you crazy? Slow down!"

"Chillax, there aren't any cops around. I want to see how fast we can go."

"Not with me in the car," Kyle said firmly.

Nelson took his foot off the pedal. "Yes, Mommy."

Another boring half hour passed before Kyle said, "This is our exit coming up."

They turned north onto US 285, the two-lane highway headed toward Carlsbad. That road was even more monotonous. Out of boredom Jason decided to clock how much time passed before they saw another car.

Fifteen minutes went by. They still hadn't encountered another car when Nelson slowed and pulled onto the shoulder, announcing, "I need to pee."

Jason scanned the desolate landscape. There wasn't a building in sight—only scrub, rocks, and sand. "Can't you wait?"

"I *vant* to pee *au naturelle*," Nelson replied, coasting to a stop.

"Leave the engine running," Jason told him, "so Kyle and I won't roast."

From inside the air-conditioned car, Jason watched Nelson hike among scrub, cactus, and yucca plants to the top of a small ridge, where the whole world could see him—if there had been anyone else around. Jason looked down the shimmering hot highway: not a car in sight.

"He's shouting something," Kyle said and rolled down his window.

"Woo-hoo!" Nelson yelled in the distance as he sprayed a stream from his shorts, back and forth across the desert. "It's fabulous!"

"He's so weird," Jason said.

After a moment Nelson stopped peeing. He just stood there with his shorts hanging off his butt. Jason rolled down his window and shouted, "Hurry up!"

Nelson turned to face the car, but rather than walk toward it, he began swinging his hips from side to side, letting his shorts drop and tugging off his T-shirt.

"What the hell's he doing?" Jason turned to Kyle.

Kyle stared blankly out the window. "I think . . . he's stripping."

Atop the dune, Nelson kicked off his khaki shorts, peeled off his underwear, and began jumping up and down, stark naked except for his sandals.

Jason blinked, incredulous, as Nelson spun in circles, waving his arms and everything else, shouting and whooping.

Kyle swung open the car door. "Nelson!" he shouted, climbing out. "Are you crazy? There are snakes out there!"

"Only mine!" Nelson laughed, shaking it at Kyle. "Woo-

**rainbow road**

hoo!" He ran in zigzags down the dune, hopping over rocks, yelling, "Try it, it's amaaaaazing!"

Jason climbed out of the car, shaking his head in disbelief. Just when he thought the guy couldn't possibly get any weirder . . .

Nelson ran up to the car, panting, and grabbed Kyle's hand. "Come on, guys! Cut loose! Jason, let yourself go!"

"Nelson!" Kyle pulled his hand away. "Would you please put your clothes back on?"

"Car's coming," Jason said.

But instead of scrambling to cover up, Nelson ran to the road's edge, waving, dancing, and calling, "Yoo-hoo!"

The car horn blared as it raced past. In the backseat, a young boy pressed his face against the window, wide-eyed and mouth agape, while the driver, a middle-aged woman in curlers, angrily punched the horn.

*That would've been just like my dad,* Jason thought, *if I'd ever pulled a stunt like this.* His old man had always squelched any show of spontaneous letting go on Jason's part.

After the car had passed, Kyle asked, "Can we go now?"

Nelson stood naked, stretching his arms toward the radiant afternoon sun. "You guys don't know what you're missing."

"Dude, put your clothes on," Jason said. He'd never really paid attention to Nelson's body before. Now, seeing him naked, he couldn't help notice. The guy actually had quite a nice little body.

Quickly Jason climbed back into the car. This entire trip was making him way too horny.

The sun was already low in the sky when the boys crossed the state line into New Mexico. Soon after, they arrived in Carlsbad.

"We're going to miss seeing the bats fly out of the caverns," Kyle said disappointedly, as Nelson drove from one campground

to another trying to find a site. Unfortunately, all were filled except for the Fam-E-Lee Values Campground, which advertised GOOD CLEAN FUN.

Inside the office Nelson asked the desk clerk, "Do you have sites that have good *dirty* fun?"

The sallow-faced woman stared at Nelson's pink hair, her lips unsmiling. "This is a family campground," she said flatly.

"We're family." Nelson smiled cheerily.

The woman handed each of the boys a page of rules. "No loud music. No alcohol. No drugs. If we get any complaints, you're out of here. Understand? Sign at the bottom and pay in advance. We have one site left."

"Isn't she a model of joy?" Nelson remarked as they bounced over one speed bump after another, past RVs and campers, squinting into the afternoon sun.

Their site waited at the very end of the sun-baked road, backed by a barbed wire fence that kept out the vast desert stretching beyond. One side of the site bordered a dry, sandy ditch. The other side housed a white minivan, a family-size tent, and a picnic table, beneath which Jason spotted a lone small boy, crouching in its shadow.

"Hi!" The boy's hand poked out from beneath the table as the boys climbed out of the car.

"Hi!" Nelson waved back, and muttered to Kyle and Jason, "He's family."

"Shut up," Jason told him. The kid couldn't be more than seven years old.

As the boys began unloading the trunk, Picnic Table Kid crawled out, revealing a tangle of curly blond hair and a ragged T-shirt that read: CAMP LIVING WATERS. He stared up silently at Nelson's pink hair and then perched a hand on one

**rainbow road**

hip, reading the car's license plate one syllable at a time.

"Vir-gin-i-a. Ith that farther than Utah?" The kid said with a lisp. "We're from Utah."

"*Definitely* family," Nelson mumbled, assembling the tent poles.

"About two thousand miles away," Kyle told the boy.

A man emerged from the neighboring tent, running a hand through his own curly blond hair as he walked over. "Esau, stop being a pest!" He dropped a hand onto the kid's shoulder and waved to the boys. "Sorry about that. He's got a mouth that won't stop. Just tell him to shut up."

"He's not bothering us," Jason spoke up, feeling sorry for the kid.

"He seems sweet," Nelson told the dad.

"Sweet?" The dad scoffed. "Sweet like a girl! He'd better start acting like a man or he's going to get his ass kicked."

The kid's blue eyes burned with shame as he quickly dropped his gaze.

"Now leave them alone," the dad said, and gave Esau a kick on the rump toward the family's tent.

Jason saw Kyle shake his head, sighing. And Nelson mouthed the words, "Ass. Hole."

The boys continued setting up camp, while the jerk dad picked on his kid inside the tent next door. It reminded Jason of how his own dad used to torment him nonstop. "How about if we go out for dinner?" he now suggested to Kyle and Nelson.

To his relief Kyle said, "I was thinking the same thing."

"Thank God!" Nelson agreed.

Night had fallen by the time the boys drove across the speed bumps out of the campground. "Who the hell would name their son Esau anyway?" Nelson asked. "It sounds like a donkey."

"It's from the Bible," Kyle told him.

"Oh, yeah. Dad seems mighty Christian," Nelson said sarcastically.

Jason drove down the town strip, looking for a place to eat. Finally they decided on McDonald's. Again. After ordering, they chose a booth by the window. They stared outside and unwrapped their burgers in silence till Kyle spoke up: "I bet Esau's lonely. I remember how lonely I used to feel. It's hard growing up different."

Jason chewed on his burger, recalling how confusing it had been not to have anyone to talk with about his feelings toward boys. But he didn't want to think about all that now. "How do you know for sure the kid's gay? He can't be older than seven."

"Oh, please!" Nelson dipped a French fry into ketchup. "I knew by the time I was three. Besides, it doesn't matter if he is or not, with that lisp and those curls, he's going to get called queer anyway. That's what's wrong with our society—if you're in any way different, you get clobbered."

"I never got clobbered," Jason said and instantly realized that was a huge lie. His dad used to pound him nearly every day. That's how he'd taught Jason to "act like a man," so that Jason wouldn't get clobbered by anyone else.

"Can we talk about something else?" Jason suggested.

Nelson gave an indifferent shrug. "Like what?"

"I don't know." After six days in a car together—and Kyle still pissed at him—what else was there to talk about?

Kyle stared out the window with a faraway look. "My dad always wanted me to be some sort of superstar athlete. He never accepted me for just me."

Nelson raised his arm to play the air violin and dabbed invisible tears from his eyes. "Yes, Kyle. We've heard you kvetch before."

Jason had to agree. He liked Mr. Meeks, who was always super-nice to him. But maybe that was because Jason *was* a star athlete.

"At least your dad doesn't treat you like some sort of leper," Nelson told Kyle. "I grew up swearing my dad couldn't really be my real dad, thinking there was some mistake—probably 'cause he treated *me* like a mistake."

Jason gazed across the table at Nelson's pink hair and million earrings. It was easy to picture his dad freaking out. And yet he felt angry at the guy. No one should treat their kid like that.

Jason kept trying to come up with something else to talk about, but all he could think about was his own dad.

"With my old man," Jason confided in a low voice so no one else could hear, "nothing I did was ever good enough. I remember my very first trophy and how my mom hugged me. But all my dad said was, 'It's about time.' No matter what I did, nothing was ever enough."

"Boy . . ." Nelson sighed. "What a bunch of losers, huh?"

Jason studied him, unsure. Did he mean them or their dads? Or both?

On the way back to the campground Nelson cranked the stereo up loud. Jason left it alone, letting the music drown out the bad feelings the dinner conversation had brought up.

He'd hoped for a cheery break after seeing that poor kid at the campground. Instead he felt more depressed than before.

With each speed bump the car hit, Jason couldn't help thinking: *That's just how this trip is turning out—one bump after another.*

# chapter 27

## jason

## kyle

## nelson

As they pulled into their campsite, Nelson noticed the lantern glowing in the tent next door. *Please don't let the dad still be yelling at the kid,* he prayed.

But as soon as he climbed out of the air-conditioned car, he heard Esau's dad continuing at it: "If you don't stop crying right now, I'll really give you something to cry about."

"Hey," Nelson whispered to Jason. "Can't you punch him out a little?"

He'd seen Jason smack a major school bully and knew he'd decked his dad. Surely he could take down Esau's dad.

Jason gazed toward the tent and rubbed his chin as though seriously considering it, but he was grinning.

"That's not funny," Kyle said. He grabbed his toothbrush, toothpaste, and towel and headed toward the bathhouse.

Jason sighed and said to Nelson, "Esau's old man would

probably press charges." He grabbed his own toothbrush and followed Kyle.

Nelson felt a little let down. So much for Jason the gay superhero. Nelson perched on the picnic table and shook a cigarette from his pack, noting it was the last one. While driving through the boring desert, he'd started thinking that maybe he should quit—especially after how Kyle had chewed him out in Texas.

But he might as well finish his pack. He lit up the cigarette and thought about Kyle. He was starting to worry about him. He'd counted on Kyle to be the one to keep cool and in control during this trip. Instead Kyle seemed like he was starting to lose it.

Kyle came back from the bathhouse still giving Jason the silent treatment, but at least he didn't sleep in the car again, like he'd threatened to that morning.

As Nelson slid into the tent beside Kyle, he could hear Esau's sobs from next door.

A woman's voice advised, "You'd better obey Daddy and stop crying or you'll make him mad."

"But I didn't mean it," Esau whimpered.

"Oh, stop sounding like a girl," his dad bellowed. "In fact, I think you *are* a girl. They must've made a mistake at the hospital. Now shut up and say your prayers. I don't want to look at you anymore."

Nelson closed his eyes and offered up his own prayers, hoping Esau would somehow turn out okay.

The following morning, Nelson woke to the commotion of Dad and Mom Esau.

"Why didn't you bring it?" Dad demanded.

"Because you didn't say to bring it," Mom responded.

Nelson pulled his pillow over his head, hoping to drown out the racket, only to hear Esau's dad bark, "Do I have to tell you everything?"

"Why don't they just shoot each other?" Nelson muttered, pulling the pillow off.

"Because of the kid," Jason's voice replied from across the tent.

Nelson glanced at Kyle's wristwatch: barely six A.M. No way. He sat up, too annoyed to sleep any longer. He tugged his shorts on, climbed out of the tent, and began searching the car trunk for cigarettes. Then he remembered he wanted to quit. Crap.

In the corner of the trunk he spotted his tin of blue corn facial scrub. He'd been meaning to do a mud mask the last few days. It might take his mind off his desire to smoke.

"I never thaw anyone with pink hair before," a small voice lisped beside him.

Nelson glanced down at the curly blond tuft beside him. "Where'd you come from?"

Esau turned and pointed a small finger beneath the picnic table. "That'th my dream houth."

Nelson glanced at the battered table and patted the kid's head. "Honey, it's a start, but you've got to learn to dream bigger than that."

Esau peered up at the tin of facial mud. "What'th that?"

Nelson displayed the palm-size tin. "Blue corn scrub mask."

Esau's eyes stared over his nose at the metal tin. "Corn? Like you eat?"

"Not exactly. You put it on your face." Nelson unscrewed the cap, revealing the coarse pale-blue cream inside.

Esau smelled it and gazed up at Nelson. "What for?"

"To exfoliate and cleanse pores." He added in his mind,

*Don't those screwed-up parents teach you* anything?

"Here, hold this." Nelson dipped a hand into the paste and handed the tin to Esau, who watched curious-eyed as Nelson smeared the scrub across his own face. "See? You make a mask and wait fifteen minutes."

Esau peered up at Nelson, his mouth hanging open. "How come?"

Nelson took the tin back, singing, "Some little desert mouse wasn't paying attention." He squatted down at Esau's eye level.

"Look, it's like this: When you get to be a teenager, the pores of your face start pooping crap and getting constipated. Isn't that something to look forward to? This is like a laxative to keep your pores clean and flowing smoothly. Get it? Good."

Esau's brows shot up. "Can I try it?"

Nelson studied the little tyke, so deprived-looking, with those messy curls and frayed sneakers. "Okay." He sighed. "We just have to make sure to get it off before the evil parents see you." He unscrewed the tin again and gently spread a scoop of cream across the boy's face, being extra careful around the eyes.

"It feelth cold like ithe," Esau lisped.

"Uh-huh." Nelson capped the tin and tossed it back into the trunk. Then he sat on the ground beside Esau. While the masks tingled their magic, Nelson watched families stir from their RVs and tents, as the sun began another blistering day. Meanwhile, the yelling continued from Esau's tent.

"Where did you put it?" Mr. Esau was shouting. "I left it here yesterday."

"Don't blame me," Mrs. Esau said. "I haven't seen it."

Esau glanced over his shoulder and returned to look at Nelson. "I like you."

Nelson shifted on his hard little patch of ground. He didn't

have much experience with kids and wasn't sure how to respond. "I . . . like you too, buddy." He stared at Esau and felt himself choking up. "Come on!" He stood up. "We'd better get that off your face before Satan's spawn come looking for you."

He grabbed his towel from the trunk and started toward the bathhouse only a few sites away. Esau hurried alongside him, trotting to keep pace. Unexpectedly, Nelson felt a tiny hand slip in between his fingers. He gazed down at the kid. Esau peered up at him, his eyes filled with trust and hope.

"Do you have dethert in Virginia?"

"No." Nelson gazed down at the mud-masked boy. "Mountains, beaches, and ocean, but no desert."

"I've never theen the othean," Esau said. "Only dethert."

*Yeah, your whole life seems like a desert.* Nelson pushed open the bathhouse door and led Esau to the washbasin. When the boy saw himself in the mirror, his entire face broke into a smile. For the first time Nelson saw him laugh, and he laughed too.

"Okay, let's get serious." Nelson wet the end of the towel beneath the faucet and crouched down to wipe the cream off Esau's face. "Now close your eyes. I want to tell you something, okay?"

Esau nodded trustingly as Nelson gently wiped the wet towel across his face, rinsing off the mud.

"Life's going to get rough sometimes," Nelson told the boy. "People will call you names and try to hurt you, they'll tell you what to feel, what to think. They'll say you're a mistake. But you're not. You know what I mean?"

Esau blinked open his eyes and shook his head. "Uh-uh."

Nelson wet the towel again, frustrated that he wasn't getting his point across. "Keep your eyes closed. Okay, just remember this one thing: It's okay to be you—exactly who you are, no matter what anyone says. Believe in yourself. Trust your heart. Be

true to who you are. Promise you'll remember that?"

Before Esau could answer, the door squeaked behind them. "What the hell?" a voice boomed.

Esau's eyes burst open. His entire little body began trembling.

"Get your butt over here!" His dad pointed to the floor, commanding. "I was looking all over for you."

Esau lowered his head and shuffled across the concrete floor to his dad.

"Didn't I tell you not to be a pest?" Esau's father cuffed the boy on the head. Esau erupted into tears.

Nelson stood from his crouch and tried to explain: "We were exfoliating."

"Leave my son alone." Dad gazed at Nelson, his eyes dark with anger. "If I see you near him again, I'll call the police." He gripped his son by the shoulder and shoved him out the door.

Nelson watched the door squeak closed and felt his mud mask cracking. A wave of fury surged into his chest. An instant later he bolted out the door, shouting after dad and kid: "No, *you're* the one the police should come after!"

He traipsed past families at picnic tables, who glanced up from their breakfasts at the pink-haired teenager with a blue mud mask.

"Why do you pick on him like that?" Nelson demanded. "He's just a little kid."

"Yeah?" The dad glanced over his shoulder, his face red from anger or embarrassment or both. "Well, he's *my* kid." He shoved the sobbing Esau toward the tent. "You keep away from him. Faggot!"

Kyle and Jason hurried from their tent as Nelson shouted back, "Asshole!"

Dad started toward Nelson, but Nelson didn't flinch. He

felt too angry to be scared. Besides, Jason had leaped up next to Nelson, yelling at the man: "Someday that boy's going to beat the crap out of you!"

"Guys?" Kyle called from behind. "Cut it out!"

"You hear me, Esau?" Jason shouted.

The little boy stood by his family's tent, eyes wide with awe at all the ruckus he'd caused.

"You grow up big and strong, Esau!" Jason yelled as Esau's mom tried to pull the boy into the tent. "When your day comes, you smack your dad, good and solid."

Esau's old man glanced over his shoulder at the boy. And Esau stared back up at him. For that one instant, Nelson saw a flicker of panic cross the man's face.

"It's okay, son." The man awkwardly laid his arm around the boy's shoulder, and guided him into the tent, no longer shoving him.

Nelson clapped Jason on the back. "That was so awesome!" But he turned to see Kyle shaking his head in disapproval. "What the heck was that all about? Are you guys crazy?"

"*He's* the crazy one." Nelson gestured over his shoulder at the dad.

"Exactly what happened?" Kyle insisted.

"Nothing!" Nelson tried to explain that it wasn't his fault. "Esau wanted a facial. And I told him to be true to himself."

"No wonder his old man got so mad." Jason sighed.

"You really think that accomplished anything?" Kyle asked.

"Yeah," Jason said forcefully. "I think it accomplished something. I bet that guy will think twice before he smacks his kid again—or before he calls someone a faggot again."

"I'm with you," Nelson agreed, punching and kickboxing their picnic table.

"Oh, right." Kyle crossed his arms. "I'm sure you really increased that guy's tolerance and acceptance of gay people."

"Look," Jason answered back. "I didn't come out just to take crap from people who think you can call someone a faggot and get away with it."

"Yeah!" Nelson jabbed the air excitedly.

"Would you shut up?" Jason snapped and returned to Kyle. "You think you can reason with people like that? The only way bullies stop is when someone stands up to them."

"You sure stood up to him," Nelson said proudly.

Kyle shook his head. "Let's just get out of here."

"Not till I do my drill," Jason said firmly.

While he went to shoot baskets, Nelson returned to the bathhouse to wash off the mud mask now flaking from his skin. It worried him to see Kyle and Jason argue, but it wasn't his fault. Was it?

When he came back to help Kyle load the trunk, he saw that Esau had reemerged from his family's tent. While his dad and mom argued and packed their minivan, the boy played by himself at the picnic table—no longer in the shadow underneath, but on top.

*Maybe there's hope for him yet,* Nelson thought.

As he, Kyle, and Jason climbed into the car to drive off, Nelson shouted, "Be yourself, Esau!"

And in defiance of his father's frown, Esau waved back.

The Carlsbad Caverns parking lot was already jammed with people when the boys arrived, even though it was barely eight. Kyle rented audio tour headsets for the three of them, and they descended into the cave's gaping entrance.

Nelson thought the stalactites, stalagmites, and curtain formations were cool, especially with the lighting effects, but after

having to circle around the millionth two-ton tourist waddling in front of him, he started getting crazy-impatient.

Kyle didn't help matters any, pausing to listen at every audio stop.

"I'll meet you guys at the cafeteria," Nelson said, hurrying on ahead.

The lunchroom at the bottom of the cave was equally crowded with kids and screaming parents. Nelson had to wait nearly twenty minutes for a Coke. Then he wandered around the gift shop, keeping a lookout for Kyle and Jason.

After a while, he decided he'd better backtrack up the cave trail. But it was too hard walking against the constant stream of people. Then when he turned back, none of the rock formations looked familiar. Had he even come this way?

After twisting down one trail and turning up another, he found his way back to the cafeteria and gift shop, but found no sign of his friends. He started sweating, unsure of what to do.

He decided to stay put in the lunchroom, wondering what could've happened to Kyle and Jason. And he was dying for a cigarette. After half hour, he decided he'd better go back to the car. But a crowd packed the waiting area for the elevators. Only after waiting another half hour did he finally reach daylight.

Unfortunately he couldn't remember where they'd parked. He walked down one broiling lane of the parking lot after another, till he finally heard Kyle shout, "Nelson!"

He and Jason were sitting in the car, doors and windows open, frowning and sweating.

"Where've you been?" Kyle demanded. "We've been waiting over an hour here, roasting!"

"I was looking for you," Nelson said feebly. "Why didn't you turn the AC on?"

"We did!" Jason started the engine. "For half an hour. You can't leave the car idling like that forever."

"I guess we missed each other," Nelson said, climbing in. He felt bad for having made them wait, especially since he'd been having a miserable time himself. "I'm sorry," he told Kyle. "So did you like the caverns?"

"Yeah," Kyle replied. "I wish I'd known I could've taken another hour."

Nelson slouched down in the seat, deciding he'd better just keep his mouth shut. But he couldn't.

"Have you guys noticed I haven't had a cigarette all day? I decided to quit."

"Great," Jason said. But Kyle merely stared out the window as the car headed downhill along the narrow, winding road.

That despondent zombie look on his face worried Nelson. Kyle usually wasn't that morose.

## chapter 28

## jason kyle nelson

Ever since Kyle had written a report on caves in third grade, he'd dreamed of one day descending the steep, dark, musty trail into Carlsbad. All his books considered them the most spectacular caverns on Earth. But his dream hadn't included feeling totally annoyed with his boyfriend and being blood-boiling pissed at his best friend.

Kyle still hadn't gotten over Jason letting that girl kiss him; it upset him that Jason had posed the question about breaking up; and it troubled him how Jason's temper so easily flared up at that little boy's dad.

In addition to all that, it infuriated Kyle how Nelson had so carelessly tried to test how fast he could speed down the interstate; how he'd stopped and totally-out-of-line danced naked in the desert; not to mention how he'd caked a mud mask on the face of some little boy he didn't even know; and on top of

everything else, how he'd gotten lost in the caverns, worrying Kyle like crazy.

Had both Jason and Nelson gone bonkers? The two of them were acting completely out of control. And Kyle didn't have a clue as to what to do about it. Instead, he simply gazed out the window at mile after mile of cactus, sand, and black rock mountains, while he shifted across the backseat to avoid the scorching sun.

"Can we stop to eat?" Nelson asked as they reached White's City, a fakey old-time Western town and water park.

"Yeah," Jason agreed. "I'm hungry."

"Whatever," Kyle told them.

Over lunch in a booth, Jason—for the first time all trip—asked to see the map. "Where are we going next?"

Kyle pointed to the route they'd originally agreed on: south to I-10, west through El Paso and Tucson, then north to Phoenix and the Grand Canyon.

"Hmm." Jason studied the map. "Hey, isn't Roswell where that UFO crashed?"

"Oh my God!" Nelson leaned over his shoulder, screaming. "We've got to go there!"

Kyle stared across the table at the two of them. "Like, you think you're actually going to see aliens? That's not the route we planned. It'll take us totally out of our way."

"No, it won't," Jason said. "We'll just go north here instead of there."

"Jason, no!" Kyle crossed his arms in frustration. Why did Jason suddenly want to switch tracks on him?

"Guys, wait!" Nelson spread his arms between them. "At times like these, I believe we should ask ourselves, 'What would Jesus do?' I think He'd definitely want to see aliens."

"Come on, Kyle." Jason's commanding eyes gazed across the table at him. "We saw the caverns like you wanted. Now this is our chance to see Roswell."

Kyle pushed his plate away, no longer hungry, and slumped against the seat. "Fine!"

As he suspected, there wasn't much to see in Roswell except "alien" souvenir shops and a free UFO museum that Jason and Nelson insisted they go to.

"It's probably free because no one would pay for it," Kyle grumbled.

An alien mannequin greeted them at the door. Beyond that, the exhibits were mostly newspaper articles with blurry photos of supposed UFOs. The museum wasn't totally lame, but it wasn't the civil rights museum either.

"I need five bucks," Jason told Kyle at the gift shop. In his hand he held an alien doll. "I want to get it for my sister."

"Five bucks?" Kyle inspected the cheaply stitched doll. "For this? We're short of money, you know?"

"Yeah, but I know she'll like it." He gave Kyle a stern look. "You know, maybe it's not a good idea for me to have to ask you for money all the time."

"Oh, yeah?" Kyle dug into his pocket, yanking out the envelope of money. "This was your idea in the first place. I never wanted to do it." He shoved the entire wad into Jason's hand and walked out.

"Let's see how long the money lasts now," he muttered to himself. He wished he'd never agreed to hold the money for Jason. And he still felt like a dope for losing his wallet.

While he leaned against the car waiting, Kyle noticed again the windshield crack made by the flying pebble. He leaned over to run his finger across the glass. Had the break

gotten bigger? Like a widening spider web, the dime-size chink now spiked out to the size of a half-dollar.

Behind Kyle, Nelson's snapping fingers and Jason's laughter sounded. He turned to see them joking and cutting up, each carrying a bag stuffed with UFO souvenirs.

"Does the crack look bigger to you?" Kyle asked them.

A silly grin crept across Jason's face. "Whose crack?"

At that Nelson doubled over, hee-hawing. "Yeah, turn around, Kyle. Let's see!"

He and Jason high-fived each other like it was the funniest joke ever.

Kyle stared in dismay at these two cackling aliens. How had this road trip mutated the boy he loved and his best friend into the gay Beavis and Butthead?

The two of them kept giggling about anal probes as they headed west on US 70 toward Picacho, until Kyle announced, "We need gas." He'd made a point of keeping an eye on the gas gauge ever since the Tennessee incident.

Nelson pulled into the next station. At one of the pump islands, a red pickup truck stood parked. A guy wearing a black cowboy hat waited in the driver's seat. A younger man in a wifebeater tank top, boots, and jeans pumped the gas.

"Yum!" Nelson smacked his lips, staring at the gas-pump guy. "He's hot!"

*He was definitely buff,* Kyle thought, but as they got closer, the steely look in the guy's gray eyes sent a chill down Kyle's spine. "Why don't you go over to the other island?"

"I want to get a better look." Nelson grinned, pulling up directly across from the truck. "Can one of you squeegee while I pump?"

"You stay here," Kyle told him. "Jason and I will do it."

"Kyle, what's your problem?" Nelson flung his door open. "May I at least have a hall pass to pee?" Without waiting for a reply, he slammed the door and strode into the station, fluffing his pink hair.

Jason wiped the windshield while Kyle pumped. Out of the corner of his eye he noticed the creepy gas-pump guy chewing tobacco. He had never actually seen somebody spit tobacco. A gooey brown stain landed on the concrete beside Kyle.

"I think you're right!" Jason's voice carried from the windshield. "The crack is getting bigger."

As Kyle lifted his gaze from the pump handle, he watched the creep's gray eyes shift from Jason to the windshield, to the FAGGS scratched into the door, and then to the rear bumper, no doubt spying the rainbow flag. Hopefully, he didn't know what it meant.

Kyle also spotted a sticker on the truck: TERRORIST HUNTER'S PERMIT—WE NEVER FORGET.

Out of nervousness Kyle offered the creep a tight, polite smile. "How's it going?"

In response, Creepy Eyes silently nodded, his clenched jaw slowly grinding the tobacco in his cheeks.

Fortunately, the gas tank finally filled. Jason climbed into the passenger seat. Kyle returned the hose. And Nelson shuffled out of the gas station in his sandals. "The men's room was too nasty," he announced, no doubt aware that the creeps with the pickup could hear him. "So I used the ladies'."

Kyle quickly replaced the gas cap as the creep spoke for the first time: "Hey, Pinky!" he yelled to Nelson. "What's that rainbow flag mean?"

"Diversity!" Kyle intervened, trying to keep Nelson's mouth shut. "It stands for diversity."

But Nelson gave the buff creep a broad smile, wink, and wave. "It means we're queer, butch."

The creep stared back expressionless as Kyle leaped into the car and yanked Nelson in after him. "Are you insane? Let's go!"

"What did he do now?" Jason asked.

"Wasn't he so frickin' hot?" Nelson exclaimed, pulling out of the station.

Kyle glanced out the window, watching the creep climb into the pickup and talk to the black-hatted driver. "He told the guys back there we're queer."

Jason turned to Nelson. "What did you do that for?"

"Because we are." Nelson opened the CD compartment and asked Jason, "Hey, can you find that song, 'Save a Horse, Ride a Cowboy'?"

"They're following us," Kyle announced.

The pickup had U-turned out of the gas station onto the highway behind them, as Kyle's heart slid into his stomach.

"So what?" Nelson gazed into the rearview. "What do you think they'll do, drive us off the road?"

"They're gaining on us," Kyle said as the truck began speeding up behind them.

Jason looked back out the rear window, then turned to Nelson. "That was really stupid, you know."

"Can't you find the CD?" Nelson replied.

Kyle glanced ahead as the road began to curve and a sign read MOUNTAIN CORRIDOR—SPEEDING FINES DOUBLED.

"Slow down," he told Nelson as the pickup drew alongside. "Just let them pass."

But the truck didn't pass. While Black Hat kept pace beside the boys, Creepy Eyes leaned out the passenger side, gesturing at Nelson to roll down his window.

"Don't!" Jason ordered. "Don't roll it down."

"Would you queens calm down? You afraid they'll toss a grenade?"

"Just don't roll down your window!" Kyle shouted. His heart was beating a million miles an hour.

"I won't." Nelson shook his head no at Creepy Guy.

In response the guy flipped the boys the finger, yelling something they couldn't hear. Nelson flipped him back.

"Dude!" Jason yanked Nelson's hand down. "Don't do that!"

Kyle leaned across the backseat toward Nelson. "Does the name Matthew Shepard mean anything to you?"

The creepy guy reached for something inside the truck. Suddenly an open beer can flew out the window and through the air, bouncing onto the hood of the boys' car. *Bang-bang-bang!* The can slammed into the windshield, spraying its golden contents before rattling over the roof. Kyle spun around to watch the can spring onto the pavement behind them.

"Crap!" Nelson shouted as beer streamed across the windshield. "Did he really just do that?"

"The crack just got bigger." Jason leaned forward to examine the glass, now splintered to the size of a fist.

"Let them go on!" Kyle ordered as the truck pulled ahead.

But as Nelson slowed the car, the truck swerved in front of them, causing Nelson to brake harder.

"Holy crap!" he exclaimed. "They really are trying to run us off the road."

"Pass them!" Jason shouted.

"No!" Kyle argued. "Just let them go."

"Gun it!" Jason shouted.

Another beer flew out from the truck, sailing through the air, and hit the windshield. Slam! The glass cracked wider.

"One more," Jason shouted, "and it's going to shatter. You'd better floor it!" Nelson swerved into the passing lane but the truck swung out to block them.

"Crap!" Nelson shouted. "They won't let me."

"Turn around!" Kyle yelled.

"Swing around to the right," Jason ordered.

Nelson yanked the wheel to the right, bouncing onto the shoulder, barely missing the truck.

"Now gun it!" Jason shouted.

Nelson floored the gas pedal as Kyle whirled around. Behind them the truck sped ahead, moving up on the left.

"Get over!" Jason shouted. "You can't let them pass. Speed up!"

Nelson clenched the wheel, squealing around a mountain curve marked 45 MPH. Kyle glanced at the speedometer: The needle was pointing at 72.

"Slow down!" Kyle shouted.

"I can't!" Nelson darted a glance in the rearview. "They're right behind us."

As they rounded the corner onto a straightaway, Kyle gripped Jason's seat to keep from falling over. How had this happened?

"They're gaining on us," Nelson said, gazing into the rearview. He slid down the seat, his foot gunning the accelerator.

"Slow down!" Kyle shouted, watching the speedometer pass 80, 90, 95 . . . as Nelson rounded one mountain curve after another. Yet the truck kept following. Kyle's heart pounded furiously.

"We're doing a hundred," Nelson announced. "Woo-hoo!"

"Watch the curve," Jason told him.

Kyle gazed ahead at a yellow arrow sign, marked CURVE 35 MPH.

Nelson jammed the brakes as the car squealed on the

**jason    nelson    kyle**

pavement. He hunched over the steering wheel, knuckles white, as he hugged the inside of the curve.

Kyle whirled around to see the truck spin across the roadway, slam through the median barricade, cross the opposing lanes, and head toward the outside edge of the mountain. He watched in horror as the truck bounced against the guardrail, nearly careening over the side, before coming to a stop, barely held back by the railing.

"They spun out," Kyle said breathlessly.

Nelson gazed in the rearview. "We lost them?"

"Yeah, they slammed across the road." Kyle glanced over his shoulder. "We should stop. They might be hurt."

"That's their problem." Jason shook his head. "We're not stopping."

"Woo-hoo!" Nelson snapped his fingers. "Ding-dong, the witch is dead. . . . Hey, I think we hit a hundred and five. That was so awesome." He raised his palm to high-five Jason.

"Are you crazy?" Kyle shouted. "We could've been killed."

"But we weren't." Jason slapped Nelson's palm.

"Oh, man!" Nelson laughed. "On that one curve, I thought we were goners."

"For sure!" Jason took a deep breath, stretching his arms. "I wish I'd seen them wipe out."

"Stop it!" Kyle shouted, his voice trembling. How could they be gloating like this?

Jason turned, his brow furrowed in concern, staring at Kyle. "What's the matter with you, Kyle? They tried to run us off the road."

"Who are you?" Kyle gazed back at him.

Jason gave Nelson a worried glance and looked back at Kyle. "What do you mean?"

Kyle felt his whole body shaking. "Who the hell are you two?"

"Kyle?" Nelson said softly. "You okay?"

"No!" Kyle shouted, folding his arms. "You nearly killed us back there, and you're joking about it? I don't know who you two are anymore, 'cause you're not who I thought you were."

Jason gazed back at him, not saying anything, then he reached his hand over to lay his hand on Kyle's knee, but Kyle pulled away.

"Leave me alone." He lay down on the seat, curling his knees up to his chest, wanting to close up and die. Why had he ever come on this trip? He covered his head with his pillow and began quietly sobbing, crying himself to sleep.

*chapter 29*

# jason kyle
# nelson

Jason bit into a fingernail, worried by how Kyle had curled up on the seat. It reminded him of how his little sister used to ball herself up when she got scared by his dad's drunken rages. Had the truck chase really freaked Kyle out that much?

Jason stared down the steep mountain valley dropping off the side of the road. "You'd better slow down," he told Nelson. "The sign said, 'Speeding fines doubled.'"

The car slowed as Nelson eased up on the gas pedal, grinning. "Can you imagine getting nabbed going a hundred and five? That's the fastest I've ever gone."

But as they wound up one hill and down another, Jason no longer felt quite so thrilled by having gone through the truck chase. Kyle was right: They could've been killed. And for what? Because of Nelson's stupid loud mouth?

"You shouldn't have said anything to those guys," Jason told him.

"Well, duh." Nelson's smile faded. "Don't you think I know that?"

"Then why'd you do it?"

Nelson's brow knitted up. "I don't know. Sometimes crap like that just pops out of my mouth. I even know while I'm saying it I should shut up. But by then it's too late. I can't stop myself."

Jason shifted uncomfortably. "So what happens if one day you can't race away at a hundred miles an hour?"

Nelson looked out the window at the black and blue mountains in the distance. "I guess I'll get my ass kicked." He pressed his lips together into a thin smile. "Don't worry. It won't be the first time."

"I'm not worried." Jason said and gazed out at the road ahead. As they descended onto the desert plain below, he thought how sometimes he also had a hard time controlling himself—not with stuff he said but with stuff he did, like getting mixed up with that girl the other night. Why couldn't he be like Kyle, always cool, always in control?

"You think maybe we should've stopped to make sure those guys were all right?" Jason asked.

"No way, dude!" Nelson shook his head. "Maybe if they'd gone over the cliff or something. They're the ones who tried to run us off."

Jason gazed into the backseat at Kyle. His chest rose and fell in sleep. "I think that really scared him. I've never seen him so upset."

"He'll get over it." Nelson's voice rang with certainty. "Sometimes he just gets a little freaked out, like my mom. He'll

be fine." Nelson was silent for the next few miles but his fingertips nervously tapped the steering wheel. "I'm more worried about me. What's going to happen once he leaves for Princeton? Know what I mean?"

Jason had tried not to think about Kyle leaving for college. All trip he'd put it out of his mind. He'd never considered that Nelson might be worried about it too.

"Yeah," Jason agreed, wondering: What would happen to him without Kyle around to guide him and help him think things through? Without Kyle to joke and just hang out with? Without Kyle to make love with?

Jason knew he was a better person because of Kyle. If it weren't for Kyle, he might never have come out to his parents, or worked up the courage to keep going to the school's Gay-Straight Alliance, or come out to his coach and team. Most importantly, he might never have accepted himself.

He only wished that he could be more the guy Kyle wanted him to be and not do so many stupid, impulsive things.

But what if he couldn't change? What if Kyle decided after this trip that he no longer wanted to be boyfriends?

Jason tried not to think about that, gazing instead at the endless blue sky stretching before them.

He put on one of Kyle's Norah Jones CDs and turned the volume low. It occurred to him that not once during the entire trip had Nelson or he asked Kyle if he wanted to play any of his music.

Now, as Jason and Nelson drove across the desert landscape, neither of them said much. But every once in a while one of them would check the backseat, eager for Kyle to wake up.

It wasn't till they approached Albuquerque that Kyle

finally stirred. Jason and Nelson exchanged a look, each too nervous to speak.

Kyle sat up, rubbing a hand across his puffy face. It almost looked as though he'd been crying.

"You sleep okay?" Jason asked.

"Yeah." Kyle covered a yawn. "Where are we? Hey, we need gas."

"I know." Nelson flicked on the blinker as he pulled onto an exit ramp. "I was waiting. I didn't want to wake you up."

At the gas station they filled the tank, took turns peeing, and cleaned the windshield. Jason examined the glass crack with his fingers to make sure it was holding steady.

"Is it okay?" Kyle asked.

"I think so, but we should do something about it in L.A."

Jason stared at Kyle, wanting to say more, afraid the windshield wasn't the only thing in need of repair.

"Hey, you guys hungry?" Nelson asked as they continued west along I-40.

Jason had lost his appetite with the truck chase, but now he was starving. "Yeah, I am. How about you, Kyle?"

"A little." Kyle nodded. "Not that much, but go ahead and stop."

"I'm sick of burgers," Nelson said. "How about that place?" He pointed to an ALL-U-CAN-EAT sign.

Inside, the restaurant swarmed with hefty parents and kids heaping their plates with mountains of ribs, fried chicken, and pizza.

Jason joined right in. But Kyle barely filled his plate. Meanwhile, Nelson piled his plate with fried shrimp, clams, oysters, coleslaw, and steamed king crab legs. "I love seafood," he announced, sitting at the table.

"You trust that?" Jason asked. "We're in the middle of the desert, you know."

"I think they have refrigerators here," Nelson replied, popping an oyster into his mouth. "This is so awesome! I'm *so* sick of McVomits."

"Dude, we're eating," Jason said. As he chewed on a rib, it worried him to see Kyle so quiet, barely picking at his pizza, apparently still shaken by the truck chase. Trying to think of some way to snap him out of it, Jason asked, "Think we can make the Grand Canyon tonight?"

"May as well," Kyle said simply.

"It's supposed to be amazing!" Jason said enthusiastically, but Kyle merely poked at a pepperoni.

"I'm going to get some more," Nelson announced, pushing away from the table.

Jason wanted to get dessert, but he stayed with Kyle. "Are you still upset? About not going back to see if those guys were okay?"

"Yeah," Kyle said, his hazel eyes stern and serious.

"But what if we'd gone back and they tried to jump us?" Jason argued.

"Well . . ." Kyle shrugged. "That's part of the risk of being responsible. Sometimes you get hurt."

"But say they weren't okay," Jason persisted. "What could we have done?"

"I don't know." Kyle sighed. "Gone for help, I guess. But it's not just that." He gave Jason a long look. "It's this whole trip. It's not what I expected." He leaned back, shaking his head, as if reluctant to say more.

Jason also pulled back, afraid to ask more, fearing what Kyle

might say: that Jason wasn't the person he'd expected. That he wanted to break up.

Nelson returned with a second plate piled even higher with fried clams, fish, and softshell crabs.

"Dude, you're eating like a pig," Jason told him.

"Oink-oink." Nelson crunched into the shell of a crab, so that the legs poked out of his mouth as he chewed. "I love these things."

Jason felt a little queasy watching him. "I'm going to get some dessert." He turned to Kyle. "You want some ice cream?"

"No, thanks," Kyle replied. But at the ice cream counter, Jason got him a scoop anyway. "In case you change your mind." He set the bowl in front of Kyle.

Nelson peered at the single-scoop ice cream dishes. "This place isn't losing any money on you guys."

When Nelson went to get dessert, Jason told Kyle in a low voice, "He's, like, stuffing himself."

Kyle glanced at the stack of Nelson's empty plates. "That's what he does when he's upset."

"You mean he's bulimic?" Jason asked. There'd been a guy on his team like that.

"Not as much as before," Kyle replied.

Nelson brought back a plate piled with chocolate cake, apple cobbler, banana pudding, oatmeal cookies, watermelon chunks, strawberry ice cream, and raspberry frozen yogurt.

"You're going to make yourself sick," Kyle told him.

Nelson shoveled a spoonful into his mouth, unconcerned. "You guys want some?"

As they walked out to the car he burped so loud it echoed across the parking lot.

"Excuse me!" He patted his stomach and told Kyle, "Let me sit in back so I can lie down."

The trip west on I-40 was unremarkable, except for an orange and pink sunset. Jason reached across the seat to gently hold Kyle's hand, but got hardly any response. And when he finally let go, Kyle moved his hand away.

Jason's heart clenched up. Kyle had never frozen on him like that. He'd gotten heated and angry. Jason could deal with that—apologize, soothe him. But now he feared he was losing Kyle and had no idea what to do about it.

He drove onward into the enveloping darkness, while Nelson burped annoyingly from the backseat.

# jason   kyle

# nelson

Nelson shifted his weight from one side of the backseat to the other. He sat up, lay down, and propped himself on Kyle's pillow, trying every possible position to make himself comfortable. He knew he shouldn't have eaten so much, but he felt like he'd been on a starvation diet all trip, the way Kyle parsed out meal money. But now, with each burp, he was glad Kyle had kept him in check.

When they stopped to pee at the Petrified Forest exit, Nelson debated whether he should make himself puke, like he used to. But he'd promised himself he wasn't going to do that anymore. He knew Kyle would feel disappointed and angry with him. And besides, it would probably stink up the whole gas station.

Once back in the car, he asked, "Hey, would you turn up the AC? It's really warm back here."

Jason cranked it up. But even though the chill draft blew over the seat to Nelson, he still felt warm. He started sweating. Then, an hour outside of Flagstaff, he began shivering like crazy.

"Hey, c-c-can you t-t-turn it down?" His teeth chattered. "It's like the North P-p-pole back here."

"We turned it down a while ago." Kyle reached his hand over the back of his seat to feel the air. "It's warmer back there than up here." He switched the overhead light on and stared down at Nelson, who lay huddled and shaking. "Are you okay?" Kyle asked.

"I think maybe I ate t-t-too much."

Kyle leaned over the seat, laying his hand on Nelson's forehead. "You're burning up!" He skipped his hand down along Nelson's face and across his chest. "And you're dripping wet." He turned to Jason. "As soon as we get to Flagstaff, we need to look for a hospital."

"H-hospital?" Nelson shivered. "I'm not that sick."

"Look for one of those blue H signs," Kyle told Jason.

As they continued down the dark interstate, Nelson stared up at the sky full of stars and started feeling nauseous, like the car was spinning beneath him. He closed his eyes as Kyle and Jason's voices drifted in and out, one moment sounding distant, like they'd stepped outside the car, and the next sounding like they were yelling in his ear.

"Come on! Get out! We're here!"

A hand squeezed Nelson's shoulder, shaking him. He opened his eyes to see Kyle and Jason. But why were they standing upside down?

"Sit up," Kyle told him. As Jason hoisted Nelson up, Kyle strapped Nelson's sandals back onto his feet.

**rainbow road**

"Where are we?" Nelson asked. His stomach wobbled, like it was about to hurl its contents.

"The hospital," Jason told him. "Put your arm around my shoulder."

"Watch his head," Kyle said, as Jason pulled Nelson to his feet.

"I can walk!" Nelson protested, tugging his arm away from Jason. But the moment Jason let go of him, Nelson felt himself sinking like a rock. Jason caught him just in time.

"I'll park the car!" Kyle shouted as Jason walked Nelson toward the door.

Unfortunately, just then Nelson's burps returned. Jason scolded him, "Dude, turn your head!"

Nelson cupped a hand to shield his eyes from the lights of the emergency waiting area.

Jason deposited Nelson in a white chair. "I told you not to eat that seafood."

When Kyle returned from the car, he pulled the health insurance card from Nelson's wallet and hurried to the registration counter. Nelson waited beside Jason, feeling so woozy and out of it he could hardly follow what was going on. He tried closing his eyes, but that only amplified the sounds around him: a screaming baby, coughs and sneezes, an old lady whose lungs rattled, a South Asian doctor shouting something about liver heat or heated liver . . .

"Here, sign these!" Kyle handed Nelson a ballpoint and some forms.

Nelson squinted at the papers. "What do they say?"

"That from now on you'll do everything I tell you."

Nelson signed where Kyle pointed. Then Kyle left again, and Nelson let his head drop onto Jason's shoulder.

"Hey, what're you doing?" Jason pushed him back up.

"I need to lie down, man." Nelson rested his head onto Jason's shoulder again.

"You can't lie down here," Jason told him, but Nelson's head was already sliding down Jason's chest and onto his lap, as Jason sighed in resignation.

"You know he adores you," Nelson mumbled.

"What?" Jason replied from somewhere above Nelson's head.

"Kyle adores you."

"Not anymore," Jason said. "Not after this trip."

Nelson didn't have the strength to argue. A dull ache had started in his forehead. So he simply said, "Yes, he does. He always will."

And then he blanked out till Kyle said, "You two look cozy."

Jason replied, "What's that for?"

"In case he throws up."

Nelson blinked his eyes open. Kyle was handing a stainless steel bedpan to Jason and said, "I'm going to phone his mom."

"You sure?" Jason asked. "It's like three in the morning there."

"Don't call her," Nelson mumbled, but he was too weak to stop Kyle. Besides, his stomach was feeling queasy again, even more than before. His throat tightened and his stomach started wrenching.

"What the heck am I supposed to do with this?" Jason muttered at the bedpan.

"I don't know," Nelson said weakly. "But I think I'm going to vomit."

Immediately, Jason propped him up. "Wait!" He whirled around, his eyes frantically scanning the room. "Come on!" He hauled Nelson to his feet, hurrying him past the old people, moms with kids, and coughing guys toward the rest room.

Nelson felt his saliva glands on overdrive as he tried to hold

his barfing down a few more seconds. Jason slammed the bath-room door open. Nelson's stomach gave a spasm. Jason rushed him toward the washbasin and Nelson started puking.

As Nelson heaved and hurled, Jason held him by the waist to keep him propped up, while with his other hand he gripped Nelson's forehead to keep it from hitting the faucet.

Nelson couldn't tell how long it lasted, but he did keep hearing Jason mutter "Whoa, dude!"—and not in an apprecia-tive way.

"I think I'm done," Nelson said at last. He felt like he'd upchucked all his bodily organs. His nasal passages burned from bile.

"Are you sure?" Jason asked testily.

Nelson nodded and Jason let go of him, but Nelson felt too weak to stand. He leaned a shoulder against the wall and slumped down toward the cold tile floor.

"Hey, what're you doing?" Jason tried to catch him.

"I'm sorry," Nelson said in a raspy voice. His eyes were sting-ing. "I should've listened to you and not eaten the seafood."

"Hey," Jason said. "You crying?"

"No." Nelson tried to choke down his sobs but that only made the inside of his nose burn more. His throat felt scratchy. His jaw hurt. His body felt like jelly.

Jason grabbed a paper towel and wiped it across Nelson's face. "Hey, come on. Let's go find Kyle. He's going to wonder what happened."

Then Jason and Kyle were leading Nelson by the elbows into a curtained alcove.

"What did his mom say?" Jason asked Kyle.

"She freaked out, said to call her as soon as he sees the doctor."

A petite nurse the size of a twelve-year-old took Nelson's

temperature and blood pressure. Then a doctor with a long black ponytail, wearing a white lab coat, hurried in. "Hey, guys. What happened to him?"

Kyle replied. "I think he got food poisoning at dinner."

"I told him not to eat the seafood," added Jason.

The doc glanced at Nelson's pink 'do. "I like your hair."

"I like yours." Nelson smiled. "Are you Indian?"

"Yep, Hopi." Doc Dude lifted a depressor to Nelson's mouth. "Open up."

"He just vomited," Jason warned him.

"That's okay," Doc said.

As soon as the depressor was out he told Nelson, "Please take off your shirt and lie back." Doc rubbed his hands together and rested them on Nelson's bare midriff. His palms felt warm.

"Tell me if this feels tender," Doc said. The statement confused Nelson as he stared up into Doc's beautiful dark eyes, barely able to concentrate on answering a barrage of questions: "Have you experienced any loss of breath? Bleeding? Seizures? Chest pain? Diarrhea? Fever? Chills? Abdominal pains? Nausea? Weakness? Headache?"

"Okay," Doc said at last. "Put your shirt back on. It looks like food poisoning." He told Nelson he'd be back to normal within twelve to forty-eight hours and wanted to put him on a saline IV and have him stay for observation for a couple of hours.

"You have to call your mom first," Kyle told Nelson. "She wants to know you're okay."

"Can't you just tell her?" Nelson pleaded, wanting to curl up.

"Come on, man." Jason pulled him to his feet. "She wants to hear your voice."

"She wants to yell at me," Nelson countered, but Kyle and Jason dragged him to the pay phone.

        **rainbow road**

His mom didn't yell. From her voice, Nelson could tell she'd been crying.

"I'm okay, Mom," he assured her and found himself crying along with her, even though it embarrassed him that Kyle and Jason were standing there watching.

He wasn't aware of much after that, except the nurse attaching an IV to his arm; trying to sleep beneath the bright waiting room lights; the doctor saying, "He can go now. Remember he has to stay hydrated. Lots and lots of water"; Jason carrying him to the car; lying on the backseat; Kyle saying, "You think the campground's going to let us in at three in the morning?"; the sound of the trunk opening; being carried into the tent; and Kyle whispering, "You scared me, buddy."

Then Nelson crashed into the deepest sleep.

# chapter 31

## jason    kyle
## nelson

Kyle lay awake in his sleeping bag, fretting about Nelson. What would happen to him when Kyle went away to college? Who would look after him?

Not that Kyle seemed to have much success at keeping him out of trouble. Kyle had felt like a failure having to tell Mrs. Glassman her son was in the ER. Hadn't Kyle promised to look after him?

"I'm really sorry," he told her over the phone. "Jason warned him not to eat the seafood, but he wouldn't stop."

"That's not your fault," she assured him. Kyle could understand that in his head, but in his heart he felt like he'd screwed up.

After all, Nelson was his most loyal friend ever. He'd helped Kyle make it through high school. He'd gotten Kyle to get over his fears about being gay. He'd encouraged him to come out to

his parents. And he'd given him the nerve to go after Jason.

What would his life have been like without Nelson? Seeing him so sick and feverish had shaken Kyle. And it made him wonder: How would he make it without Nelson when he had to leave for college?

Of course they'd stay friends, talk on the phone, and hang out during school vacations, but that was way different from spending almost 24/7 together, like during the past four years.

On the other side of Kyle's sleeping bag, Jason rolled over, and Kyle's thoughts wandered to how both good and confusing it had been to watch Nelson and Jason become better friends during the trip.

He'd enjoyed watching them get closer. But it irked him how Nelson accepted Jason after he did stuff Kyle didn't like— such as kissing that girl or getting into a spat with Esau's dad—or when they egged each other on, like with the truck chase.

This whole trip had been confusing when it came to Jason. It felt like Jason had changed. Every day he was revealing sides of himself that Kyle had never realized were there. Although Kyle had known Jason was bi, impulsive, stubborn, and had a trigger temper, he'd never been confronted with all of who Jason was on such a daily basis.

Kyle had thought this trip would be their honeymoon. Instead he'd learned his dream lover snored, took dumps, and sometimes got really, really stinky after basketball practice. Granted, those were all pretty superficial things, but when combined with the deeper stuff it made Kyle question: was Jason really The One?

From the sleeping bag beside Kyle, Jason's throat gurgled a gentle snore and Kyle covered his head with his pillow, tired and worn-out.

Almost immediately he fell into dreams where he was running through the desert, beneath the scorching sun, except . . . was he naked? He brought his hand down to cover his privates, sprinting so no one would see him. His heart thundered with every step. His lungs ached as if ready to burst. He stumbled, ready to collapse, exhausted. Except in his gut he knew he had to get someplace important. Someone was in danger. They needed him urgently. If he didn't get there it would be too late. He sprinted faster, panting, his throat parched.

The desert became hospital hallways, lined with doors and medical files. Kyle burst through one door, turned, ran down another hall. His heart beat harder, from dread.

Then a heaviness came over him. Beneath the bright light of a room so cold it made him shiver waited a gurney. On top of it lay a sleeping bag with a body inside. And Kyle knew he was too late. The person he'd come to save had died.

He reached for the zipper, hand trembling, and slowly pulled it down, revealing the familiar soft brown curls. Inside the bag lay Jason, stiff and silent, eyes closed, his lips silent and lifeless. A wave of grief crashed down on Kyle. His heart ached as he collapsed to his knees, crying.

His own sobbing woke him, coughing and choking inside the tent. Across the darkness of night he reached for real-life Jason, but Kyle's arms landed on empty floor. No sleeping bag. No Jason.

Kyle sat up, trying to clear his sleepy brain. Where was he? He remembered driving through the desert . . . a hospital, but . . . had Jason really died? If not, where *was* he?

"Jason?" Kyle's heart pounded as he groped for his glasses, but he was too panicked to find them.

"Jason?" he called again, climbing over Nelson and tugging on the zipper to the door.

Stepping outside, his foot hit something. A voice shouted, "Hey!" and Kyle tumbled to the ground.

"Damn!" Jason cursed. "You kicked me."

Kyle pushed himself off Jason's lumpy sleeping bag. "What the hell are you doing out here?"

"Man!" Jason rubbed his side. "That hurt."

"Well, you scared the crap out of me," Kyle replied, sitting up beside him.

"Sorry," Jason said quietly. "I couldn't sleep."

"You were *sleeping* out here?" Kyle gazed around at the blurry sand and stone of the campsite.

When the boys had arrived at the campground around three A.M., they'd found a night check-in box. The only site available was little more than a patch of rock and dust everyone else at the campground had passed up. In addition to the bleakness of the setting, it was now really cold.

"It's freezing!" Kyle wrapped his arms around the thin sleeves of his T-shirt. "Why didn't you tell me you were coming out here?"

"You were sleeping."

"Well, you scared the crap out of me," Kyle repeated, and turned to climb back into the tent. At least now he knew Jason wasn't dead. But as Kyle was about to step inside, Jason's hand rested on his calf. "Did you notice the stars?"

Kyle stopped and glanced up. "I don't have my glasses on." But even without his specs, he could see a million points of light twinkling against the black desert sky. The brilliance of it took his breath away.

"They were really bright a while ago," Jason said softly. "They're starting to fade a little now. You can see over there where the sun's going to come up."

Kyle looked in the direction Jason pointed and wrapped his arms around himself more tightly, shivering from both cold and awe.

"Hey," Jason said, almost whispering. "You want to climb in?"

Kyle glanced down at the sleeping bag. "We can't both fit in there." Besides, even though he was glad Jason wasn't dead, he still felt distant from him.

"Come on," Jason whispered, unzipping his sleeping bag halfway.

"Jason! I'm cold, I'm sleepy, and we both won't fit in there."

"Don't be so stubborn." Jason tugged on Kyle's leg.

"*Me?* Who's being—? Okay, fine. You'll see."

Jason lay back as Kyle crouched in, slipping his legs beside Jason's.

"Here, squeeze up next to me," Jason said, and somehow managed to zip them both up inside the bag. He wrapped his warm arms around Kyle. His chest pressed so close against Kyle's back that Kyle could feel Jason's heartbeat.

"The ground's rock-hard out here," Kyle complained, not wanting to feel so close to Jason. His thoughts were too mixed up inside. When Jason didn't say anything, Kyle gave a sigh. "I don't know, Jason."

"About what?" Jason replied, planting a warm kiss on Kyle's ear.

"About *us*," Kyle clarified. "This trip hasn't turned out like I'd thought."

He felt Jason's lips pull away. This obviously wasn't the best conversation to have with both of them wedged in together. But they had to have it sometime.

"Has it turned out like *you* thought?" Kyle asked.

"No, not exactly." Jason's voice sounded guarded. "I

thought we'd have more time together, just you and me. And there's a lot of stuff I hadn't expected."

"Me too," Kyle said, and then he was quiet. He wanted to say more—a lot more—but how? How could he tell the boy in whose arms he lay—the boy he'd thought he loved with all his heart—that his feelings were changing?

"Are you still mad about the guys with the truck?" Jason asked.

"No . . ." Kyle hesitated, trying to sort out his words. "That just really scared me."

Jason was quiet a moment, then he asked, "Are you still angry I yelled at Esau's dad?"

"No, but that scared me too." Even now, lying beside Jason, it confused Kyle how this boy who'd been so consistently gentle with him could so easily show such aggression with someone else.

"You know I'd never hurt you, Kyle," Jason whispered reassuringly.

"I know." Kyle sighed. "It's not that."

"Are you still mad about that girl?"

"Oh, yeah!" Kyle exclaimed. "I'm *still* angry about that."

Jason let out a breath. "I said I'm sorry, Kyle. Tell me what else I can do. I'll do it."

Kyle stared up at the stars, wishing he had an answer. "It's not just that, Jason. It's . . . I'm just not sure about us anymore."

Behind him, he felt Jason's chest contract, as if Kyle had accidentally struck him. And this time around, Kyle wasn't sure what to answer when Jason asked, "So does that mean you want to break up?"

# chapter 32

## jason

## kyle

## nelson

Inside the sleeping bag, Jason's heart beat anxiously as he waited for Kyle's response. He was certain that this time Kyle would want to break up.

After all, he didn't blame Kyle for being angry with him and having doubts about their relationship. Jason had doubts too. The difference was that Jason's doubts usually focused on himself. For in spite of being a star basketball athlete and good at other sports, he was well aware of his failings.

To begin with, he wasn't anywhere near as smart as Kyle. And even though other people told him he was good-looking, when he looked in the mirror he saw were imperfect teeth and huge eyebrows. His feet were too big. He hated his nose. He knew he sometimes had a temper problem, and it scared him that he might turn out like his dad, angry and bitter. He still

couldn't forgive himself for the way he'd hurt Debra. And he felt like a screwup for having lost his basketball scholarship. In sum, there were times when he hated himself. How could he expect Kyle to want to be involved with him?

As they'd dated, every time Kyle told him something sweet, like "I believe in you," "You're a role model," or even "I love you," Jason had often thought, *That's what you think. Wait till you really get to know me and realize how confused and messed-up I am.*

But he'd kept silent, hoping that what Kyle was saying might be true.

Now he realized: no such luck.

As he'd feared, during the course of their road trip Kyle had unavoidably glimpsed who Jason really was. No wonder Kyle doubted their relationship. He probably wanted to climb out of Jason's sleeping bag and run as fast and as far away as possible.

"Jason," Kyle replied at last, "would you please stop asking me if I want to break up every time we have a discussion? That doesn't help."

Jason squirmed in the sleeping bag. Clearly that wasn't the response he'd expected. Was Kyle avoiding his question? "Kyle," Jason insisted, "I want to know the truth. Do you want to break up?"

"No," Kyle said sharply. "If I wanted to break up, would I be scrunched up in here with you? Do *you* want to break up?"

"No!" Jason replied, his thoughts spinning. "But then why did you say you're not sure about us anymore?"

"Because I'm not!" Kyle began shifting his body around in the cramped sleeping bag, turning to face Jason. "I'm scared and angry with you and really hurt by what you did. But that doesn't mean I want to break up."

Jason stared into Kyle's face, only inches away, and struggled to understand. If Kyle felt so bad with him, why did he still want to be with him?

"I don't get it," he told Kyle. "If not being sure about us doesn't mean you're thinking about breaking up, then what does it mean?"

"It means . . ." Kyle's eyes closed for a moment as if he were trying to sort out his thoughts. "I guess I had this image of you as this guy I'd always wished I could be: strong, athletic—"

"But you *are* athletic," Jason interrupted.

"Not like you, Jason. I'm basically a math nerd who can swim a good freestyle."

"But you learned to shoot baskets," Jason insisted.

"Because you taught me! Now would you please be quiet and listen?"

Jason pressed his jaw shut, although it hurt hearing Kyle put himself down.

"It's like I got caught up in this image of you," Kyle continued, "after you came out, with all the media and fan mail you got. I know it sounds dorky, but it's like you were some sort of god. I remember at prom everyone watching me dance with you. I felt like the luckiest guy on earth. Then when you got invited to California, I felt for sure I was going on a dream trip with this hero everyone adores. I guess I kind of put you on a pedestal."

Jason's eyes searched Kyle's face, trying to understand. "Kyle, I'm far from perfect."

"I know . . ." Kyle's eyes shifted away, embarrassed. "At least I thought I did. So much has happened so fast on this trip. It's like I'm jet-lagged, and we've only been driving."

He smiled, but Jason didn't feel like joking. "So then, where does that leave us?"

Kyle drew in a deep breath and let it out. "I had a dream you died." He brought his face close, laying his head on Jason's shoulder. "I know I don't want to break up. I'm just no longer sure where this is going."

Jason felt the warmth of Kyle's breath. "Do you have to know?"

In his chaotic family, Jason had never known what would happen from day to day. He'd kind of gotten used to that.

Kyle raised his head and studied Jason as though he'd just asked something really profound. "You mean like those old guys said, 'Take it one day at a time'?"

That wasn't exactly what Jason had been thinking, but it made sense. He tried to recall: What had the old guys said was their secret? Trust . . . communication . . . and what was the third thing? He couldn't remember.

"Kyle, I'm trying to do the best I can. I don't mean to screw up. Please don't give up on me. If we break up, I'll feel like a total failure. You're what I always wanted."

Kyle sank into him. "And you're what *I* always wanted. I just wish. . . . Why can't we feel close like this all the time?"

As Jason thought about the question, he realized he'd also learned a lot about Kyle on this trip—like the fact that he didn't always respond well to changes. But that was okay. They kind of balanced each other out.

He leaned toward Kyle and began kissing him, gently at first, but as Kyle responded, their kisses became more fervent. They held their bodies close, pressing together and feeling each other's growing excitement. But their passion was thwarted by the stirrings of campers down the road and the approaching dawn.

"Hey," Jason whispered. "Let's go see the sun rise over the canyon."

"What about Nelson?" Kyle asked.

"He'll be all right. He needs to sleep. Come on. Just you and me."

Kyle's brow knitted up, as if thinking. "Okay, but let me leave him a note . . . and some water."

Once they were in the car, it was a twenty-minute drive through the crisp dawn chill from their campground to the canyon's South Rim.

"Do you think we'll make it in time?" Kyle asked as they entered the park.

They followed a line of cars, all apparently with the same purpose, to the parking lot and then hurried with the other tourists to the viewing platform at the canyon's edge.

Jason pointed out a bench for Kyle to stand on and better see above the crowd. Then he positioned himself on the ground below Kyle, draping Kyle's arms over his shoulders, not caring if anyone saw them.

Together they watched the eastern sky turn blue, then gray, then pink, then orange, till the sun first appeared—a tiny white dot of light between a butte and a mesa.

Then as the orb turned golden, its first rays burst forth, turning all heads west. The crowd inhaled a collective gasp as a show of flame blazed steadily across the canyon's rock layers— orange, burgundy, crimson, and gold—while shadows withdrew like a tide down to the canyon's floor.

The grandeur of the spectacle made Jason's drama with Kyle seem so insignificant by comparison. After all, if this magnificent gorge had been formed one drop of water at a time, maybe there was hope for Kyle and him, one day at a time.

# jason          kyle

## nelson

Nelson woke sweating atop his sleeping bag, his mouth feeling dry as the desert. He glanced around the sun-hot tent. What time was it? Where was he? Where had Kyle and Jason gone? Slowly, he recalled last night's events: getting sick . . . the hospital . . . the adorable doctor . . . crying over the phone with his mom . . .

Beside his pillow someone had placed a bottle of water. Kyle, no doubt. Nelson guzzled it down. Then he crawled forward to gaze out the mesh door.

Across the campground road, in the shade of the bathhouse, Kyle and Jason sat on the sidewalk, playing cards.

"Hey!" Nelson shouted weakly. "What time's it?"

The boys looked up from their card game and Kyle glanced at his watch. "Eleven thirty!"

Nelson collapsed back onto his pillow, wiped out from weakness. A moment later, Kyle and Jason leaned in the door.

"Did you drink some water?" Kyle asked.

"You look like crap," Jason told him.

"I feel like crap. How long have you guys been up?"

Kyle gave Jason a conspiratorial glance. "We went to watch the sunrise."

"Why didn't you wake me?" Nelson grumbled. "I wanted to see that."

"You needed to sleep," Jason told him. "We'll go back for sunset."

Nelson stared at Kyle and Jason. At least it seemed they were getting along better.

After he'd taken a shower, the three of them drove to Grand Canyon Village. They spent most of the day trying to escape the heat by hanging inside the AC of the visitor's center, the cafeteria, and the lodge lobby. They were still beat from the night before and took turns sneaking a nap wherever they could. And all the while, Kyle kept prodding Nelson to drink more water. "The doctor said you have to stay hydrated."

Around five o'clock, it finally began to cool outside and the boys wandered to the trail overlooking the canyon.

"That's it?" Nelson peered over the edge. "It's just a big hole."

But the sunset was pretty awesome, and it was sweet to see Kyle and Jason holding hands as they watched it.

Early that night all three of them crawled into their sleeping bags. And early next morning they set out on their final stretch to L.A.

Nelson found the drive through western California really, really boring: mostly more desert and bleak jagged mountains— pretty much the same as the last three states they'd left behind.

Then *bam!* As they crossed the San Bernardino Mountains, the first L.A. suburbs appeared in ambush. Except they didn't

look like Nelson expected: with green lawns and kidney-shaped swimming pools, like in movies. Instead, concrete strip malls spread out in every direction, seemingly forever.

"L.A.! We made it." Jason punched the horn at the sight of downtown's skyscrapers, shouting, "Woo-hoo!"

"Hey!" Nelson pretended to scold him. "That's my job. Woo-hoo!"

"You need to take Highway 101." Kyle guided them from the backseat toward the school. In spite of his directions, they almost overlooked the old Spanish-style stucco building wedged between a warehouse and a film lab.

"It's not exactly Beverly Hills High," Nelson remarked as they parked in front.

But inside, the Harry Hay School appeared newly remodeled. Hammers banged from down the hall. Phones rang. Several families waited in the lobby. Among them, an African-American mom clutched her hands. A dad gazed uneasily toward the ceiling. Beside them sat an uncertain-gender teen dressed in jeans and baggy shirt. His/her head gleefully bobbed to the music from headphones.

Nelson wondered, *What would it have been like to go to an alternative high school like this? To be able to go through the day without being called a gazillion names? To not have to fight a principal who tried to block them from starting a Gay-Straight Alliance?*

"We're here to see the principal, Ms. Yamamoto," Jason told the receptionist.

"Do you have an appointment?" she asked.

"This is Jason Carrillo," Kyle answered. "He's speaking at the opening tomorrow."

From behind the receptionist's filing cabinet, a boy with brilliant pink hair appeared. Nelson's jaw dropped. As their

eyes met, he couldn't help but smile, as did the boy.

"You're Jason?" the boy asked, walking over to Nelson.

Nelson felt an immediate, almost electric connection. The boy looked to be about his age. They were the same height and thin build, though the boy had brown eyes, tan skin, and lips so tender-looking Nelson wished he could kiss them. Right then and there.

"Um, no." He pointed. "*That's* Jason. I'm Nelson."

The boy's eyes shifted briefly to Jason but came back to Nelson. "I'm Manny." He extended his hand. "That's short for Manuel."

"Hey, I like your hair." Nelson grinned, feeling the warmth of Manny's palm.

"Yeah, I like yours, too." Manny laughed.

"I'm Kyle." They shook hands and Jason followed. "Wha's up?"

But Nelson noticed Manny didn't shake their hands anywhere near as long as he'd shaken his. *Could Manny possibly be interested in me?* Nelson wondered. *Nah. Surely anyone that cute already had a boyfriend.*

"We're really excited you guys are here," Manny said. "Ms. Yamamoto said to let her know when you arrived. You guys want a Coke or something? How was your trip?"

The boys told him about the trip as Manny got them sodas from the teachers' lounge. Then he explained that he was work-ing at the school temporarily, to help with the opening. The following week he'd start community college.

While he spoke, Manny kept smiling at Nelson. Nelson's heart sped up. He glanced away, excited. If Manny already had a boyfriend, why would he be flirting with him like that? Could he possibly be single?

The school's principal, Ms. Yamamoto, turned out to be

nothing like Nelson's principal, hyper, hard-ass Mueller. Behind her boxy little rectangular glasses she seemed calm and easygoing. "Thanks for driving all the way across the country," she told the boys, and they all responded, "Thank *you*."

"So, are you all set with your speech?" she asked Jason.

"Um . . ." Jason cleared his throat. He shifted his feet across the floor. "Not yet."

The question made even Nelson squirm. Like Kyle, he'd also worried about when Jason would get jamming on his speech. But like Jason, Nelson had also managed to put it out of his mind.

Ms. Yamamoto didn't seem fazed. "Well, just speak from your heart," she told Jason. "Tell the kids your story. Share your experience. You have lots of fans here. I know you'll do fine." She smiled reassuringly. "Now I imagine you're tired and want to get settled. We have a dinner arranged with some of the school's board and faculty this evening. Manny will help guide you around."

Manny grinned at Nelson, his teeth so beautifully white against his cinnamon-colored skin that it made Nelson wonder, *Why are you torturing me like this?*

He felt a little jealous when Manny sat beside Kyle in the backseat, guiding them through streets with familiar TV names: Melrose, Santa Monica, Sunset Boulevard.

At the hotel Manny helped them unload the trunk and carry their bags. And inside their eighth-floor room he drew the curtains to the picture window. "If it wasn't for the smog, you'd have a great hillside view of the city—all the way to the ocean."

Jason squinted, trying to peer through the haze. "I always wanted to see the Pacific."

"We can go tomorrow, after your speech." Manny grabbed

the ice bucket off the counter. "I'll get you some ice." He glanced at Nelson. "Want to come with me?"

"Sure!" Nelson leaped off the bed.

"I figured they'd like a moment alone," Manny whispered as they left Kyle and Jason in the room. "They're a couple, right?"

"I think so," Nelson replied, half-joking. "I'm not sure, after this trip."

Manny grinned. "How about you? Do you have a boyfriend?"

"No . . ." Nelson answered, his heart racing ahead of him. "Do you?"

"Not anymore," Manny replied, as they reached the ice machine. "We broke up twenty-seven days ago. It was pretty serious. We'd been together over three months. I guess I'm what you call 'relationship-oriented.'"

While Manny looked at him, Nelson tried to calm his breath. Was this boy for real? Could someone this cute, this nice, this sweet, his own age, and so sexy, actually be single and interested?

"How long will you be here?" Manny asked as ice plunked to overflowing in the bucket.

"We head back the day after tomorrow," Nelson said sadly.

"No way!" Manny exclaimed. "You drove this far to leave so quickly? Why don't you stay longer? I'd love to show you around and hang out."

Nelson gazed at this smiling pink-haired angel and his voice nearly broke as he explained, "Kyle and Jason have to return for college. And it's my car, so I have to go back with them. Besides, Kyle lost his license, so I have to help drive."

"Oh," Manny said, his smile fading.

Then they walked silently back down the hall till Manny said, "You should at least get your windshield fixed before you head

back. My uncle owns a salvage yard. I wouldn't want anything to happen to you."

Nelson held the door as Manny brushed past him into the hotel room. For an instant their hands touched, and Nelson thought his heart would break from longing.

# chapter 34

## jason          kyle
## nelson

Kyle had perceived the spark between Nelson and Manny the moment it had ignited.

He watched their two pink-haired heads step from the hotel room for ice and whispered to Jason, "They're so perfect for each other."

"That's so funny about their hair." Jason grinned. "What did those two old guys in Texas say? Similars stay together."

"Not just the hair. The way they look at each other. They're like magnets."

"Except for one detail. They live a continent apart."

"That sucks," Kyle agreed, cupping his hands behind his head as he lay on the bed. He'd always wanted Nelson to have a boyfriend. Manny seemed ideal.

"I've never seen so many Mercedes and Beamers," Jason commented, staring out the window at the billboards and traffic

on Sunset Strip. "I feel like a rock star being here."

Kyle gazed at Jason. He looked so radiant in the afternoon sunlight, the AC unit gently blowing his curls back. "You sort of are."

Jason glanced back at him, a knowing look on his face. "Come back to Earth, Kyle. I'm not a rock star."

"You're right. I'm sorry." Kyle patted the double bed. "Come lie down."

Jason kicked off his sneakers and lay beside Kyle, wrapping his arm across his chest. "I'm kind of starting to freak out about my speech."

*Finally,* Kyle thought. It had driven him crazy all trip how Jason kept putting it off.

"We can work on it after dinner," Kyle suggested. "I'll help you with it."

He kissed Jason, first on the cheek, then on the lips. It felt so great being able to stretch out with him in a real bed again. No sleeping bags. No rain pelting the roof. No sun roasting them alive. No squeaky sofa bed. No noisy campers next door. . . . Now if only they could have some time alone together.

Jason must've been thinking the same thing because in the middle of kissing Kyle he murmured, "Think we can get Nelson to go out with Manny tonight?"

"That shouldn't take much," Kyle replied, just as Manny and Nelson came back with the ice.

"Hey, guys!" He waved at them on the bed. "I'm going to let you get ready for dinner—and pick you up at seven. Let me give you my cell number in case you need anything." He jotted down his number and handed it to Nelson. "Do you guys have a cell?"

Kyle darted a glance at Nelson, who was turning red as the

carpet. To spare him any embarrassment, Kyle said, "It accidentally got wet."

"I know that sucks," Manny replied. "Once mine fell in the toilet. Talk about embarrassing."

Kyle, Nelson, and Jason exchanged a look.

"Anyway," Manny continued, "I'll see you later." He gazed at Nelson. "Call me if you need anything."

Nelson walked him to the door. When he returned, he threw himself onto the other bed, pounding the mattress with his fists and kicking his feet. "It isn't fair!" he screamed. "Why does he have to live three thousand miles away?"

"I think he really likes you," Kyle said.

"Don't tell me that," Nelson protested, then added, "Do you really think so?"

"Dude, totally!" Jason agreed. "His eyes are, like, glued to you."

"But why?" Nelson sat up on the bed. "With all the cute boys out here? I swear everyone looks like a model. And you know they're all gay. So why would he be interested in *me*?"

"Because!" Kyle propped himself on his elbow. "You're as cute as anyone out here. You're intelligent. You have a great sense of humor . . ."

"And you both have the pink hair thing." Jason grinned.

"You're good-looking," Kyle continued, "and a heck of a great guy. Why wouldn't he like you?"

"I wish I could have a smoke." Nelson nervously fidgeted with the nightstand pen, uncapping and capping it. "Except he doesn't smoke. I don't think anyone out here smokes."

"I think he's great," Kyle said.

"Don't say that!" Nelson fell back on the bed, then sat up again. "He is, isn't he?"

**rainbow road**

"Apart from being supercute," Kyle replied, "he's so genuine. He's really sweet."

"Ugh, this sucks!" Nelson jabbed his hands into his hair, tugging on it. "What am I going to do?"

"Enjoy getting to know him," Kyle replied. "What else can you do?"

"Why don't you guys go out after dinner?" Jason suggested, nudging Kyle.

"Yeah!" Kyle agreed. "Have fun with him. Just be safe."

"Oh God, I wonder what he's like in bed." Nelson fell back again, staring up at the ceiling. "I've never done it with a Latino guy."

"Dude, we're the best!" Jason smiled proudly.

"What should I wear tonight?" Nelson sprang to his feet and began yanking clothes from his bags. "What's even clean? We've got to do laundry."

Each of the boys tried to find clean clothes for dinner, in between taking turns showering and calling their moms. While Jason showered, Kyle told his mom about the Grand Canyon and she asked, "How are things going with Jason?"

"Better," Kyle whispered into the phone. "We had a real good talk. Except now he's stressed about his speech tomorrow. I kept telling him to work on it during the trip."

"You're a good writer," his mom said. "Offer to help him."

"I did!" Kyle screamed a whisper. He felt almost as stressed as Jason about the speech.

At dinner the conversation didn't help his jitters either. A big bearded man on the school board asked Jason, "All set for your big day tomorrow?"

"I can't wait to hear what you have to say," interjected a woman with black spiky hair, the school's librarian.

"Do you speak often in front of groups?" said a woman with a minister's collar, also on the board.

"We're expecting a pretty big crowd." Ms. Yamamoto smiled calmly.

"Some city council members will be there," commented a bald English teacher.

Kyle reached beneath the table to reassure Jason—and himself—by holding his hand. Both their palms dripped with sweat.

After everyone said their good-byes, Manny asked the boys, "You guys want to go out?"

"We really need to work on Jason's speech," Kyle replied. "Why don't you and Nelson go out?"

Manny's face became a total grin. "You want to?" he asked Nelson and Nelson beamed. "Sure!"

After Kyle and Jason got back to the hotel room, Jason kind of freaked out.

"The frickin' city council's going to be there tomorrow!" He kicked his shoes off, tossing them across the room.

"Not the entire council," Kyle said, trying to calm Jason. But in truth Kyle was equally stressed. "Let's concentrate on what Ms. Yamamoto said," he suggested, sitting down at the writing desk.

"Speak from your heart?" Jason rolled his eyes and threw himself onto the bed. "What the heck does that mean?"

"She told you to share your experience." Kyle pulled out the hotel writing paper from the desk drawer. "Can you hand me that pen?"

Jason tossed him the ballpoint from the nightstand. "What experience?"

"Well, tell them what it was like for you growing up knowing you were gay, that sort of stuff."

"Dude!" Jason glared at him, grabbed the remote control,

and turned the TV on. "Are you forgetting I was in the closet till last year? These kids are *out!* They probably all have pink, or green, or purple hair. They're the ones I used to watch get beat up and I was too chicken to say anything." Jason angrily flicked from one TV channel to another. "You want me to tell them that?"

"Jason, would you turn that off, please? I'm trying to help you."

Jason clicked the tube off, grumbling. "I never should've said I'd do this."

"Why don't you tell them," Kyle pressed, "why you finally decided to come out?"

"Yeah, right." Jason crossed his arms. "You mean tell them I used to think about guys when I was doing my girlfriend? The city council would *love* that."

"No," Kyle said, growing more and more annoyed. "I mean tell them why you decided to come out to your coach and team, so you could be a role model. Tell them about the letters you've gotten from all over the country."

Jason shook his head. "Kyle, I came out because I was sick of hiding. That's the reason. Just because everyone says I'm a role model doesn't make me one. You're putting me on a pedestal again."

Kyle tapped the pen against the desk, pondering: Was Jason right? Or was he just being belligerent?

"I never should've agreed to this," Jason repeated.

"Well, it's too late now!" Kyle snapped, losing his patience. "Do you want me help you with this or don't you?"

"I feel like a fraud," Jason grumbled.

"But you're not!"

"Oh, that's right, I forgot." Jason smirked. "You think I'm a god."

"Fine!" Kyle threw down the pen. "You don't want my help. You just want to feel sorry for yourself!"

Jason bit into his lip, giving him a hard-jawed look. Then he got up off the bed and started to change his clothes.

Kyle watched him. "Where are you going?"

"To find a court." Jason shoved his sneakers on. "I didn't practice this morning."

"Jason, it's almost midnight! Can't you miss one single day of your stupid practice?"

Jason shot him an angry look and grabbed his basketball from atop the dresser.

Kyle crossed his arms, wishing he hadn't said "stupid." He knew Jason's practice was important. But Jason's being so contrary pissed him off. Plus, there was another reason for his frustration: "I thought we were going to bed together before Nelson got back." He'd even made sure to hang the DO NOT DISTURB sign outside the door.

Jason hesitated, his eyes shifting from Kyle to the bed. "I'm too mixed-up inside." He turned to leave.

Kyle realized it was pointless to try and stop him. As the door closed, he grabbed Jason's strewn clothes off the bed and hurled them onto the floor. He wasn't sure what ticked him off more—that Jason had copped out on his speech, that he'd rejected Kyle's help with it, or that he'd bailed on their chance to make love.

Kyle flicked the TV on again and surfed through the channels, trying to take his mind off Jason. Yet he kept listening for the doorknob, wishing Jason would hurry back.

About an hour later Kyle felt himself drifting off to sleep. He got up, stripped to his briefs, turned the TV off, and debated whether to set the alarm for the next morning in case

Jason forgot. Wasn't it Jason's responsibility to show up for his speech? But Kyle set the alarm anyway.

Angry but also tired, he quickly fell asleep. Sometime during the night, he felt Jason's arm slide around him. And in spite of his anger, Kyle let it stay there.

# chapter 35

# jason kyle

## nelson

For Jason, shooting hoops wasn't just exercise or a pastime. Basketball was how he dealt with stuff: pressure at home, stress at school, and especially his anger—at his dad, with friends, with himself. And tonight he felt majorly disappointed with himself. He *had* to shoot hoops more than ever.

At the hotel's front desk he asked, "Where's the nearest basketball court?"

The clerk gave him a weird look, but fortunately one of the bellhops overheard and pointed him to a school six blocks away.

As Jason headed toward the court, he felt bad for walking out on Kyle. But on the trip he'd realized how he needed time to get away and be by himself—to build up a sweat and burn off stress—especially at times like now, when he felt like he was exploding inside.

He knew he shouldn't have put off writing his speech. But

he'd been so nervous about it. And with each day that passed, he'd grown more nervous.

He didn't want to let those kids down tomorrow. He didn't want to let himself down. But what could he possibly tell them?

He knew Kyle had been trying to help. If Jason had any sense he would've accepted Kyle's help. Heck, why not just let Kyle write the whole speech? He'd probably write a better one than Jason ever could. But Jason had wanted to write this speech himself, without Kyle's help.

Now here he was, shooting baskets at midnight, with barely enough light from streetlamps to make out the curve of the rim against the white backboard. In a few hours he was supposed to address some huge audience, and he had no idea what to say.

He'd needed to find out: Was he really the wonderful role model Kyle thought he was? He now had his answer: He'd screwed up. Big-time.

When Jason got back to the hotel, he quietly stepped into their darkened room. He found Kyle asleep—and Nelson wasn't back yet. Jason's pulse quickened. He wanted so badly to feel Kyle's arms around him. Would Kyle still want to make love?

Quickly, Jason took a hot shower. Then he slid beneath the bedsheets, slipping his arm around Kyle's bare waist. To his relief, Kyle didn't rebuff him.

But just then the doorknob clicked, followed by Nelson's giggles and whispers.

"Thanks again. See you tomorrow."

The door closed softly, and Nelson's footsteps padded across the carpet to the other bed.

Jason let out a deep sigh, holding Kyle in his arms, and wondered: How, with so much pent-up emotion, would he ever get to sleep?

Next morning Jason woke to the radio alarm blaring reports of freeway delays. As he shut it off, he heard the shower being turned off and saw that Kyle's side of the bed was empty. In the other bed a lump beneath the covers indicated Nelson was still sleeping.

Jason walked to the window and pulled the curtains open. He jumped back, startled. Where yesterday was haze and smog, today the city stretched clearly in front of him as far as he could see. In the distance shimmered the blue Pacific.

"Oh my gosh!" Kyle exclaimed, emerging from the bathroom with a towel round his waist. "You can see forever."

Jason watched his expression, trying to discern if he was still angry. "I'm sorry about last night," Jason said. "Thanks for setting the alarm."

"No problem." Kyle kissed his neck, smelling clean and soapy. "You want me to order room service?"

"I'm not hungry. I think I'm too nervous."

"How about at least some juice and yogurt?"

"Okay."

"You ordering food?" a voice croaked from beneath Nelson's covers.

Kyle ordered breakfast and somehow all three of them managed to eat, shower, and get half-ready by the time Manny showed up.

Jason had brought his blazer, a dress shirt, and tie for the event. Kyle used the hotel room iron for Jason's shirt, and Nelson showed him how to tie something called a half-Windsor, which looked more stylish than the knot Jason had learned to tie. Manny found a shoeshine cloth in the bathroom toiletry basket and polished Jason's dress shoes.

All the attention should've made Jason feel great. But instead

he felt like a loser for how he was about to disappoint them.

Nelson drove toward the school, with Manny beside him giving directions. Jason sat in back with Kyle, biting his nails till Kyle gently pulled his hand away from his mouth.

A block from the school they began to see parents with their teens walking toward the entrance. A TV news van stood parked outside the door.

"There's going to be TV here?" Jason asked. No one had mentioned that.

"There wasn't supposed to be," Manny replied.

Then Jason saw the reason for the news van: a half-dozen protesters, holding up placards: GOD HATES FAGS. STOP BRAIN-WASHING OUR KIDS. REPENT OR BURN. The signs normally would have angered Jason, but in his current nervous state, they rattled him further. It didn't help any when Nelson leaned out the window, blowing kisses at the protesters, shouting, "God is love!"

While Nelson parked the car, Manny led Kyle and Jason inside. Ms. Yamamoto was waiting for them, her cheery, peaceful smile unnerving Jason even more.

Inside the auditorium they sat in the front row. The program started with a bunch of boring speeches about every child's right to a safe school setting in which to learn, free of harassment and name-calling, blah, blah, blah . . .

According to the program Jason wasn't scheduled to speak till the end.

"We saved the best for last," Manny whispered from the seat beside him.

Jason squirmed in his chair, roasting inside his blazer. As he watched the woman blabbing at the podium, he tugged at his tie, wanting to bolt out of there. Meanwhile, Kyle patted him on the back, as if trying to soothe him.

Nelson didn't join them till the fourth speech. "What took you so long?" Kyle whispered.

"I was proselytizing the picketers." Nelson grinned. "I think I made one convert."

Jason couldn't tell if Nelson was serious. He never knew with him. But then Jason suddenly got an idea. Why hadn't he thought of it earlier?

"Nelson!" he whispered. "I want to talk to you a minute." He climbed over Manny and led Nelson to the hall outside the auditorium. "Look, I can't do this. You're the one they should've invited. You've got to do it."

Nelson's brow creased with confusion, but then a smile crept across his face. "Finally!" He snapped his fingers. "Someone gets it! That's what I said from the start. Of course I'm the one they should've invited."

Jason let out a huge sigh of relief. He felt like a loser for wimping out, but at least he wouldn't be a total failure on stage in front of everyone.

Except Nelson stopped snapping his fingers and looked Jason squarely in the eye. "But I'm *not* the one they invited. They invited *you,* Jason. And you've got to get up there." His blue eyes drilled into Jason, and in spite of his goofy pink hair, he looked like the most determined man on earth.

"Maybe you'll make a huge fool of yourself, but if that's what it takes for you to accept that a lot of us look up to you—then that's what you've got to do, because I'm not getting you out of this."

The auditorium door swung open. Applause sounded from inside as Manny leaned out into the hall. "Jason, you're up next!"

Nelson reached up to Jason's shoulder and spun him toward the auditorium door. Jason gave up resisting, as his heart

slipped to his stomach. Manny led him backstage, where Jason stood stiffly, waiting for the current speaker to finish. He was beyond worry now, his mind blank with fear.

He didn't hear his introduction or the applause, only Ms. Yamamoto saying, "Jason Carrillo," and then he was behind the podium, staring at three hundred waiting faces.

"Um . . ." He cleared his throat, and suddenly remembered to say, "Thank you."

At least that was a start.

"Um . . ." he continued. "You would think after playing so many basketball games in front of hundreds of people, I wouldn't be so nervous, but I think this is one of the scariest moments of my life."

Several people laughed, probably feeling sorry for him, and he laughed too, from nerves.

"I guess the difference is, when I'm on the court I've got a team, whereas here I'm all . . ."

He stopped himself as he gazed down toward the front row at Kyle, Nelson, and Manny. Kyle was smiling up at him with his big hazel puppy-dog eyes. And Jason realized that even if he made a total ass of himself, for reasons beyond his understanding Kyle would still love him, not one bit less.

Meanwhile Nelson was giving him a serious look, as if commanding him to keep going.

And next to Nelson, Manny leaned forward anxiously, his face full of expectation, his knuckles white as they gripped the seat.

"Actually," Jason continued, "I guess I'm not alone here either. I was originally supposed to be, but my boyfriend and"—he glanced at Nelson—"one of our friends decided to come with me. They have no idea how glad I am right now that they're here."

The audience laughed at that, and Jason saw Manny's grip

relax on his chair. Nelson gave Jason an approving nod. Kyle beamed at him even more admiringly. And Jason breathed a little easier.

"Like probably all of you," he told the audience, "at some point when I was a kid, I started figuring out I was gay. Although I had little girlfriends, I was also curious about boys. When I was ten, I decided that since I'd kissed girls, I wanted to find out what it would be like to kiss a boy."

The audience laughed, though Jason hadn't meant to be funny.

"Unfortunately my dad came in on us. He gave me the biggest beating I'd ever had in my life."

Jason's voice grew more serious and the audience became still.

"You probably saw that sign outside." Jason pointed toward the street. "'Stop brainwashing our kids.' Well, I was one of the ones brainwashed. That beating convinced me there was something wrong with me for wanting to kiss another boy like me."

Jason glanced down at Kyle again, and he felt as much adoration for him as he saw reflected in those eyes.

"I think for me the worst part of growing up gay was the loneliness that followed that beating. I became a prisoner locked up with my feelings. Of course I knew there were other kids, those like you. I heard the names you got called. I saw you getting beat up. And I'm ashamed to say I stood by like a coward, afraid to speak up, for fear my own secret would come out. And I hated myself for that."

Jason swallowed hard. Where were all these words coming from?

"Another sign outside says, 'Repent or burn.' I think in my case it happened the other way around: I spent most of my childhood burning inside. . . ." He paused and took a deep breath.

"I've repented now, and I'm standing up for myself, and for you, and for thousands of others like us all across America."

The audience burst into applause at that, startling Jason.

"As I drove across the country with my boyfriend and best friend . . ."

Was he actually calling Nelson his best friend?

" . . . we met some amazing people: a whole community of gay guys and women in the Middle of Nowhere, Tennessee, living free and being themselves. . . ."

Wait a minute, hadn't he thought they were weird? From where were all these new thoughts coming?

"We met this transgender girl who's just so happy being able to be herself as she always knew she was meant to be. And these two old guys in an RV, just loving each other and growing old. And I realize the reason I'd been so afraid to come out was for fear I'd be all alone."

He scanned the audience. "But I get it now. I understand why it's so important to come out, and speak out, and reach out, and to have schools like this. And also, why those people outside with the signs are so afraid of us. Because when we stop being alone, we get what I had on the court: a team to play with, to work with, to encourage each other, and to be there for one another, stronger than any single one of us could ever be."

The crowd roared into applause again, once more surprising Jason, so much so that he lost his train of thought. He felt like there was something more he should say, but all the clapping had brought his nervousness back and he decided: better quit while ahead.

Then he remembered to say "Thank you," and as he glanced down at Kyle and Nelson, he suddenly realized what else he wanted to say.

**jason**   nelson   kyle                                          225

"Before I leave, I want to introduce you to my boyfriend, Kyle, and our best friend, Nelson. Without them, I would never have gotten here."

At that the crowd stood in ovation. Kyle gazed up at Jason, and it was all Jason could do to keep from choking up and making a sobbing fool of himself in front of all these people.

Then he was out in the lobby, feeling like he really was a rock star, crushed by little freshmen and sophomores on their first day at this new gay school, asking him to sign their notebooks— kids with green hair and purple hair, with earrings and nose rings, kids he wasn't sure were boys or girls—all excited and hyper and giggling, as kids were meant to be, in a school where they could be themselves without being called names or fearing they'd get pounded. And as Jason signed autographs and looked into their smiling faces, he imagined a future world in which boys and girls like him would no longer be afraid of—and miss out on—getting to know such kids.

Then somehow Nelson managed to squeeze through the crowd and stood beside him, eyebrows arched, and asked, "Best friends, huh? When did that—?"

Before he could finish, Jason wrapped his arms around him, whispering in his ear, "Thanks, buddy."

# jason   kyle

# nelson

At the luncheon following the speech, Nelson sat beside Manny, who kept asking the boys, "Is there anything you guys need?" So when Manny pulled out his Chap Stick, Nelson naturally asked, "Can I borrow it?"

He'd never before felt so immediately close and comfortable with any guy in his life—not even Kyle. And it both thrilled him and scared the crap out of him.

When they were leaving the school, Nelson squeezed Kyle's arm and whispered in his ear, "Explain to me again: Why's he acting like he likes me so much?"

"Because you're very likeable." Kyle patted Nelson's shoulder. "Just let that in."

Driving back to the hotel, they made their plans for the afternoon. After changing clothes and stuffing all their dirty laundry in bags, they drove to Venice Beach.

"Wow, there it is!" Jason exclaimed as he headed off with Kyle to enjoy the ocean.

Meanwhile, Nelson went with Manny to his uncle's salvage yard to have the windshield repaired.

"I can't believe you drove it that way." Manny examined the splintering crack.

"I can't believe it held," Nelson said. "But it did."

They charged the repair with the credit card from Kyle's dad. When Manny's uncle told them the car was ready, he also handed Nelson a billfold. "I found this wedged inside when I moved the front seat."

"No way!" Nelson screamed. It was Kyle's wallet, with the two hundred dollars and his license. He'd be legal to drive again.

"This is so amazing," Nelson kept repeating as they drove to do laundry at Manny's apartment. They were unloading the dirty clothes bags from the car when Manny's housemate came out to help them.

"Hey, you must be Nelson." He extended his hand. "My name's Ernesto. Manny told me about you this morning."

Nelson shook hands, grinning. "Whatever he said, I deny it."

"Yeah," Ernesto said. "He told me you were pretty funny."

They talked and joked for a few minutes before Ernesto said good-bye and headed off to work.

"We've been best friends since grade school," Manny said as he led Nelson into the living room and dropped the laundry bags. "Ernesto's seen me through all my dating, my drama, my different-colored hair . . ."

"Just like me and Kyle," Nelson observed, plopping onto the orange futon.

"Except he's straight," Manny said, sitting beside Nelson.

"You're best friend's *straight*?"

**rainbow road**

"Is that okay?" Manny asked.

"Yeah, of course! I wish *I* had more straight guy friends. But they usually get way too nervous around me."

Manny's cell phone rang and he told Nelson, "Hang on a minute. . . . Hello?" he answered and laughed into the phone, grinning at Nelson.

While Manny talked on the cell, Nelson looked around the apartment. On one wall hung a huge abstract painting that he really liked, with broad swaths of bright colors. Manny had told him he liked to paint.

"Is that one of yours?" Nelson whispered, pointing, and Manny nodded back.

Nelson liked the whole apartment. The white walls gave it a clean look, the wood floors gave it warmth, the bright colors made it interesting, and a vase of flowers gave it life. It was exactly the type of place Nelson would like to live in when he finally moved out from his mom's.

Just then an outrageous thought popped into Nelson's head. But immediately he tossed it out for being too crazy.

"That was Ernesto." Manny gave a huge grin as he folded up his cell. "He said he approves."

"Of what?" Nelson asked, suspecting the answer, but wanting to be sure.

Manny leaned forward to kiss Nelson and whispered, "Of you."

They'd kissed the night before, but even so, as Manny's tender lips landed on his, Nelson felt like it was the first time. He kissed Manny back, his tongue gently rolling against Manny's and breathing in his sweet smell, like oranges and ocean and sunshine all mixed together.

As they kissed, Nelson wasn't certain what would happen

next, but he knew what he'd like to happen. And when Manny slid his warm hands beneath Nelson's T-shirt, tugging it off, Nelson helped him along, though he regretted having to stop kissing even for an instant.

And then Manny was bending over Nelson, his hair like a big pink carnation as he dropped flower-petal kisses across Nelson's chest. And as Nelson moaned softly, he couldn't help wishing it was night, so Manny wouldn't see how unbuff he was.

But then Manny's face drifted up, his eyes intent with longing. "You have such a beautiful body."

Not wanting to argue, Nelson tugged Manny's T-shirt off and gazed at the smooth tan chest, so dark compared to his own, and ran his fingers along the taut skin.

"*You* have such an awesome body," Nelson echoed.

Once again the boys began kissing, more ardently than before, as they pressed their naked chests together. And Nelson clung to Manny as though holding something priceless and long sought.

"Want to see my bedroom?" Manny whispered, and Nelson grinned. "I don't know. Let me think about that. Hmm. Okay!"

Manny laughed and led him by the hand to the bedroom and another abstract painting—this one in silvers, blues, and greens that reminded Nelson of ships, and waves, and the sea. In the corner of the room Nelson spotted a basketball. That surprised him, but he quickly forgot about it as Manny pulled him onto the bed, unstrapping his sandals.

Then they were lying down, one moment side to side, the next on top of each other, their hands touching and groping, as if discovering places never before experienced, and all the while kissing, making Nelson glad he'd borrowed Manny's Chap Stick.

Then they were naked, gazing bashfully at one another.

And it felt to Nelson as though he were staring in the mirror and liking the reflection that peered back at him: smiling, warm, and accepting.

But the mirror clouded a moment as Nelson remembered that tomorrow they'd have to part. Then Manny reached his hand out. And their passion returned as a wave, pulling them up to its crest, then flinging them against the shore. Ebbing and flowing, their ardor peaked and waned, as they kissed and touched, exploring nooks and crannies, tearing open condoms, entering one another, feeling closer than ever, and then lying quietly together, hearing only their heartbeats.

"I feel so happy." Nelson rested his head on Manny's bare chest. "And sad at the same time."

"Me too." Manny ran his fingertips across Nelson's back. "That's how I feel."

"This sucks *so* much," Nelson continued in a low voice.

"Totally," Manny agreed, then added, "But it doesn't have to."

Nelson propped himself on one elbow. "What do you mean?" The crazy idea he'd had earlier came back to him. Was Manny thinking the same thing?

"I mean . . ." Manny traced a finger down the center of Nelson's chest. "Why don't you stay longer—here, with me?"

Manny *had* been thinking the same thing.

"But what about Ernesto?" Nelson cautiously asked.

"Um . . ." Manny blushed. "That's why we kind-of-sort-of arranged for him to meet you. He and I talked about it this morning. He said it's okay so long as you help with rent and food."

"You mean it?" Nelson asked, a little blown away. A part of him felt like jumping up and down on the bed in excitement, while another part wanted to bolt out the door in panic. Was Manny nuts? "But you hardly know me."

Manny gave his head a thoughtful shake. "That's true, but . . . I think you're a lot like me, and I know myself. It's like I know what you're thinking half the time before you even say it." A sly grin crossed his face. "Like right now, I bet a part of you wants to run out the door. Am I right?"

Nelson felt his face grow warm. This was way too scary. Was he ready to risk getting involved with someone who knew what he was thinking?

"Look." Manny sat up to face Nelson. "I've met your friends. You and I made love. I think you can tell a lot about a person by their friends and how they make love. And I've never made love like that with anyone."

He took hold of Nelson's hand. "I like you a lot, Nelson. I want to get to know you more. If you think I'm nutsy and it won't work, I understand. I'll leave you with Kyle and Jason and say thanks. But if you'd like to stay a week or a month, however long you want, I'd really like to spend that time with you."

Nelson listened quietly, holding on tight to Manny's hand, his heart racing, as he fought the urge to bolt.

"Just think about it," Manny said soothingly. "Okay?"

Nelson swallowed hard and nodded.

After that, they peeled the sheets off the bed and added them to the other loads of all three boys' skanky clothes from the road trip. Then they showered together and once again ended up making love. After all the clothes were dry and folded, Nelson helped put the sheets back on the bed and asked about the basketball in the corner. "Do you play?"

"Sometimes. I played intramurals in high school. That's how I first heard about Jason. I was surfing the Web and read about him coming out. Then when Ms. Yamamoto told me they were look-ing for a last-minute speaker, I immediately thought of him."

**rainbow road**

As Nelson listened, he thought how if it hadn't been for Jason coming out, he might never have met Manny. And he remembered what BJ had said about his destiny.

"How about you?" Manny asked eagerly. "Do you play?"

"Um . . . not a lot," Nelson said evasively, a plan forming in his mind. "Holy crap! Look what time it is. Kyle's going to be so pissed!"

"No, he won't." Manny grinned as they carried the fresh laundry back to the car. "He told me when we dropped them off to take as long with you as I needed."

"He did?" Nelson asked, stuffing the laundry in the trunk.

And when they arrived back at Venice Beach, Manny was right: Kyle wasn't mad at all, waiting patiently with Jason at the café where they'd all agreed to meet.

As the four of them ate pizza and watched the sun sink behind the Pacific, Nelson said, "I like L.A."

Then Manny guided them back to the hotel and said good night, agreeing to come back to say good-bye in the morning. But before he left he asked Nelson, "Are you going to think about what I said?"

"Like there's any chance I might *not* think about it?" Nelson replied, kissing him good-night.

"Okay, guys, we've got to talk," Nelson told Kyle and Jason before they'd even gotten into the hotel elevator. "I'm totally falling for this guy. He asked me to stay out here—oh, crap! I forgot!" He pulled Kyle's wallet from his pocket. "Guess what his uncle found!"

Kyle grabbed the wallet in disbelief. "Where?"

Nelson stepped out of the elevator, Kyle and Jason following. "Between the seats."

"Now I *really* feel stupid," Kyle said.

"Since you have your license again," Nelson explained, "you and Jason could drive back without me, except . . . I don't know if I want to stay out here. I mean, that would be crazy. Wouldn't it?"

"Not if you're in love with him," Kyle replied, opening the door to the hotel room. "Did you discuss HIV status, like you promised me?"

"Yes, Mother!" Nelson collapsed onto his bed. "He's negative."

As Kyle and Jason sat on the bed facing him, Nelson continued, "I need you guys to tell me something: When you two are together do either of you ever feel like bolting from the room?"

"No." "Yes." Kyle and Jason both answered at once, and Kyle turned to Jason, grinning. "Yeah, I know you do."

"How?" Jason asked.

"Because you bolted the first time I kissed you."

"Oh, yeah." The color rose in Jason's cheeks.

"And every time we get into an argument you ask if I want to break up. It's like you want to run away."

Jason's brow rose up embarrassed-like and Nelson asked him, "So how do you deal with wanting to run away from someone you love?"

"Well . . ." Jason scratched his knee thoughtfully, still blushing. "By going to shoot baskets, I guess. That's sort of like running away, but not. And even if you run away, if you really like someone, you come back." He gazed at Kyle with a sappy look that reminded Nelson of those two old farts in Texas.

"What should I do?" Nelson wailed.

Jason shook his head. "Only you can decide that, dude."

"I think you should stay with him," Kyle said.

"But you're always the practical one," Nelson retorted. "I'm supposed to be the impulsive one."

"I guess you've rubbed off on me." Kyle grinned. "In this case I think you should follow your heart."

Nelson fell back on the bed and took a huge breath. "What would I tell my mom?"

"The truth," Kyle replied. "That you've fallen in love and want to see where it goes. But you'd better call her soon, because it's already one in the morning there."

"Crap!" Nelson sat up. He drew a deep breath, grabbed the phone, and dialed. While waiting he tugged at his shirt, damp with sweat.

His mom answered at the third ring. "Nelson?" How did she already know it was him? "Are you okay? What happened?"

"Nothing happened. I'm fine. I just need to talk to you about something."

"Nelson, you're scaring me. Tell me what happened."

"Chill, Mom. It's a good thing. I met a guy. His name's Manny."

Nelson proceeded to tell her how they'd met, about the school and Jason's speech, and about how Manny had guided them everywhere. His mom listened quietly, until she finally said, "That's great, honey, but why are you calling me at one in the morning?"

"Because . . ." Nelson inhaled deeply breath. "He's asked me to stay out here with him."

A pause, then his mom asked curtly, "For how long?"

"Um . . ." Nelson looked toward Kyle and Jason for strength.

"I don't know . . . a week, a month . . ."

"Wait!" his mom barked, sounding suddenly wide awake. "How would Kyle and Jason get back?"

"They'll drive the car back."

"But then how will *you* get back?"

"Um . . . I hadn't thought that far ahead." Immediately, he knew that was the wrong thing to say.

"You haven't thought how you'd get back?" His mom's voice grew loud. "Nelson, you do not have permission to stay out there."

"Mom?" Nelson's own voice grew louder. "I'm not asking for your permission. I'm telling you."

He looked to Kyle and Jason. Jason nodded enthusiastically, but Kyle motioned him to calm down.

"I really like him, Mom. And he likes me. I like it out here. I feel like I belong. And I want to try this."

"Nelson, you just met him. Of course he seems wonderful. But you can't just decide to stay three thousand miles from home. Come back first, we'll talk about it, then if you still want to, you can visit him . . ."

Her plan sounded reasonable. But that wasn't how Nelson wanted to do it. "No, Mom." He sat up straight. "I'm staying here."

"Nelson!" his mom shouted and went into a rant about how she'd trusted him with the car, yadda, yadda, yadda . . . till she asked, "Is Kyle there? Let me speak with him."

Nelson held the receiver out to Kyle. "She wants to talk to you."

Nelson could see the lump in Kyle's throat as he took the phone.

"Hi, Mrs. Glassman. Sorry to wake you. . . . Yes . . . Yes . . . I know . . . Yes . . ."

Nelson leaned forward, trying to imagine the conversation and dreading the worst. Would Kyle cave in to her?

"No, ma'am, he's a very nice young man, the same age as

**rainbow road**

Nelson. I think he'll be good for him. . . . Yes, I know you do. . . .
I think they'll be fine. I wouldn't say that if I didn't mean it. . . .
Yes . . . I think that would be great. Okay, I'll put him on. Good
night. Sorry to wake you."

With a weird grin on his face, he handed the receiver back to
Nelson, who covered the mouthpiece, whispering, "What did
she say?"

When Kyle didn't answer, Nelson put the receiver to his
ear. "Yeah?"

"If you're determined to stay out there, then I'm coming
to visit."

"What?" Nelson leaned into the phone, stunned. "You'd
do that?"

A visit seemed so clingy, so kidlike, but . . . He'd missed her,
and he'd like for her to meet Manny, and she could bring some
of his stuff and . . . it suddenly struck him: She was agreeing
that he could stay in L.A.

After hanging up the phone, Nelson just sat there, feeling a
little dazed. "Well, I guess this means you guys are going back
without me." He walked over to the window and stared at the
city lights of . . . his new home?

He turned to Kyle and Jason. They stared at him expec-
tantly. He knew he'd miss them like crazy. Yet a surge of excitement coursed through his arteries.

"Woo-hoo!" He leaped onto their bed, snapping his fingers,
bouncing Kyle and Jason up and down on the mattress. Then he
recalled one more thing he needed to complete this journey.

He jumped from the bed and grabbed Jason's basketball. "I
want you to teach me."

# chapter 37

## jason    kyle

## nelson

At first Kyle didn't understand why it was suddenly so important to Nelson to learn basketball. Only as they walked through the night streets with Nelson jabbering about Manny and asking Jason's advice did it occur to Kyle to ask Nelson, "Does Manny play basketball?"

Nelson answered with a sheepish grin, "Yeah."

At the court Kyle watched Jason patiently walk Nelson through the steps for a right-handed layup, demonstrating each move, while Nelson ran from the ball, covering his head.

But in less than an hour, Nelson scored the first basket of his life. Jason jumped and woo-hooed with him, snapping his fingers too.

And Kyle began to sense that the events on the court were about more than simply Manny. The two boys' interaction had become a parting tribute from Nelson to Jason, and from Jason

to Nelson in return; a reconciling between two very different boys who'd become unlikely best friends.

By one that morning Nelson had mastered a fairly decent layup, and Jason offered up finger snaps at every play.

Once back in their hotel, still hyper with energy and sadness, the boys recalled stories of their trip together. Nelson led them in the steps of Britney's "Boys." And even after they'd turned out the lights they kept talking for another hour before they were finally willing to sleep.

Yet at nine next morning Kyle somehow managed to answer the door when Manny showed up with doughnuts.

Nelson pulled the bedcovers over his head. "I don't want to scare you away."

But Manny yanked them down, telling him, "No such luck."

"Then I guess I'm staying." Nelson grinned, puffy-eyed from lack of sleep.

"For real?" Manny asked, his voice anxious with hope. "Don't kid me about that. You're really staying?"

"Yeah." Nelson shrugged. "Be careful what you ask for. My mom's coming to check you out."

"Huh?" Manny said, bewildered.

"Speaking of check out," Kyle reminded everyone. "We need to get moving."

The three of them took turns showering, in between doughnuts and sorting through clothes for what was whose.

In the garage Manny had parked next to the boys' car, and Nelson moved his stuff over.

"Hey!" Jason held up Nelson's doll. "You want your Aladdin?"

"Nah," Nelson told him. "Keep it for good luck!" Then he turned to Manny with a look of sudden recognition. "Did anyone ever tell you you look like Aladdin?"

"Well . . ." Kyle announced to Nelson. "I guess this is it." Except how would he say "Laters" to his best friend ever? Then he remembered that kooky Horn-Boy in Tennessee.

Slowly he placed his hand over Nelson's heart and looked into his blue eyes. "I wish you peace, joy, love, and lots of hot, groovy lovemaking." Then he hugged Nelson, harder than he ever had in his life.

"You're worse than my mother," Nelson exclaimed as he hugged him back.

"I know." Kyle let go, grinning, and trying not to cry. "Don't be surprised if you get a visit from me, too."

"You'd better come visit!" Nelson swung an arm around Kyle again, his own eyes puddling up.

"Take good care of him," Kyle told Manny, giving him a hug too.

And naturally, Jason also gave them hugs. "Hey, remember!" he told Nelson, as he climbed into the driver's seat and tossed an imaginary basketball through the open window, emphasizing his follow-through.

"Right, Coach," Nelson saluted. Then he turned to Manny. "Hey, you want to shoot some hoops later?"

Everyone waved and Kyle watched through the rear window as Nelson wiped his cheeks. Then Kyle's vision blurred, as tears misted his contacts and he lost it, choking up while Jason held his hand.

An hour later the boys cleared the San Bernardino Mountains, leaving L.A. behind. Jason remarked, "It seems so quiet without him."

Kyle knew he meant Nelson, but he thought it wasn't just Nelson's absence that made it so quiet, it was knowing their journey would soon end.

They'd planned a straight shot along I-40, to make it back East in four days. But late that first afternoon, in the middle of Arizona, Jason took an exit onto a deserted side road, explaining, "I have to pee."

A mischievous grin played on his face as he pulled the car over, and Kyle was right there with him.

The two quickly stripped off shorts and tops, staring "dare you" into each other's eyes. Then they were running naked through the sandy, scrubby desert as they danced and jumped and shouted "Woo-hoo!"

That night in New Mexico they finally made love again, beginning a little fiercely, like starved animals, but then their moves became gentler and more tender, holding one another, as if welcoming each other home.

Their second night, when they unloaded their tent in Oklahoma, Kyle came across the can of Nelson's blue corn facial mask. He remembered the little boy Esau and noticed some cream remained inside.

"I pray the little guy's safe and healthy," Kyle told Jason.

"And I pray he's getting big and strong," Jason said. "So someday he can whip his dad's butt."

"In honor of Esau and Nelson . . ." Kyle raised the can ceremoniously in the air. Then he turned to Jason. "I think we should use this stuff up."

They smeared fingers of icy paste across each other's faces. Kyle's skin tingled as he watched his boyfriend become a primitive-looking tribesman. And as they gazed across their campfire exfoliating, they became possessed with the desire to dance like wacky Faeries, encircling the charcoal flames.

By the third night, in Tennessee, it was raining so hard they decided to splurge on a cheap roadside motel.

"How about that one?" Jason pointed. Next to the highway, a neon sign blinked: MOTEL ROMEO.

Kyle had heard of such places. His cheeks grew warm as he grinned at Jason.

On their motel room bed waited a pair of mints and condoms. Mirrors lined the ceiling. "Just like in Graceland." Kyle laughed.

But after they made love, Kyle felt more sad than happy, knowing this would be their last night together until . . . when? In three days he'd leave for Princeton. How could he be certain he and Jason would be able to survive weeks apart? He couldn't. But hadn't they weathered two weeks together and become closer than ever before?

He reached for Jason's hand, recalling what the two older guys had said was their secret. Trust. Communication. And commitment.

On the fourth day they reached I-81 and crossed into Virginia. Late that afternoon they turned into Kyle's driveway, trumpeting the horn as his parents hurried out from the house.

His mom and dad hugged them almost equally, as though they were both their sons. Kyle's dad helped unload the car, while his mom set out plates steaming with turkey and gravy, mashed potatoes, and creamed corn, their first home-cooked meal since New Orleans.

Between ravenous mouthfuls, Kyle and Jason recounted stories from their journey, each filling in where the other left off.

"And the sunrise on the Grand Canyon!" Kyle exclaimed.

"That was *so* amazing!" Jason continued.

"That's what I was going to say." Kyle grinned.

"I know." Jason smiled back across the table.

And Kyle recalled another table, one with a boot vase full of flowers during lunch halfway across the continent.

Now he softened his gaze, trying to picture Jason in twenty years, his hair starting to gray and tiny wrinkle lines forming at his eye corners. He imagined their life unfolding as a road before them. And he wondered: Would they one day celebrate their own RV journey?

He realized he was getting ahead of himself again, but every time Jason smiled at him, Kyle couldn't help seeing a lifetime ahead.

# for more information about . . .

## organizing a peer group

GLSEN (Gay, Lesbian and Straight Education Network)
90 Broad Street, 2nd Floor
New York, NY 10004
Phone: (212) 727-0135
Fax: (212) 727-0245
www.glsen.org (Please visit this Web site to find the chapter in your region.)

The Gay, Lesbian and Straight Education Network strives to ensure that each member of every school community is valued and respected regardless of sexual orientation or gender identity/expression. GLSEN believes that such an atmosphere engenders a positive sense of self, which is the basis of educational achievement and personal growth. Since homophobia and heterosexism undermine a healthy school climate, we work to educate teachers, students, and the public at large about the damaging effects these forces have on youth and adults alike. GLSEN recognizes that forces such as racism and sexism have similarly adverse impacts on communities, and we support schools in seeking to redress all such inequities. GLSEN seeks to develop school climates where difference is valued for the positive contribution it makes in creating a more vibrant and diverse community. We welcome as members any and all individuals, regardless of sexual orientation, gender identity/expression, or occupation, who are committed to seeing this philosophy realized in K-12 schools.

GLSEN combats the harassment and discrimination leveled against students and school personnel. GLSEN creates learning environments that affirm the inherent dignity of all students, and, in so doing, teaches them to respect and accept all of their classmates—regardless of sexual orientation and gender identity/expression. GLSEN believes that the key to ending anti-gay prejudice and hate-motivated violence is education. And it's for this reason that GLSEN brings together students, educators, families, and other community members—of any sexual orientation or gender identity/expression—to reform America's educational system.

GLSEN's student organizing project provides support and resources to youth in even the most isolated of places, supporting students as they form and lead gay-straight alliances—helping them to change their own school environments from the inside out. A Gay-Straight Alliance (GSA) is a school-based, student-led, noncurricular club organized to end anti-gay bias and homophobia in schools and create positive change by making schools welcoming, supportive, and safe places for all students, regardless of sexual orientation or gender identity. GSAs help eliminate anti-gay bias, discrimination, harassment, and violence by educating school communities about homophobia and the lives of youth, and supporting lesbian, gay, bisexual, and transgender (LGBT) students and their heterosexual allies.

## issues with parents

PFLAG: Parents, Families and Friends of Lesbians and Gays
1726 M. Street, NW, Suite 400
Washington, DC 20036
Phone: (202) 467-8180
Fax: (202) 467-8194
www.pflag.org (Please visit this Web site to find the chapter in your region.)

Parents, Families and Friends of Lesbians and Gays promotes the health and well-being of gay, lesbian, bisexual, and transgendered persons and their families and friends through support, to cope with an adverse society; education, to enlighten an ill-informed public; and advocacy, to end discrimination and to

secure equal civil rights. Parents, Families and Friends of Lesbians and Gays provides opportunity for dialogue about sexual orientation and gender identity, and acts to create a society that is healthy and respectful of human diversity. PFLAG is a national nonprofit organization with a membership of over 80,000 households and more than 440 affiliates worldwide. This vast grassroots network is developed, resourced, and serviced by the PFLAG national office, located in Washington, D.C., the national Board of Directors, and the Regional Directors' Council. The parents, families, and friends of lesbian, gay, bisexual, and transgendered persons celebrate diversity and envision a society that embraces everyone, including those of diverse sexual orientations and gender identities. Only with respect, dignity, and equality for all will we reach our full potential as human beings, individually and collectively. PFLAG welcomes the participation and support of all who share in, and hope to realize, this vision.

## violence and hate crimes against gays and lesbians

The New York City Gay & Lesbian Anti-Violence Project and the National Coalition of Anti-Violence Projects
240 West 35th Street, Suite 200
New York, NY 10001
Phone: (212) 714-1184
Fax: (212) 714-2627
Bilingual hotline based in the New York area: (212) 714-1141
www.avp.org (Please visit this Web site to find a branch and phone contact for your region.)

The New York City Gay & Lesbian Anti-Violence Project (AVP) is the nation's largest crime-victim service agency for the lesbian, gay, transgender, bisexual, and HIV-affected communities. For twenty years, AVP has provided counseling and advocacy for thousands of victims of bias-motivated violence, domestic violence, sexual assault, HIV-related violence, and police misconduct. AVP educates the public about violence against or within our communities and works to reform public policies impacting all lesbian,

gay, transgender, bisexual, and HIV-affected people. The NCAVP is the nationwide network of anti-violence projects of which the New York's AVP is a part.

## human rights campaign

1640 Rhode Island Avenue, NW
Washington, DC 20036-3278
Phone: (202) 628-4160 or 1-800-777-4723
Fax: (202) 347-5323
www.hrc.org

As America's largest gay and lesbian organization, the Human Rights Campaign provides a national voice on gay and lesbian issues. The Human Rights Campaign effectively lobbies Congress, mobilizes grassroots action in diverse communities, invests strategically to elect a fair-minded Congress, and increases public understanding through innovative education and communication strategies.

HRC is a bipartisan organization that works to advance equality based on sexual orientation and gender expression and identity, to ensure that gay, lesbian, bisexual, and transgender Americans can be open, honest, and safe at home, at work, and in the community.

## hiv (human immunodeficiency virus) and aids (acquired immune deficiency syndrome)

Centers for Disease Control
CDC-INFO (Formerly known as the CDC National AIDS Hotline)
1-800-CDCINFO (1-800-232-4636) In English and en Español
www.cdc.gov/hiv/hivinfo/nah.htm

The Centers for Disease Control and Prevention (CDC) is recognized as the lead federal agency for protecting the health and safety of people at home and abroad, providing credible information to enhance health decisions,

and promoting health through strong partnerships. CDC serves as the national focus for developing and applying disease prevention and control, environmental health, and health promotion and education activities designed to improve the health of the people of the United States.

Behavioral science has shown that a balance of prevention messages is important for young people. Total abstinence from sexual activity is the only sure way to prevent sexual transmission of HIV infection. Despite all efforts, some young people may still engage in sexual intercourse that puts them at risk for HIV and other STDs. For these individuals, the correct and consistent use of latex condoms has been shown to be highly effective in preventing the transmission of HIV and other STDs. Data clearly show that many young people are sexually active and that they are placing themselves and their partners at risk for infection with HIV and other STDs. These young people must be provided with the skills and support they need to protect themselves.

## teen sexuality

Advocates for Youth
2000 M Street, NW, Suite 750
Washington, DC 20036
Phone: (202) 419-3420
Fax: (202) 419-1448
www.advocatesforyouth.org

There is much to do to improve adolescent reproductive and sexual health in the United States and in the developing world. Recent declines in teenage pregnancy and childbearing are threatened by growing political battles over adolescent sexuality. Societal confusion over sex and a growing adult cynicism about youth culture further fuel the debate. To date, conservative forces have successfully censored sexuality education in over one-third of American schools, confidential access to contraception is under attack in the United States and routinely withheld from adolescents in the developing world, and adolescent access to abortion is almost a thing of the past. Concurrently, poverty, homophobia, and racism continue to con-

found the battle against HIV, leaving gay, lesbian, bisexual, and transgender (GLBT) youth, youth of color, and young people in the developing world particularly vulnerable to infection.

Advocates envisions a time when there is societal consensus that sexuality is a normal, positive, and healthy aspect of being human, of being a teen, of being alive. Advocates for Youth believes that a shift in the cultural environment in which adolescents live—from one that distrusts young people and their sexuality to one that embraces youth as partners and recognizes adolescent sexual development as normal and healthy—will yield significant public health outcomes for youth in the United States and in the developing world. To ultimately have the largest impact on improving adolescent sexual health, Advocates believes its role is to boldly advocate for changes in the environment that will improve the delivery of adolescent sexual health information and services.

# gay and lesbian teen suicides

The Trevor Helpline: 1-866-4U-TREVOR (1-866-488-7386) and 1-800-850-8078
www.thetrevorproject.org

The Trevor Helpline is a national 24-hour toll-free suicide prevention hotline aimed at gay or questioning youth. The Trevor Helpline is geared toward helping those in crisis, or anyone wanting information on how to help someone in crisis. All calls are handled by trained counselors and are free and confidential.

The Trevor Helpline was established by the Trevor Project in August 1998 to coincide with the HBO airing of Trevor, hosted by Ellen DeGeneres. Trevor is the award-winning short film about a thirteen-year-old boy named Trevor who, when rejected by friends and peers as he begins to come to terms with his sexuality, makes an unsuccessful attempt at suicide.

When Trevor was scheduled to air on HBO, the film's creators began to realize that some of the program's teen viewers might be facing the same kind of crisis as Trevor, and they began to search for a support line to help them. When they discovered that no national twenty-four-hour toll-free

suicide hotline existed that was geared toward gay youth, they decided to establish one and began the search for funding.

## gay and lesbian teen services on the internet

Youth Guardian Services, Inc.
101 E. State Street, #299
Ithaca, NY 14850
Phone: 1-877-270-5152
Fax: (703) 783-0525
www.youth-guard.org

Youth Guardian Services is a youth-run, nonprofit organization that provides support services on the Internet to gay, lesbian, bisexual, transgendered, questioning, and straight supportive youth. At this time the organization operates solely on private donations from individuals.

The YOUTH e-mail lists are a group of three e-mail mailing lists separated by age groups (13–17, 17–21, 21–25). The goal of these lists is to provide gay, lesbian, bisexual, transgendered, and questioning youth an open forum to communicate with other youth. The content ranges from support topics in times of crisis to "chit-chat" and small talk. Each list is operated by a volunteer staff made up of members who are in the same age group as the list subscribers.

The newest addition to the YOUTH Lists is the STR8 List for straight and questioning youth aged twenty-five or younger who have friends or family members who are gay, lesbian, bisexual, transgendered, or questioning. The list provides a safe space and supportive environment to talk with other straight youth in similar situations about the unique issues facing straight youth who have friends or family members who are gay, lesbian, bisexual, transgendered, or questioning.